WITHDRAWN
LVC BISHOP LIBRARY

the **HEIGHTS,** the **DEPTHS,** AND *everything* **IN BETWEEN**

the **HEIGHTS,** the **DEPTHS,**
AND *everything* **IN BETWEEN**

Sally Nemeth

Alfred A. Knopf   *New York*

THIS IS A BORZOI BOOK PUBLISHED BY ALFRED A. KNOPF

This is a work of fiction. Names, characters, places, and incidents either are the product of the author's imagination or are used fictitiously. Any resemblance to actual persons, living or dead, events, or locales is entirely coincidental.

Copyright © 2006 by Sally Nemeth

All rights reserved.

Published in the United States by Alfred A. Knopf, an imprint of Random House Children's Books, a division of Random House, Inc., New York.

KNOPF, BORZOI BOOKS, and the colophon are registered trademarks of Random House, Inc.

www.randomhouse.com/kids

Educators and librarians, for a variety of teaching tools, visit us at www.randomhouse.com/teachers

Library of Congress Cataloging-in-Publication Data
Nemeth, Sally.
The heights, the depths, and everything in between / Sally Nemeth. — 1st ed.
p. cm.
SUMMARY: In 1977, best friends Lucy Small, a seventh grader from Wilmington, Delaware, who is five feet ten inches tall, and Jake Little, a dwarf, try unsuccessfully to go unnoticed during their first year of junior high school.
ISBN-13: 978-0-375-83458-5 (trade) — ISBN-13: 978-0-375-93458-2 (lib. bdg.)
ISBN-10: 0-375-83458-3 (trade) — ISBN-10: 0-375-93458-8 (lib. bdg.)
[1. Best friends—Fiction. 2. Friendship—Fiction. 3. Size—Fiction. 4. Junior high schools—Fiction. 5. Schools—Fiction. 6. Wilmington (Del.)—History—20th century—Fiction.] I. Title.
PZ7.N437735He 2006
[Fic]—dc22
2005033273

Printed in the United States of America

10 9 8 7 6 5 4 3 2 1

First Edition

For Lily, Carter, Kendra, Audrey, and Owen,
my favorite book lovers

Contents

PROLOGUE

When we were little, my best friend Jake and I saw eye to eye. Then I grew, and he didn't. I grew a lot. He didn't grow at all. He never really will. He's a dwarf, and I'm a freak of nature. I swear, you should see us. He looks like everyone else except he's got these short arms and legs and stands about four feet tall. I'm thirteen years old and five foot ten. Since fourth grade, I've been the tallest girl in my class, but at five foot ten I'm taller than all the boys too. It's ridiculous. And Jake and me together? It's no wonder that we turn heads. Heck, I'd look too. I don't think I'd yell, "Hey, look everybody, the circus is in town!" but that's just me. Unlike some people, I was taught some manners.

We live in a subdivision in Delaware called The Heights. If you ask me, this is someone's idea of a joke. Not Delaware. Well, okay, yes, Del-a-*where*? For your information, Delaware is one of the thirteen original American colonies. It's smack up against the east coast, between Pennsylvania, New Jersey, and Maryland, and is about the size of your living room. The joke is this: the highest height in Delaware is just 442 feet above sea level. No one's getting woozy from the altitude here, that's for sure.

But this is where we live, in a house that looks like the house three doors down from ours and so on and so on. The developer who built this place had a limited imagination, so on every street, the Cape Cod is followed by the Tudor, which is followed by the Western ranch house. Cape Cod, Tudor, Western ranch, Cape Cod, Tudor, Western ranch, over and over. It's like some kind of awful housing theme park. But it's home.

Jake and I both live in Western ranches, three doors down from each other. Our folks bought the houses in 1970, the year they were built. Back then, each dirt yard had a single stupid sapling stuck right out in front, and nothing else. Since then everyone's planted grass, hedges, flower beds, climbing roses. It's the only thing that makes each house different.

Jake's mother has a gardening obsession. Every bit of possible space is planted, pruned, and weeded within an inch of its life. She's even got one of those corny pom-pom bushes called a "topiary" that looks like a cross between a shrub and a French poodle. In general, she's into perfection, which has always been kind of hard on Jake.

Our yard . . . okay, I'll be kind. It was my dad's dream to live in a brand-new house that no one had ever lived in before and to make it his own. Well, for a while it was his dream. He took off a year and a half ago in January. He's sent letters and postcards every week and calls when he can, but it's not the same as having him here. Mom tries to garden. She really does. But since Dad left, the yard has suffered. Last spring she planted plants the nursery labeled "hardy," and in the fall we pulled their shriveled stumps from the ground. Neither of us has anything approaching a green thumb. We do, at least, have grass.

The "dad thing" is something Jake and I have in common. His dad is gone too, but for different reasons than mine. My dad has been off "finding himself"—or at least that's what my mother tells me. They got married young, and she says he always felt like he never got a chance to find out who he really was, so he had to go off and do that without us. *I* always knew who he was: my dad. But I guess he's a lot of other things too, and he's got to figure that all out. And then he'll be back. I've had bad days when I'm not so certain, but sooner or later, we'll all live under the same roof again.

Jake's not quite so lucky. His dad married someone else, someone with kids of her own. They live in North Carolina, which isn't so awfully far, but it's not so close either. Jake goes to stay with them for two weeks each summer. When he leaves, he's always happy to go, like it's going to be some kind of great adventure, but when the two weeks are up, he's always glad to come home.

Here are the two best things about The Heights. Thing 1: It used to be a farm, and Mr. Lukens, the old farmer who sold off his land to the developer, kept a few acres for himself. He's got a couple of Shetland ponies, some milk cows, and loads of barn cats, and he doesn't mind kids hanging around so long as we don't try to ride the ponies or tip the cows. Thing 2: Our street, Cliff View Drive—no cliff, no view— backs up on a graveyard. No lie. We walk through our back-yards and there we are, in a graveyard. Most people think this is creepy. We don't. Hands down, the graveyard's got the best roller-skating roads in the neighborhood, the only trees big enough to climb, and Otis, a genuine crabby old grave digger who chews tobacco and spits a lot. Some of the graves date all the way back to the Revolutionary War, but you can hardly read the stones, they're so worn down. There are a bunch of Civil War graves, though, that you can still read. Back then, they wrote a lot of stuff about the person who died. One stone even has the name of every battle the guy fought in—Gettysburg, Antietam, Bull Run—before he was wounded at the battle of Spotsylvania Court House and died. It's pretty darn cool, if you ask me.

The other really cool thing is that once you walk through the graveyard and past the old Methodist church, you're in Pennsylvania. Sometimes I like to just stand there, straddling the line, one foot in each state, like some kind of colossus. At five foot ten, feeling like a colossus isn't much of a stretch, but you know what I mean. It makes me imagine I could walk across the country, giant step by giant step, striding over state lines, great plains, and mountain ranges until I stand on the California coast and dip my big big toe in the Pacific Ocean. It's stupid, I know, but the thought of it amuses me.

It's summer now, and Jake is gone, so I've got a lot of time to think about stupid things, and to think about things that are not so stupid. Like last year. Last year was no joke. Last year Jake and I started junior high, and since then, everything's changed. Everything. This summer, I've been thinking about that a lot.

Oh yeah—my name. Lucy. Lucy Small. Yep—I'm five foot ten, and my last name is Small. Jake's last name is Little. Lucy Small and Jake Little. Other people think it's kind of tragic. I think it's hilarious. What choice do I have? In grade school, on the playground, the girls would jump rope, singing, "Lucy Small, Lucy Small, Lucy Small is ten feet tall." Jake had a worse time of it, but even *he* saw the humor. It's true what they say: you gotta laugh, or all you do is cry.

Chapter 1
The Dog Days

We were ticking down to the dog days of summer. The grass, once green as, well, grass, was beginning to go brown and felt scratchy and crackly underfoot. Trees all over the neighborhood that just days ago seemed full and proud now looked droopy and kind of embarrassed, leaves fading and wilting in the late August heat. Full-color fall hadn't arrived yet, but the beginnings of it were creeping up on us like a sneaky peacock. Right now, though, everything just seemed worn out, dried up, bored with itself almost.

Jake and I, though we hated to admit it, were a little bit bored too. Jake's annual trip to North Carolina had come and gone. He'd been back for three weeks, and the most I could get out of him about it was this: "It was okay."

Mom and I had gone to the shore for our yearly vacation. We'd spent a week in a tiny cottage at Rehoboth Beach, and six of the seven days it had rained. We'd come back home feeling cranky and moldy.

Even the neighborhood pool had closed for the season, the water drained out, the lifeguards gone back to college. Newspaper advertisements warned there were only days left to hit the back-to-school sales before the Labor Day barbecues began.

Yes, summer was just about done, and the first day of school loomed large. Jake sat above me in the highest branches of our favorite maple, smack in the middle of the Calvary Methodist Cemetery. I was well below him, reclining on a big hammock-shaped branch, the leaves motionless in the hot, muggy air. I hate to be obvious, but the day was as still as the grave.

"It's what I hear," said Jake knowingly. "If you can't find your classroom, forget it. Ask an eighth or ninth grader for directions and they'll get you totally lost on purpose."

"Then I'm screwed." I didn't need any help getting lost; I have a lousy sense of direction. My dad always said I could get lost on my way from the fridge to the stove.

"Maybe we'll be in the same classes. Safety in numbers."

"Maybe." I wasn't hopeful about this. Jake and I hadn't even been assigned to the same homeroom. The chances of our class schedules being the same seemed remote.

"Hey, you guys, coming up," a horribly cheery voice rang out. It was Cheryl Egby. She lived down the street in a Tudor with a pinky-pink rose garden. A year behind us, she was now heading into sixth grade, where she would absolutely rule the school. She was the kind of kid who practically had the words "born to win" stamped across her forehead.

I looked down to see her hoist herself up into the bottom branches of the tree, her blond ponytail bouncing behind her as if it had a life of its own. Gracefully, she launched herself from limb to limb like the perky little gymnast she was, reaching me in no time flat.

"Whatcha doing?"

Jake looked at her witheringly. "Sitting in a tree in the middle of a graveyard, Cheryl. What does it look like we're doing?"

"Duh. I *know* that. Whatcha doing later? My mom's taking me shopping for new school clothes." She looked as proud as a toddler who'd just pooped in the potty for the very first time.

Needless to say, shopping for clothes was an exercise in torture for both me and Jake. His mom was forever hemming pants and shortening shirt sleeves. My mom, on the other hand, was always looking for clothes with hems she could let down, sleeves she could lengthen. Nothing ever fit, nothing ever would.

"We're going to Strawbridge & Clothier in Philadelphia," she crowed. "I'm getting a Pandora skirt and sweater set and some Pappagallo shoes. Mom already said. Where are you going for school clothes? Wilmington Dry?"

I fought the urge to boot her out of the tree. Jake saved me from myself.

"Lucy's going shopping in New York."

"Really?" She sounded skeptical. Could I actually be taking a shopping trip to New York? Would she have to be jealous? She looked like she was just about to buy it, but Jake had to take it a step too far.

"Then after New York, Paris."

"You are *not*." Even Cheryl wasn't so gullible.

"I don't really care about clothes, Cheryl," I lied. My clothes always looked altered. It was impossible to hide, and the best thing to do was to act like it didn't matter one bit.

"How can you not care about clothes? I mean, you're starting *junior high*."

"Like that changes everything?"

9

"Well, it does, and I've got a little fashion tip for you. Stop wearing shorts under your dresses. Nobody's going to see your underpants when you're hanging upside down on the jungle gym. There's no more recess in junior high."

"I know that."

"Oh yeah? How come you're wearing shorts under your sundress right now?"

Clearly, she was a moron. *"I'm up a tree,* Cheryl."

Jake snorted with laughter, a little pig sound coming out of his nose. That started me laughing, then he laughed harder, then I laughed even harder, then we were roaring. It really wasn't that funny, but it was one of those things where every time you wind down to going, "heh, heh, heh," you set yourselves right back off again. Cheryl wasn't laughing.

"You guys are too weird," she huffed. "If you don't make a little effort, you're going to be complete freaks in junior high." And with that, she neatly swung herself out of the tree and trotted off home like a prize pony.

Our laughter wound down real quick. Because it was true. We were bound to be the junior high freak show. Elementary school had been tough enough, but at least we'd grown up with all those kids—they'd seen us all their lives.

Caesar Rodney Junior High combined students from five different elementary schools in the district, and we were going to be mixed in with kids we didn't know at all: kids who had never even seen us before. For a while, we sat in the comforting embrace of the maple tree without saying a word.

Suddenly the stillness of the day was shattered once again, this time by the roaring sound of a backhoe rumbling out of the cemetery maintenance garage.

"Hey. It's Otis," said Jake, craning his neck to see.

We looked down to see Otis, the grave digger, driving the backhoe, wearing faded coveralls, his cocoa-colored face shaded by a battered red cowboy hat decorated with blue jay feathers.

We'd had a love-hate relationship with Otis since we'd first moved in. Fascinated by the perfect rectangular holes he dug, we'd hover around, gaping at the sheer walls of earth going six feet straight down. Though he enjoyed our appreciation of his work, mostly he didn't want us hanging around. He made a sport of being grouchy, threatening us with unspeakable horrors and nightmares if we were to actually witness a burial. We didn't entirely believe him, but we couldn't exactly doubt him either: terrible things just might happen if we watched him bury the dead.

"Let's get out of here," I said.

"You go on. I'm gonna stay and watch."

"We've seen him dig a hundred graves."

"So?"

Jake was clearly in a mood now. I decided to let him be. "Fine. Whatcha doing later?"

He sighed mightily. "Nothing. My mom's got a date. You?"

"Dunno. Come by?"

"Yeah. Maybe." He sounded unconvincing. His mom's dates always made him melancholy.

"Okay. See ya maybe." And with that, I carefully picked my way down the tree. I did not possess any great natural grace, but at least I could run fast, and once on the ground I sprinted like a giraffe, past Otis and his infernal machine and into the relative peace and quiet of my own backyard.

Chapter 2
Small Joy

Our backyard didn't look any better than the front. In fact, it looked much worse. In back of the house, the grass struggled to grow in a complete lack of shade, taking hold in the spring only to burn up in the summer. Dad had planted a couple of small chestnut trees, which managed to thrive until tent caterpillars took them over last fall. Mom and I, armed with brooms, squeamishly knocked the huge spidery cocoons from branches, bringing a squirming rain of wormy things down on our heads. I don't think either of us stopped shaking for hours after. Now the trees stubbornly clung to life, bracing themselves for the next wave of invaders.

I came through the sliding glass door into the den, the room where we'd spent a lot of our time as a family, watching TV. Over the past few years, there had been a lot to watch, most of it not so nice: war, assassinations, riots, impeachment. Until recently, I'd been too young to really understand any of that. But my parents were always glued to the news, and since it was our one and only television set, I watched too. Now, 1977, one year past our nation's bicentennial, things had calmed down considerably. A good guy, a peanut farmer with a funny family, was living in the White

House, reassuring us in his soft Southern drawl that the long national nightmare was over.

Mom was in the kitchen, staring into the open fridge, looking as though some great cosmic answer sat right inside, if only she could suss it out.

"Mom?"

She startled a bit. She hadn't heard me come in. "Oh, Lucy. I was just going to . . ." She trailed off, losing her train of thought.

"Fix lunch?"

"Tuna salad. Yes. That's exactly what I was going to do. You know, sometimes I swear if I had another brain it would be lonesome."

She pulled celery, mayonnaise, mustard, and sweet pickle relish out of the fridge. She really was somewhere else entirely. "Mom, I don't like sweet relish."

She looked at the jar in her hand. "Since when?"

"Since always." It was Dad who liked sweet relish so much, and that jar had been in the fridge since he'd gone.

"See? Brainless." She put the jar back in the door of the fridge and started opening and draining cans of tuna fish.

Mom's a pretty woman. Not gorgeous. Pretty. She's got reddish shoulder-length hair, honest-to-God green eyes, and an athletic build. And she's five foot six, which means that I, her darling daughter Gargantua, tower over her. Dad's six-four. I blame this all on him.

Mom's name is Joy, and until recently, it fit her perfectly. She used to joke that when she filled out forms that asked for her last name first, she always felt as though she was lying when she wrote down the words "small joy." But lately, it's been true. When she thinks I'm not watching, I catch her

13

looking completely sad and forlorn. I'm never quite sure what to do, so I look away. It feels like I'm prying.

She dumped the cans of tuna into a bowl and began to wash and dice celery, her heavy knife going *snick, snick, snick* through the crispness.

"Lucy, we can't put it off any longer."

"Put what off?"

She didn't even bother. She knew I knew. "It's Saturday, Monday's Labor Day, Tuesday *I* go back to work and *you* go back to school. Today is *it*."

The horror. Maybe I could stall her. "How about Sunday?"

"Uh-uh. Sunday's no good. We're shopping for school clothes today, and that's final."

Now the next phase of negotiations began. "I just saw Cheryl Egby and she's going to Strawbridge's in Philadelphia with her mom."

"I don't know why Lois Egby drags her butt into Philadelphia when there's a perfectly good Strawbridge's here in Wilmington."

"Beats me."

"It has almost everything the Philadelphia store has except sales tax. I guess some people don't need to save money."

"Can we go there too?"

Mom looked at me like I was nuts. "Philadelphia?"

"No. Strawbridge's."

"Absolutely not. It's completely overpriced."

Of course, Strawbridge's had the latest of everything, and unless you wanted to look hopelessly out of it, that was where you shopped. "Can we buy just one thing there? Just one?"

Mom sighed. We did get checks from Dad, but they were sporadic and unpredictable, and she had to make them last. "Maybe for Christmas, honey. But not right now."

"So if we're not going to Strawbridge's, where are we going?" It wasn't like I didn't know the answer.

Mom looked up at me and smiled. "Where else? The Dry. Do you want your bread toasted?"

Thank you, no, I did not. Nor did I want to go to The Dry, but it was a losing battle. After lunch, it was off to the Land of Last Year.

Wilmington Dry Goods was a charmless place. A cavernous former warehouse, it held bins piled high with last year's fashions, all sold at deep discount. Hukapoo, Landlubber, Levi's, Ladybug—everything you might want, but nothing current. Nothing up-to-the-minute. When I was younger, I enjoyed the search. Finding your size, your color, your desire in a jumble of fabric was like coming up with the sky blue Easter egg tucked way away in the bushes. Now it was simply a chore.

And it was definitely a place you didn't want to run into anyone you knew. Not that there was any shame in shopping at The Dry. Everyone shopped there, even snotty Cheryl Egby. But there was something undignified about pawing through the bins, your head buried in the pile, your butt up in the air.

So I let Mom do it.

She dug through a bin of Landlubber jeans, pulling out possibilities, checking the size, tossing them back on the heap, digging again. All of a sudden, she noticed my total lack of participation.

"Lucy. A little help here."

I scanned the store. No one I knew. Good. I bent over and started tugging on a pants leg buried deep in the mound of jeans. It wouldn't budge. I pulled with both hands, hard, just as a woman on the other side of the heap let go of the other leg. Wham! I landed right on my keister, jeans in hand, the rest of the pile toppling down on my head. Princess Grace, yep, that was me.

"Lucy?" Mom came to my aid at the very instant the woman who'd been pulling on the pants came around the bin to help. She looked at Mom, searching her face, then broke into a smile.

"Joy? Joy Walsh?"

"Annie?"

"Oh my God, it's been . . ."

"Since high school!"

"How *are* you?"

"Mom?" I sat on the floor between them, jeans strewn all around me.

"Oh, honey, I'm sorry." She pulled me to my feet. "This graceful thing here is my daughter, Lucy."

Annie-whoever-she-was looked up at me. "My, my, you're a long drink of water," she said, stating the obvious. She turned to Mom. "I guess you're not Joy Walsh anymore."

"Joy Small. I got married while I was in nursing school. You?"

"Sophomore year of college to Ray Stratton. Remember him?"

Mom nodded, but I could tell she didn't.

Annie rattled on. "Had my first kid right away. He's around here somewhere. . . ." She scanned the room, eyes

16

landing on a boy way across the store who stood by a bin of high-top sneakers, yakking with his pals. "There he is. Billy! Come here! There's someone I want you to meet!" She waved him down like the ground crew at an airport.

Kids never really want to meet their parents' friends. We do it because it's polite and we have to, but really, after the initial introduction, we might as well be wallpaper.

Billy Stratton ambled over, coolly running a hand through his longish brown hair, his lanky body getting taller and taller as he approached. Could it be? A boy I could actually look up to?

"Joy, Lucy, this is my son, Billy. He'll be a ninth grader at Caesar Rodney, *and* he's captain of the basketball team."

He was at least six foot two, and gorgeous.

"That's wonderful. Lucy's starting seventh grade there."

"You don't say. Well, Billy, you'll have to show Lucy the ropes, won't you?"

"Yeah, sure, Mom," he said, with a complete lack of interest.

This was excruciating. It was never going to happen. The gorgeous ninth-grade captain of the basketball team wasn't going to have the time of day for me.

"That's my boy. You go on back to your friends now." She reached up and ruffled his hair as he jerked his head away, running his hands back through it, undoing the damage.

"See ya at school," I said, like the biggest twit on earth.

"Yeah, sure." And with that, he turned and went back to his buddies, who were goofing on him even as he approached.

Mom and Annie continued to play catch-up: marriage, family, work, husbands, years gone by. Mom left out the part about Dad being gone, though. I didn't blame her.

Wilmington Dry didn't quite seem the place to go into such detail.

As they blabbed on and I became wallpaper, I glanced over toward Billy Stratton and his friends. Just as I looked at Billy, he looked back, our eyes met, and then I don't know what possessed me. I did something I instantly regretted: I raised my hand and gave him a tiny wave. He looked at me in disbelief, rolled his eyes, shook his head, and said something to his friends, who then, naturally, all turned toward me and waved back, laughing and shoving each other, the way boys do. What an idiot. If I could have, I'd have crawled to the center of the Landlubber bin and never come out again, ever.

Chapter 3
A Sleepless Night

"Lucy, stand still," Mom said through a mouthful of straight pins. "You keep moving around and I'm going to stick you."

It was late, and I stood on a kitchen chair, bleary with fatigue. Mom was on her knees in front of me pinning up a skirt, her ancient black Singer sewing machine set up on the table. Our trip to The Dry had been exhausting but successful: four shirts, three skirts, two pairs of jeans, a coat, and one dress, all immediately pounced on by Mom and her trusty seam ripper. She'd yanked out hems and cuffs and was busy with the task of lengthening everything.

"I'm tired, Mom."

"Stop whining."

"I'm not whining."

"You are."

Answering with "I'm not" would just be more whining in Mom's book. "Aren't you tired too?"

Mom took the pins out of her mouth and looked up at me. "Exhausted."

"Can't we do this tomorrow?"

"We won't have time to do it tomorrow."

"But tomorrow's Sunday." We weren't regular church-goers. What else there was to do on a Sunday?

"Aunt Jenny? Barbecue? Ring a bell?"

Right. Aunt Jenny. Dad's older sister. Before Dad's departure, we had only visited with her occasionally. But now she insisted on including us in everything, and I do mean everything. Mom thought she did it out of guilt, but I felt like she just didn't want to lose Dad entirely, and having Mom and me around somehow kept her closer to him.

"How about Monday?"

Mom stuck the pins in her tomato-shaped pincushion. "Okay, fine, we're done."

"Are you mad?"

"Do I seem mad?"

Mom's mood was a subject better left unanswered lately, but I gave it a shot. "Not exactly. Just tired."

"Give me the skirt. Let's call it a night."

She stiffly rose to her feet as I scooched the skirt around so I could undo it with ease.

Mom rubbed her low back, kneading out the kinks. "I'm sorry if I seem so crabby. It's just . . . you know."

I did know. Dad. Or the lack thereof. I handed her the skirt.

"Mom. Do you think . . ."

"What?"

Nah. I didn't want to get into it, the sore subject of Dad. "Do you think we could stop by the river on our way up to Aunt Jenny's?"

"On the way back, maybe, just for a bit. Go on to bed, Lucy. And no reading under the covers, okay? You'll ruin your eyes."

She didn't need to tell me. I'm a big reader, but I wasn't awake long enough to get through a full paragraph of my current library book, let alone pages and pages, lit dimly by flashlight.

"Lucy. Lu-cy."

As I lay deep in a dreamy sleep, the voice seemed far away, like a ghostly echo.

"Loooo-sssseeeey."

The voice hissed, beckoned. I stirred, opened my eyes, tried to focus.

"Let me in."

Suddenly there was a terrible scratching on my window screen, something trying to get me. I sat right up, *very* awake. A scream caught in my throat. I clutched the covers, frozen up against the headboard. By day I played in the graveyard with no fear, but by night, who knows what evil lurked out there, skulking around in the dark? I'm serious. I was terrified.

"Lucy!"

Jake. Who else? Furious, I got up, marched to the window, and raised up the screen. "What are you doing? You scared the crap outta me."

"Sorry." He hoisted himself up, his short legs scrabbling on the windowsill as he clambered through. "My mom's still out on her date," he whispered. "I'm bored."

"So you decided to come over and scare me to death?"

"I said I was sorry. Jeez."

"What time is it?"

"Midnight."

"And she's still out?"

Jake shrugged. Who were we to question the dating habits of the divorced parent?

"Your mom's date—was he nice?"

Jake launched right in, like he'd been stewing over it for hours. "Okay, first thing, while Mom was mixing martinis, he squatted down low so we could have a man-to-man talk."

"Oh no." There was nothing Jake hated more.

"*Then,* when they were *just* about to leave, he reached down and patted me on the head like a good dog."

Okay, I take it back. Jake hated *that* more than anything.

"I wanted to kick him in the shins."

We sat facing each other on my twin beds, contemplating Jake's violent urges, my knobby ankles poking out of my pajama bottoms. As tall and gawky as I always felt, it was hard to put myself in Jake's shoes, condescended to daily, treated like a harmless little pet. It was a wonder he didn't go through life in a constant rage, bruising kneecaps right and left.

"Can I crash in your guest room?" he asked.

"Won't your mom flip out if you're not there?"

"Probably," he said, unconcerned.

"You better get your butt home," I warned. I could picture it now: Mrs. Little, peering into Jake's room to find an empty bed, an open window, frantically calling the cops, the fire department, the National Guard.

"I haven't been home for hours."

"Where have you been?"

"In the tree."

"*At midnight? Alone?*" The thought of it was horrible. "I wouldn't be caught dead out there at midnight."

Jake waited a second until I realized what I'd said. Then we both started to laugh, shoving our fists in our mouths to keep the sound from escaping.

"You're such a dope."

"I don't believe I just said that."

"I'll never let you forget it."

"That's kind of you."

"Anytime. I'm outta here."

"Okay. 'Night, Jake."

"G'night. Don't let the vampires bite." And with that, he climbed back through the window.

I closed the screen and tried to go to sleep again, but every time I nodded off, I'd jolt back awake. A vision of myself alone, in the middle of the graveyard in the middle of the night, kept popping into my head. Gravestones as far as I could see, and some seething presence looming up behind me, coming ever nearer in the dark. I'd run and run and get nowhere, scream and scream without sound. At first light, finally, I was able to sleep.

Chapter 4
Enough Cole Slaw to Go Around

Aunt Jenny's fussy. There's no other way to say it. She and her husband, Uncle Pete, both much older than my dad, never had kids of their own, so their small house is pristine, their yard perfect. A place for everything, and everything in its place. I swear, you'd pick up a glass to take a drink and she'd wipe the sweat ring from the table, almost every darn time. Luckily, we were eating outside.

They lived up near Chadds Ford, Pennsylvania, a pretty town famous for the Wyeth family, three generations of painters and illustrators who lived there too. But Aunt Jenny and Uncle Pete didn't travel in artistic circles, as they liked to say, and knew the Wyeths only as folks they saw at the post office every now and then.

Uncle Pete manned a grill full of burgers as Aunt Jenny brought out bowl after bowl of side dishes: cole slaw, potato salad, bread and butter pickles, tomatoes and onions, baked beans—enough food for an army, even though there were only seven of us there. Besides the four of us family, the neighbors, Ira and Rebekah Simon, were there with their toddler, Bernard, whom they'd nicknamed Beanie. This was something he'd curse them for when he got to be my age, I guarantee you that. Beanie was into absolutely everything. Aunt Jenny watched him like a hawk.

"My goodness, Jenny, you think there's enough to go around?" kidded Mom.

"Mama and Daddy were going to come," Aunt Jenny explained, her eyes fixed on Beanie as he tore up fistfuls of grass, "but Daddy was feeling poorly and you know Mama doesn't drive anymore."

"I said I'd go get her," said Uncle Pete, flipping a burger, which sent up a sizzle of flame.

"I know you did, dear, and it was a very sweet offer, but Mama didn't want to leave Daddy alone when he wasn't feeling so good."

"What's wrong with him?" asked Mom. I could see her brace herself for a litany of woes.

"What isn't? The man's seventy-six years old. Take your pick of ailments. He's going downhill every day."

"Jenny, I swear, the way you talk you'd think your dad had one foot in the grave," Uncle Pete said.

Aunt Jenny decided to enlighten the Simons. "First it was kidney stones, then his blood pressure, then his hip, his prostate, cataracts, and now his heart. One thing after the other, bam, bam, bam, like dominoes." She glanced over in Beanie's direction. "Ah, ah, ah, Beanie. Those are *flowers,* honey."

Beanie was gleefully ripping the heads off Aunt Jenny's petunias. His mother, a bland-looking woman, wearily rose and scooped up the squirming child. She sat him on her lap and handed him a spoon, which he immediately started banging on the table.

I was overwhelmed by guilt. I hadn't seen my grandparents, Grandy and Gamma, since my birthday in March, when they'd driven down from their house in Lancaster County to celebrate. Since then, they'd invited me up to stay the weekend with them a couple of times, but I'd had other things to do, so I'd turned them down. When I was younger, I loved to go stay and see all the neighboring Amish people with their old-fashioned clothes and horse buggies. But since I'd discovered that the Amish sold their goods on Saturdays at a farmers' market within walking distance of our house, that draw was gone, and weekends spent with Grandy and Gamma were slower than molasses. Still, as their one and only grandchild, I should have made the effort.

With Beanie banging away, Aunt Jenny immediately changed gears. "Joy, what do you hear from Richard?"

It wasn't like her to talk about Dad in front of people who weren't family, but I think Beanie's assault on the picnic table was unhinging her.

"I got a letter from him just the other day," Mom said.

This was news to me.

"He's in Oklahoma."

"Oklahoma," Aunt Jenny sniffed. "What in the world is he doing there?"

"Working on an oil rig."

This was astonishing. It was hard to imagine my dad, a chemist who wore horn-rimmed glasses and a lab coat to work, dressed in a hard hat and work boots, covered in crude.

Uncle Pete seemed thrilled. "An oil rig? Well, I'll be damned!"

"That does sound exciting," added Ira, his first contribution to the conversation.

Aunt Jenny took a dim view. "Exciting? I think it sounds

dreadful. All that schooling and he's doing manual labor? What on earth is he thinking?"

Wham! Beanie's fist came down on the long wooden spoon stuck in the bowl of cole slaw. Almost in slow motion, it flipped up in the air, flinging a mound of the stuff all over, spraying everyone at the table with goopy cabbage. I looked over at Aunt Jenny, her mouth open in shock, her hair dripping with slaw.

"Oh, I'm *so* sorry!" Rebekah leapt to her feet, Beanie slung under one arm. She grabbed a napkin and started to dab at Aunt Jenny, who batted her hands away.

"No, no, no. *Please.* Let me." Aunt Jenny snatched the napkin from Rebekah's hands as everyone else wiped the cole slaw from arms, faces, clothing, suppressing giggles. Finally, Mom let loose with a good laugh that set off Ira and Uncle Pete and me. Beanie, held by his mom like a sack of potatoes, started to chortle as well. Only Aunt Jenny and Rebekah seemed to miss the humor.

"Is there anything I can do?" Rebekah asked pleadingly.

"Lock that kid in a cage," said Aunt Jenny, "and throw away the key."

Rebekah looked at her, unsure if she was kidding. Then Aunt Jenny looked up and gave her a big smile. Rebekah relaxed and giggled a bit. "Oh boy, for a second there, I thought you were serious."

"Who says I'm not?" said Aunt Jenny in a joshing tone.

Rebekah set Beanie down on the ground and reached for the bowl of cole slaw. "I'll go refill this."

"That's all there is," said Aunt Jenny, still swabbing down the front of her summer shift, looking at the rest of us, "but obviously there was enough to go around."

That set us all off laughing again. Yes, Aunt Jenny was fussy. But she was also a good old gal.

The Brandywine River ran nearby Aunt Jenny and Uncle Pete's house, and it was truly a beautiful thing, winding its way through rolling farmland, past fieldstone walls and old gristmills with water wheels that turned antique grindstones. As a family, we used to canoe down the river. Paddling barely at all, Dad steering us through the mild current, a full picnic basket on board—it was the perfect lazy day.

The river was running low, and rocks normally submerged lay exposed to the sun. Barefoot, I easily stepped from stone to stone, reaching a flat-topped boulder midstream, where I sat dangling my toes in the cool water. Mom sat on the bank of the river, sunning herself on this next-to-last day of summer. I looked at her, drowsy and relaxed as she soaked up the rays, her reddish hair flashing in the sunlight. I knew she was still attractive, but because she was my mom, it was hard to see her that way. I thought about Jake, and his mom going out on dates with men who were not his father. And I wondered if this was something Mom had ever considered doing. I mean, Dad was technically gone, and though they were still married, he seemed like someone we barely knew anymore, despite the letters and postcards and phone calls. I didn't like to think this way, but sometimes it was hard to avoid.

The stream ran on underneath me, the sound of it soothing as I thought of Mom and Dad and why things were the way they were. After a while, I stood up, stepped my way back across the river, and sat by Mom on the grassy bank.

She was picking dandelions and winding them into a chain. Even at rest, she liked to have something to do with her hands.

"Mom?"

"Yes, honey?"

"Why didn't you tell me about Dad?"

Mom sat for a moment, weaving her flowers as I watched a dragonfly hover over the river, its wings iridescent with color. "Sometimes your dad writes letters that are just for me."

"Okay, but couldn't you have told me about Oklahoma?"

"He said he was sending you a postcard, and I thought you should hear it from him yourself."

This didn't sound good. "Hear what?"

She looked at me, weighing her words. "He likes it out west. There's a job opening in California that he's been waiting for. He thinks maybe we should join him there."

"What?"

"I know it's hard for you to imagine, living in a whole different place. It's hard for me too."

"But—what about school, and Grandy and Gamma, and . . ."

"Don't worry, Lucy. Nothing's going to happen anytime soon. There's a lot of stuff your dad and I still have to work out between us."

"What about me? I mean, this is something just *you* two get to decide?"

"Actually, honey, it is."

"That's not fair."

"No, it's not. But, like I said, it's nothing to worry about right now."

Mom closed the circle of her dandelion garland and placed it on top of my head, like a little yellow crown. "There. You look like a princess."

I have never in my life looked like a princess, but the way Mom gazed at me, I could almost believe it was true.

"A Renaissance princess," she said, smiling.

Whatever *that* was.

The river ran on, unimpressed.

Chapter 5
Labor Day

I woke to the sound of Mom's Singer, chattering away in the kitchen like a crazed hamster on a wheel. I stretched, yawned, thought about going back to sleep, then remembered it was Labor Day, my last day of freedom. I hopped out of bed, made my way to the bathroom, and looked in the mirror at my hair, tangled like a rat's nest from my nighttime tossing and turning. I'm a very active sleeper; ask anyone I've ever shared a bed with. I roll, I sprawl, I kick, I hog blankets, and I'm told I snore like a grizzly bear, but that last little bit of information came from Dad and he's known to exaggerate.

After my morning "ablutions," which is an old-fashioned word Gamma likes to use for washing up, I pulled on shorts and a T-shirt and made my way to the kitchen. Mom sat hunched over her sewing machine, the fabric of my new pleated skirt flying under the bobbing needle. She finished the hem, trimmed the loose thread, and pulled the skirt from the machine.

"Morning, sleepyhead."

"Morning. What time is it?"

"Almost eleven-thirty."

The last day of summer vacation and I'd slept most of the morning away.

"Did Jake come by yet?"

"No. You two have plans?"

I shrugged. "Just hanging out."

"Well, maybe he slept in too. I'll fix you some breakfast and then you can go wake him up."

I sat while Mom bustled around the kitchen, scrambling eggs, toasting toast, pouring juice. I envied the way she moved, each motion taking up only exactly as much time and space as it needed. I wondered when, if ever, I'd have that grace.

"Did you decide what you're going to wear to school tomorrow?"

Even though, like I've said, I pretended not to care, that first-day-of-school outfit was a big deal, but you couldn't look like you'd tried too hard. I was hopeless at it.

"I don't know. Depends on the weather."

"It's supposed to be just like today."

The day was already hot and muggy. Forget about anything long-sleeved, which ruled out everything we'd bought at The Dry. I munched my toast and pondered.

Mom leaned over and kissed me on top of my head. "Whatever you wear, honey, I know you'll look fabulous."

Sometimes parents are just blind.

When I walked up to Jake's house, his mom was out front in the garden, whacking away at a shrub with a scary pair of hedge trimmers. Mrs. Little is the kind of woman who'd be hard to describe if she ever went missing: five-five, light brown hair and eyes, average face. Her first name was Dorothy, but everyone called her Dotty, which was about as bad a nickname as I could imagine. She was sharp as a tack, and whenever she focused on me, I always started to fidget. Absolutely nothing got past her.

"Morning, Mrs. Little."

"It's twelve-fifteen, Lucy."

"Oh. Well, afternoon, then. Is Jake up?"

"He is, but he's not going anywhere today. He's grounded. If you want to talk with him, he's out back, weeding."

Grounded? On the last day of summer? This was cruel and unusual punishment. I had to get the details. I started heading to the backyard.

"Oh, and Lucy?"

I stopped.

"Tell your mother I need to talk to her."

Uh-oh. This sounded ominous. I nodded and made a bee-line for Jake, who was squatting in the dirt, sulkily yanking weeds from the backyard flower beds. I hate to admit this, but even to me, sometimes Jake looks like he belongs in a fairy tale. This was one of those times. With the last of the sunflowers and hollyhocks towering over him, Jake looked like something straight out of the Brothers Grimm.

He heard me crunching toward him on the gravel path. "Hey," he said, squinting up at me in the sunlight.

"Hey. How come you're grounded?"

"Ah. You spoke with the Commandant," he said, rising, dusting off his knees. Mrs. Little was not only hard to fool; she was strict.

"Yeah. What happened?"

"The other night, when I paid you a visit? Mom and I got home at *exactly* the same time. She and her dream date

33

pulled into the driveway right when I was sneaking under the garage door."

"Ouch."

"She was trying to keep it together in front of Mr. Right, but, boy, was she pissed. She let me have it as soon as he split."

"I can't believe she grounded you on the last day of summer vacation. It stinks."

"I hate her. For the past two days, I've been her slave. Yesterday, she made me clean out the basement. At least today I'm outside."

"Hey—you didn't tell your mom you came over to my house that night, did you?"

Jake looked at me like I was dumb. "Of course not. Why?"

"She said to tell my mom she wants to talk to her."

"You *know* I'd never say anything to get you in trouble. Right?"

"Yeah. Likewise." Under heaps of parental pressure, Jake and I had never ratted on each other and never would. "I wish you weren't stuck here."

"Me too. Whatcha gonna do today?"

"I dunno. Maybe go up to see Mr. Lukens. . . . She's really gonna make you work all day?"

"If I ditch, she'll ground me for life."

"Okay, well, see you at the bus stop tomorrow."

"Yeah. See you."

And with that, he went on with his weeding, and I went on my way.

Between The Heights and Mr. Lukens' farm are a small creek and a dense but narrow woods that keeps Mr. Lukens from seeing what the modern world made of his hundred acres. He sold his land after his wife died, when it was clear that his children had no interest in farming. Every morning before dawn, he milked his three cows and delivered the milk to a small dairy. Then he whiled the rest of the day away with small chores. For the most part, his workdays were over by lunchtime, and he was bored enough to entertain the likes of me and Jake.

I made my way through the woods toward the cluster of farm buildings. As I stepped across the creek, I heard voices shushing each other overhead. I looked up to see a crookedly built platform in a big oak tree, and sitting on the platform, the neighborhood bad boys: Mark Morelli and Chaz Givens, with a black-haired boy I didn't know. They were a year ahead of me in school, though Mark was even older, having been held back. All of them were smoking cigarettes they'd probably pilfered, flicking the ashes on their jeans and rubbing it in.

"Whatcha lookin' at?" asked Mark defiantly.

I'd known them for years and they didn't rattle me. "Buncha baboons in a tree."

Chaz started to jump up and down and go "Ooo-ooo-eee-eee-ah-ah!" like an ape. He, like Mark, was no genius.

"Shaddup," said Mark, annoyed.

"You shut up!"

"No, *you.*"

They had now exhausted their witty conversation and socked each other on the arm, Chaz putting a little too much into his rabbit punch.

"Ow, ya jerk!" Mark rubbed his arm.

"Sorry, man," said Chaz, actually looking a little guilty.

"You guys build that thing?" I asked.

"No. It grew here. Whaddya think?" said Mark sarcastically.

"Where'd you get the stuff to build it?"

"We swiped it from a construction site over by Gary's," explained Chaz proudly. "They just left everything out, so we figured they really wanted us to have it." He stubbed out his cigarette and flicked the butt toward me, missing by a mile.

"Who's Gary?"

"I am," said the boy with black hair. "Who are *you*?"

Chaz piped up. "She's the Jolly Green Giant."

Chaz and Mark got a good chuckle out of that one, and I thought they were actually going to die laughing after Mark said, "But where's the Little Green Sprout?"

Oh, what a hoot.

"You guys are hilarious," I sneered. The Jolly Green Giant and the Little Green Sprout were cartoon characters in a vegetable commercial, and Jake and I had been tagged with those names on the playground as soon as that stupid ad showed up on TV. I turned to walk off, when Gary called out.

"Hey. For real. What's your name?"

I turned, faced him. "Lucy. Why?"

"I dunno. You wanna come up?"

The invitation floored me. I couldn't imagine why he was asking me to climb up and join them in their tree house. I looked at him, and he looked back, betraying nothing. He was a tough-looking kid, a couple years older than me and definitely no one I should be hanging around with, but strangely, he made me feel a little bit like I couldn't breathe quite right. I almost said yes, but with the company he was keeping, it was only a matter of time before I became the butt of their dumb jokes again.

"Not today." As I turned to go, I thought I saw some disappointment on his face, but I could have been wrong.

Mr. Lukens was over by the barn, sitting on a straw bale, wearing his usual bib overalls, plaid shirt, and fedora, which is a kind of hat men wear in old gangster movies. But on Mr. Lukens, the hat looked just right, his wrinkly face peering out beneath the brim like someone from another time. Curled up on his lap was his favorite barn cat, a calico named Callie. He said she was the best mouser he'd ever seen, and she understood him like nobody on earth, except for his late wife.

"Hi, Mr. Lukens."

"Lucy. Haven't seen you in a while. Did school start?"

"Tomorrow."

"Oh. Big day, huh?"

"I guess."

"First day of school's always a big day. Where's your better half?"

If Jake had shown up alone, Mr. Lukens would have asked him the same question. "He's doing yard work for his mom."

"Aw, he's a good son, that boy. A good son."

I didn't want to change his high opinion of Jake, so I didn't tell him that Jake was working for his mom because he'd been grounded. Callie stood up, stretched, yawned, and curled back up again, purring like a motor scooter.

"Callie's getting tubby. She been eating lots of mice?"

"Nope. Callie's been a hussy. Gonna have a litter of kitties any day now. You want one?"

Almost everyone in the neighborhood had a cat courtesy

of Mr. Lukens—except us. Dad was allergic. But maybe now I could talk Mom into it.

"Maybe. I'll ask."

"Late in the season for her to be havin' babies. If she didn't have a warm house to sleep in, they'd all freeze over the winter."

"You let her in the house?" The only animal he'd ever let in the house was his old retriever, Rex, who'd gone to doggie heaven a couple years back.

"Callie just helped herself one day. Walked right in like she owned the place. And you know what? Now she does!" He seemed incredibly proud of Callie for ruling the roost. She looked proud of herself as well. Proud and fat. "You let me know about that kitty, okay? Gonna be a pretty litter. Right, little mama?"

He stroked Callie as she looked up at him in complete agreement—hers would be the prettiest brood of barn kittens ever to be born on Mr. Lukens' farm. No doubt about it.

I eventually got tired of trying to entertain myself, and though it was sad it had to end, my summer vacation was over. Wandering home, I found Mom in the backyard talking intently with Mrs. Little. They didn't hear me come through the house, and I didn't exactly announce my arrival. Instead, I hid behind the curtains of the sliding glass door and eavesdropped. It was a rotten thing to do, but I really couldn't help myself. Honest.

"I'm just not sure what to do about him," said Mrs. Little, obviously conflicted.

"How long has it been going on?" asked Mom, concerned.

"All summer."

"Really?"

Whatever this was, it was news to Mom.

"Really. I think it's serious."

Oh boy. Were they talking about Jake? Was it possible he'd been sneaking out all summer and hadn't told me?

"If you were in my shoes, Joy, what would you do?"

"Well, I think you're doing the right thing. I mean, if you think it's serious, it's definitely time that they met."

"They did. It didn't go well."

They? Jake and . . . Just then, the phone rang.

"Oh, hold that thought." Mom headed toward the sliding glass door on her way to answer the phone. I dashed for the front door, trying to make it look like I was just coming home as Mom came through the den on her way to pick up the kitchen phone.

"Hello? Oh, Gladys, we missed you two at Jenny's yesterday."

It was Gamma. Mom started going "uh-huh, uh-huh," as I loudly shut the front door and came into the kitchen, winded from my guilty sprint. "Oh, Lucy just came in. You want to talk to her? Okay." Mom gestured me over, covering the mouthpiece of the phone. "It's your Gamma. She wants to wish you luck on your first day of school."

Mom handed me the phone and I talked to Gamma and Grandy for a while, their clueless good wishes reassuring me that I'd be the greatest success Caesar Rodney had ever seen. And truthfully, it was nice to hear, even though they were completely unaware of the harsh realities of junior high.

Chapter 6
It Begins

My locker wouldn't open. In homeroom we'd all been handed our secret combinations and warned not to give them out to anyone. *Or else.* We had to memorize them and then destroy the slip of paper they were written on. But there I was, turning the dial over and over—six right, twenty-six left, sixteen right—with no results. The hallway was louder than a stampede, with herds of students heading for their next class: screeching cheerleaders in uniform, calculator dweebs in black-framed glasses, laid-back girls in peasant skirts and long feathered hair, greaser boys in T-shirts and ripped-up jeans, swaggering jocks, khaki-clad preps, and finally Jake, swallowed up by the crush of taller kids. He came to me, cutting through the chattering crowd, risking life and limb. I stood there, my arms loaded with books and lunch bag, my face flushed with frustration. Honestly, I was almost in tears.

"What's up?"

"I can't get this damn thing open!"

"Gimme your combination."

I hesitated for a split second, then realized how stupid that was. I gladly handed him the super-secret slip of paper.

"Six, twenty-six, sixteen—that's easy to remember."

"Say it a little louder so everyone can hear."

"In this racket?"

He went to work on the sticky lock, turning it over and over, just as I had, with the same results: none. It would not open for either of us. The hall was beginning to empty out as students filed into their classrooms.

"Just—go on. You're gonna be late for your next class."

"You are too."

"I'll just take all this junk with me." I hoisted my books, lunch, and shoulder bag and, of course, toppled the whole pile to the floor. My denim ring binder sprung open, scattering perfect white pages across the hallway. "Dammit!" This was not how my first day was supposed to go.

Jake scrambled around, gathering pages, and as we squatted down, a pair of beat-up boots and grimy Levi's stopped right in front of me. I looked up. It was Gary, from the tree house, wearing a black T-shirt and a jean jacket with the sleeves ripped off. He looked like the baddest juvenile delinquent on earth.

"Hey, Lucy."

"Gary?"

The few remaining students in the hallway glanced at him sideways, as though looking right at him might draw his attention to them instead of us.

"Having some trouble?"

Yes, I was. I was, once again, having some trouble breathing. I couldn't answer, so Jake piped up.

"We can't open her locker."

"What's the combination?"

"Six, twenty-six, sixteen." Jake volunteered my secret code without hesitation. I glared at him as Gary stepped up to the task.

"Sticky one, huh?" he said, smiling crookedly at me.

I nodded in agreement. I still wasn't breathing quite right. He twirled the dial fast around and around, spinning through all the numbers, then slowly, with great delicacy, right six, left twenty-six, right sixteen, and just before he lifted up on the latch, he gave the locker a quick whack with the side of his fist. It sprung right open. He turned to me and grinned.

"There you go."

"How'd you know to do that?" Jake asked him.

"This was my locker last year."

"No lie?"

"No lie. Different combination, same locker. So what's your name?"

"Jake Little." Jake braced himself for the laughter that usually followed, but it didn't come. Gary just looked at him like the name wasn't a joke unto itself. Jake smiled. "You?"

"Gary Geary." Gary waited too, for the inevitable, and Jake didn't disappoint him.

"What, your folks couldn't think up a first name?"

"Ran out. I had three older brothers."

"Three brothers? Cool."

"You?"

"Only child."

"Cool."

The hallway was now almost empty and I'd stashed all my books in my locker except my notebook. I hesitated before shutting the door, and Gary noticed.

"Don't worry. I'll swing by next period and make sure you get it open."

"Thanks."

"No problem. What you got next?"

"Spanish."

"Oh. I got biology."

Jake looked at his class schedule. "Me too."

Gary looked over Jake's shoulder at his schedule. "Right on. We're in the same section."

"Aren't you . . ." Jake hesitated. Gary did seem older than us, but you didn't just flat out ask someone if they'd flunked.

"Got held back once in elementary school and again last year. Gotta do seventh grade over."

"That's a drag."

"Well, maybe this year I'll get it right."

The bell rang loudly, jarring us all.

"Damn. Let's go!" He dashed off down the hall with Jake hot on his heels as I ran off in what I hoped was the right direction. As I looked back over my shoulder, I could see Jake's short legs spinning to keep up with Gary's long stride, the two of them running together, laughing all the way.

"Buenos días! Cómo se llama?" The teacher, a petite, brown-haired woman, greeted me brightly.

I looked down at her blankly. I had no idea what she was saying. With the same cheerful voice, she repeated herself in lightly accented English.

"Good morning. What is your name?"

"Oh. Lucy Small."

There were a few predictable twitters from the class as

the teacher scanned her class list. "Lucy Small, Lucy Small, ah—here it is!" She marked her attendance book with a check mark. "*Me llamo Señorita De Leon.* My name is Miss De Leon." She pointed at the board, where she'd written her name in Spanish with a funny little squiggle over the "n" in *Señorita.*

I was beginning to get the hang of this. She was going to repeat everything. I thought it must get old for her.

"*Sientase allí, por favor.* Sit over there, please." She indicated an empty desk.

Tired of being the focus of attention, I gratefully slid into the chair and set my notebook on the carved-up desk.

"Okay. We were just in the process of giving everyone their Spanish names," she informed me. "Where were we?" She looked down, consulting her class list. "Ah. Raquel Perlman."

The class erupted in giggles. "Raquel" was the name of a busty movie star. Pale and myopic, Rachel Perlman looked just mortified. Unfazed, Señorita De Leon moved right along.

"Antonio Rossi."

Not such a stretch for Anthony. If she was already on the R's . . .

"Lucia Small."

Lucia. The way she pronounced it sounded dangerously close to Lucille, which is definitely *not* my name. My name is Lucy. Period. Okay, Lucy Ann, if you really want to know. But Lucia was a heck of a lot better than Raquel. I could live with it.

"Kwame Thompson? Hmmmm." She was stymied. Kwame sat patiently while she mulled it over. He was a kid I didn't know—we hadn't gone to the same elementary

44

school. "There is not a similar Spanish name, so we will call you Paco." Kwame seemed pleased. Paco was a cool name. Paco Thompson. I was a bit envious.

"*Bueno.* Please turn to chapter one in your textbook and repeat after me."

The learning had now officially begun.

Gary and Jake were waiting for me by my locker in the din of the hallway. Kids were walking a wide path around Gary, avoiding eye contact, while at the same time gaping at Jake.

When people stared at me and Jake, I always pretended like I didn't notice, but Jake often glared right back up at them, and he was doing it now. Most kids got immediately uncomfortable and looked away, but a few kept gawking. Gary zeroed in on them.

"What the hell are you looking at?"

That hurried them right along. If I hadn't already met Gary, it would have scared me off too. He was definitely menacing. Jake spotted me, my head above the crowd.

"Hey, Lucy."

"Hey."

"We're here to make sure you can open your locker by yourself."

"Thanks." I stood there like a dope. It was that breathing thing again.

"So . . . open it," said Jake, startling me out of my stupor.

I stepped up to the locker as Gary directed me through the delicate operation.

"Spin it all the way around a few times. Yeah. Like that."

He was standing right behind me looking over my shoulder, so close we were almost touching.

"Now the combination."

I turned to look him right in his blue, blue eyes and I realized he was exactly my height. The combination went flying out of my head.

"I can't believe this. I just forgot it."

Jake looked up at me like I was a big dummy. "Six, twenty-six, sixteen."

"Right, right." I carefully dialed the numbers.

"Now whack it," Gary advised.

I gave the locker a quick punch. It sprung open.

"There you go." Gary seemed a little disappointed by my rapid success.

"Thanks."

"You think you can handle it now?"

"Yeah. I think so," I said, still not entirely sure.

"Okay. See you around."

"Yeah. Okay. See you."

"Later, Jake." Gary gave Jake a nod.

"Later," said Jake, nodding back.

I watched Gary lope off until he turned a corner, then I looked down at Jake, who was eyeing me strangely.

"You like him, don't you?" he said, almost accusingly.

I felt all kinds of different things about Gary but wasn't going to admit that to Jake. "I don't even know him."

"He's a good guy. We're gonna hang out."

"Oh, your mom's gonna love that."

"Like I care." His weekend punishment had left Jake with no mercy for his mother.

"What've you got next?"

"Math. You?"

"English."

"Okay. See ya at lunch?"

"Yeah. Save me a seat." And with that, I dumped my Spanish textbook in my locker and closed it with a bang.

English was uneventful. Reading was assigned, grammar reviewed, and the first weekly vocabulary list was handed out. I already knew all the words.

By the next class, American history, it appeared that Kwame Thompson and I had identical schedules. He plunked himself down next to me, pulled out a wide-toothed hair pick, and began to delicately fluff up and pat down his "natural."

"Sick of me yet?" he said, grinning.

"I don't know. What do you have after lunch?"

"Biology. You?"

"Biology."

"Lemme see your schedule," he said, pocketing his pick. He compared it to his own schedule, nodding. "Uh-huh. Uh-huh." He handed mine back. "Except for gym, home ec, and shop, we've got the exact same classes, and we've even got those at the same time."

Girls took home economics, boys took wood shop, and gym classes were segregated by sex. Gym was on Monday, Wednesday, Friday; home ec and shop on Tuesday, Thursday.

"I wish I didn't have to take home ec," I said.

"You want to take shop?"

"No. I just think it's kinda dumb, cooking in school."

"You already know how to cook?"

"No."

"Well, you should."

"Why?" I said defensively. "Because I'm a *girl*?"

"No. Everybody should know how."

"Oh yeah? Do you?"

"Sure. My folks have funny work schedules, so me and my big sister Stephanie do some of the cooking. I'm Kwame."

"I know. I'm Lucy."

"Lucia."

"Paco."

"Right. Paco." He smiled. He liked that name better, I think, than Kwame. "You're so tall. You ever think of modeling?"

The question took me by surprise. "No."

"You should. They're all Amazons."

I had no idea what an Amazon was, but it didn't sound like something I wanted to be.

Kwame looked up and his smile faded. "Oh boy."

I followed his gaze. Gary had squeaked through the door just before the teacher closed it and was scanning the room for a seat. He saw me and nodded. I gave him a little wave.

Kwame leaned over and whispered, "You know him?" He sounded a little bit amazed.

"Kinda. Why?"

"Okay, everybody. Quiet down." The teacher, Mr. Haley, had written his name on the board.

"I'll tell you later," said Kwame.

Gary spotted a seat in the back row and was heading for it when Mr. Haley stopped him.

"Mr. Geary, for our second time around together, I'd like you in the first row."

Gary turned, gave Mr. Haley a shrug, like it didn't matter to him one way or the other, and sat himself at a desk directly under Mr. Haley's nose. Immediately he slumped, like sitting up straight was far too much effort.

"As you can see, I'm Mr. Haley"—he helpfully pointed to the chalkboard for the idiots among us—"and this is American history. Please look at your schedules and make sure you're in the right place at the right time."

There was a flurry of activity as people double-checked their schedules. One girl sheepishly stood up, grabbed her books, said " 'scuse me," and scooted out of the room.

"Happens every year. Okay. I'd like all of you to pull out your textbooks, open to the first chapter, and read a paragraph aloud as I call your names."

This seemed like a colossal waste of time.

"Starting with Mr. Geary."

Gary looked at Mr. Haley and shook his head slightly, not in refusal, but like he couldn't believe he was being asked to do such a thing.

"Go on." Mr. Haley stood right in front of Gary, looking at him like he wanted to get this over with too.

I couldn't for the life of me figure out what the big deal was until Gary started to read. Or tried to. The words came haltingly out of his mouth like a first-grader. Anything longer than two syllables had to be worked through, sounded out. There was a hushed silence in the room that was worse than whispers and laughter. Gary struggled along, his face scrunched up with effort. After two agonizing sentences, Mr. Haley moved on to the next student, and the whole room relaxed.

Gary sat, a hard, defiant look set on his face, but I could have sworn he was near tears. I hated Mr. Haley instantly for putting him on the spot like that.

Gary Geary was fourteen years old, and he could barely read.

* * *

The noise in the hallways between classes was nothing compared to the lunchroom. Sitting next to Jake at a table full of geeks, I had to shout to be heard.

"He can't read."

"Really?"

"Really. That jerk Mr. Haley made us all read aloud and Gary could barely do it."

"Well, that explains why he's still in seventh grade."

"I can't believe no one ever taught him how."

"He's not dumb."

"I didn't say he was."

"Yes, you did."

"No, I didn't."

"Can I sit with you?"

I looked up. There was Kwame, standing with his tray, looking as alone as a person can look in a room full of people.

"Sure."

Relieved, he sat down across from me and looked at Jake. Jake looked back. I realized I was going to have to do the honors.

"Kwame, Jake. Jake, Kwame."

Jake nodded. Kwame nodded. Introductions over, Kwame looked at his lunch tray.

"What *is* this?" he asked suspiciously.

"It's supposed to be Salisbury steak," Jake answered.

"Says who?"

"The lunch calendar."

"Uh-huh. Well, from here on in, I think I'm brown bagging."

"You and me both," said Jake agreeably.

50

"I was telling Jake about Mr. Haley making everybody read aloud."

"He does that every year," said Kwame. "My sister told me. He just wants to see if everybody can."

"You'd think a person wouldn't get out of elementary school if they couldn't read," I said.

"You get to a certain age, they just pass you on, no matter what," he said. "Like Gary Geary. He was a year ahead of me in elementary school."

"You went to elementary school with him?" asked Jake.

"Uh-huh," Kwame said, tentatively tasting his food. "And when my sister Stephanie was in high school, she was in the same year as his brother."

"Which brother? He's got three," said Jake.

"Only two now. One's dead and the other two are gone."

"Gone where?"

"One's off somewhere in the Air Force and the other one is in jail."

"You're kidding." I didn't know anyone who even *knew* anyone in jail, let alone had a relative there. And a brother dead? This was something.

"I'm not lying. I heard—"

"Hey, Lucy. Hey, Jake."

Kwame looked up to see Gary looming over him. He swallowed hard. Gary sat down right next to him.

"Hey, Gary," said Jake, pleased as punch to see heads around us swivel to take this in. "No lunch?"

"I don't know about you, but I can't eat that crap." He reached in the pocket of his jean jacket and took out a crumpled paper bag. Out of the other pocket, he took a small carton of school milk. The paper bag held a squashed bologna sandwich and a bag of potato chips, smashed to smithereens. The Salisbury steak actually looked good by comparison.

Kwame sat as still as a mouse next to a coiled snake. He brought his fork to his mouth in slow motion, as though that might make him invisible to the menace sitting beside him. Gary, munching his mushed-up sandwich, noticed Kwame immediately.

"You went to my elementary school, didn't you?" he asked.

"Mm-hmm." Kwame nodded slightly.

"What's your name?"

"Kwame. Kwame Thompson."

"You got a sister, right?"

"Stephanie."

"Yeah. She used to hang out some with my brother Luke."

"She did?" Kwame turned to face him, surprised.

"She bought that old beater VW and brought it to the garage. Luke fixed it up for her. She still got that thing?"

"Yeah."

"Haven't seen her since . . ." He stopped himself. "Haven't seen her in a while. I guess it's been running fine."

"You have a garage?" Jake asked. Aside from his mother's dumpy beige station wagon, he truly loved cars.

"Geary's Garage, out on Naaman's Road. You never drove by it?"

"Is it the one that's always got motorcycles out front?" Jake asked, in awe.

"That's it."

"Damn." Jake was beyond impressed.

52

Gary had finished his lousy lunch. "I'm gonna sneak outside. Have a smoke. Wanna come?"

Even Jake, who could sit in the graveyard alone at midnight, wasn't that daring on the very first day of school. "Nah. Maybe later."

Maybe later? I looked at him in disbelief. Jake didn't smoke.

"Okay, cool. See ya."

"See ya."

Gary tossed his trash into a bin and, after some words with the lunch monitor, headed out into the hallway. He seemed almost like some character in a movie, with all the tragedy in his family. It made me want to know everything about him, and also made me wish we'd never met. I hadn't known Gary a full day yet, and already I was all turned around.

Chapter 7
The Runt

Jake wouldn't shut up about Gary. It was all he could talk about, all of the time. Gary had a dirt bike. Gary could tune up a car. Gary knew how to drive. He knew everything about Gary but the really important stuff, like what had happened to his brothers. And of course he wouldn't come right out and ask Gary anything like that. I swear, for all their constant jawing, boys really don't know how to talk at all.

I knew a vague thing or two from Kwame, who, unlike other boys, talked about real stuff, even if most of it seemed secondhand. In fact, he was a bit of a gossip, but I figured that was fine so long as I remembered not to tell him anything I didn't want anyone else to know. But other people didn't have much to do with him anyway. He was an odd duck, for sure—a bit too interested in girl stuff for most guys and, honestly, for most girls too. For example, every day he had something complimentary to say about my outfit, which was nice. But then he'd give advice like "You gotta stop wearing those flats" and "You need to play up your height," which I was definitely not going to do.

Another person who wanted me to play up my height was Mr. Bartell, the boys' PE teacher who coached both the boys' and girls' basketball teams. He zeroed in on me during my first gym class, standing there in my dippy one-piece gym uniform, which was—surprise—too short and was about to cut me in half. He told me I could get out of gym class if I made the basketball team, and then I could use the gym time to do my homework in the library.

Personally, I thought basketball was a bore. In elementary school, the gym teacher always made me stand under the basket the whole darn game waving my arms around over my head. This was supposed to stop anyone from scoring, but it didn't. I felt like a complete lunkhead, with my arms up in the air like I was being robbed or something. Nope. The game was dull. So I told Mr. Bartell I'd think about it, just to be polite.

But anyway, by the time the first week of school was over, Gary had already been caught smoking and had been given two weeks' detention for it. I figured that, like most kids, he'd have been grounded for the weekend, but no, he wasn't. He was going to meet Jake on Saturday at the tree house and then the two of them were going to ride Gary's dirt bike. I had not been invited, and even if I had, I'm not sure I'd have gone. Well, okay, I would have.

So on Saturday morning, as I sat eating my Cheerios, I decided I'd go to the farm to see if Callie had had her kittens yet. To get there, I'd have to go through the woods and past the tree house. And if the boys just happened to still be there . . .

"Lucy. Your dad is on the phone," Mom said, coming into the kitchen from her bedroom. "You want to talk to him?"

I don't know why Mom bothered to ask. I always wanted to talk to Dad. I grabbed the wall phone in the kitchen, winding myself up in the cord as we talked.

"Dad?"

"How's my Lucy Goosey?"

"Fine."

"And your first week of school?"

"Okay."

"Just okay?"

"Well, it just started, you know? I mean, Spanish is good. And English. Biology's okay, home ec is stupid, math stinks, and I hate my American history teacher."

Mom was doing stuff around the kitchen, listening to my end of the conversation while pretending not to.

"Why?"

"He's kind of a jerk. Where are you?"

"Oklahoma still, but I'm leaving in a few days."

"Really?" I held my breath. I couldn't bring myself to ask if he was coming home; I'd been disappointed before.

"I'm going to California. There's a job opening there I've been waiting for."

"Mom said." I tried to sound cheerful, even though I wouldn't be seeing him anytime soon. "Where in California?"

With a huge clatter, Mom dropped the frying pan she was scrubbing in the sink. She sighed and then picked it back up again, scouring it with purpose.

"Pasadena. What do you think about that?"

"Isn't that where they have that parade?"

"Yep. New Year's Day. Want to be the queen of the Rose Parade?"

I laughed. "I don't think so."

"Come on. I can see it now. My Lucy on a big flowered float, in a rhinestone tiara, waving to the crowds like Miss America."

"Miss America's dumb."

"Dumb? Huh. Well, yeah, I guess you're right. Miss America is pretty dumb. You hang in there with that history teacher, okay? He might turn out all right."

"Okay, Dad."

"Can I talk to your mom again?"

"Sure."

"Love you, honey."

"Love you too." I spun myself out of the phone cord and offered the receiver to Mom, but she waved it off, drying her hands.

"I'm going to go take it back in the bedroom. Hang up when you hear me get on the line."

As soon as Mom picked up the extension in her bedroom, I clicked the button on the phone cradle to make it sound like I'd hung up, and then I listened in. I'm not proud of it, but once again I was eavesdropping. I'm really not that kind of person, honest. There was just stuff I needed to know, and no one was telling me anything. I put my hand over the mouthpiece so they couldn't hear me breathe and glued my ear to the receiver.

"Joy, I'm sorry, but you know I wasn't happy."

"I know, but will this job in California make you happy? Or will it be the next one, or maybe the one after that?"

"I don't know."

"Well, we can't drag ourselves across the country, following you from city to city while you figure yourself out."

"Did I ask you to?"

"No. But in a way, I wish you had."

"Would you have come?"

"No."

"Then, honey, I can't win for losing."

Mom started to cry. At that point, I knew I had to stop. As quietly as I could, I hung up for real and left the house. I didn't want to be around when Mom got off the phone.

Jake sat alone in the tree house, his short legs swinging impatiently in the air. He'd heard me coming, my feet crunching twigs and leaves as I made my way through the woods. The hopeful look on his face disappeared as soon as he saw that it was me and not who he'd been hoping for: Gary the Magnificent.

"Hey."

"Hey."

"Thought you were riding Gary's dirt bike."

"Yeah, well, it was sort of a maybe thing anyway," Jake lied unconvincingly. He was usually much better at it than that.

"Really?"

"Yeah. I mean, he still might come."

"What time were you supposed to meet him?"

"Before lunch."

It was almost noon, but there was still hope.

"You gonna wait here all day?"

"No," he said defensively. "Why?"

"I'm gonna go see if Callie had her kittens yet. Wanna come?"

"I don't know," he said, wavering. Jake was the only boy I knew who really liked cats.

"Oh, come on. You said Gary was a maybe anyway."

Suddenly Jake looked up, sharp as a hawk, his eyes

searching behind me. Then I heard it too: twigs snapping underfoot. Someone was coming. My heart started to race as the footsteps approached, then . . .

"Hey, sprout, whatcha doin' in our tree house?"

It was Mark and Chaz. Like me, Jake had known them forever, and their tough-guy talk didn't work on him either.

"Waiting for Gary. He told me to meet him here."

"Did not."

"Did too."

"Did not."

"Did too."

This could go on all day. I decided to put an end to it quickly. "He did. I heard him."

"Oh yeah?"

"Yeah. And it's *his* tree house too," I said, staring down at Chaz. Sometimes being five-ten has its advantages.

"Well, he ain't coming," Chaz informed me, planting his fists on his hips like the Jolly Green Giant did in the commercials. "Ho-ho-ho."

Ooooh, I wanted to pop him one.

"We were going to ride his dirt bike," Jake said, trying to hide his disappointment.

"Us too, but he ain't coming. Said his mom made him help out at the garage or something."

"Is Gary grounded?" I couldn't help sounding smug. Maybe even super-cool Gary got punished.

"Who cares? But he ain't coming, so why don't you just beat it. Both of you."

Jake looked bummed. I could tell he thought Gary's invitation was only for him, but it was clear the plans had always included Chaz and Mark. "Aw, screw it." Jake turned and started to climb down, using boards nailed to the tree trunk as a ladder to the ground. Just as he was halfway down, Mark had to open his trap again.

"You can't ride a dirt bike anyway, runt. Your feet won't reach the pedals."

If I hadn't seen it myself, I wouldn't have believed it, but Jake turned and launched himself from halfway down the tree trunk like some kamikaze, a flying bundle of mad-as-hell hitting Mark square in the chest, tackling him to the ground.

"Oof!" Mark started to cough, the wind knocked out of him as Jake straddled him, pummeling Mark with his stubby arms.

"Take that back! You take it back!"

"Hey, hey!" Chaz moved in to try to pull Jake off Mark, but Jake was surprisingly strong, clinging to Mark long enough for me to give Chaz a shove.

"Leave him alone!" I yelled.

"Butt out, Lucy!" sneered Chaz, shoving back.

"You butt out!" I shoved him again.

The sound of a dirt bike screamed through the woods. Like the sheriff in a western come to break up a bar fight, Gary charged up to the scene. Distracted by the roaring engine, Jake paused in his fury and looked up just long enough for Mark to get one hand loose and sock him right in the mouth. Jake, almost unsaddled by the punch, went back at Mark like a ferocious little animal. I'd never seen him in a frenzy like that before, and it scared me.

"Jake!" I hollered, trying to bring him back to reality.

"Yo! Knock it off!" said Gary. He climbed off his bike and

pulled Jake off Mark, pinning his arms behind his back. Jake flailed and kicked at him, out of his head with anger. "Jake, man, what's going on?"

"I'm gonna kill him."

"Hey, hey, hey! Enough!"

"I'm gonna kill that jerk."

"Stop it! I hear enough of that crap at home, okay?" Gary meant business. You could hear it in his voice. Jake calmed down almost immediately.

Mark was on his feet, dusting off his jeans and his pride.

"What the hell?" Gary looked at Mark and Chaz, who both shrugged.

"Dunno. Little man here just went psycho," explained Mark, leaving out the details.

Gary looked at me. I wasn't going to say a word. I could tell this was a boy thing. This one was entirely Jake's call, but Jake wasn't giving anything up. He wasn't going to tell on Mark for being such a jerk. I didn't get it, but then I didn't really have to.

Gary let Jake go. Jake reached up and touched his lip. It was bleeding.

"You okay?"

"Yeah."

"Lemme see."

Jake didn't like to be babied. It didn't matter by who. "I said it's okay." That ended the discussion. "So are we riding, or what?"

"Nah. Gotta work for my dad this weekend. Just rode by to tell you. I'll see you guys Monday." And with that, Gary mounted his dirt bike, revved the engine, and roared off, leaving us in his dust.

"See? I told you Gary couldn't ride today," said Mark amiably. He seemed to be completely over Jake's fury.

"Yeah, yeah, you told me." Jake seemed over it too. "So what are you guys gonna do?"

"Hang out in the tree house. You?"

"Dunno."

"Wanna hang?"

The fight had somehow earned Jake some respect, and apparently I was now forgotten. The invisible girl.

"Yeah. Sure."

The three of them climbed to the platform, not saying a word to me until they were up there looking down. Like an afterthought, there I was, still on the ground, looking up.

"You're not coming up?" asked Jake. It was sort of an invitation, but really wasn't. I could tell he wanted to hang with the boys, and that didn't include me.

"Nah. I'm going to the farm. I'll talk to you later." And as I walked away, I heard the hiss of a match lighting and smelled sulfur. I looked back to see Chaz pass a lit cigarette to Jake. Jake took a drag, blew out the smoke expertly, and passed it on to Mark. My best friend in the world was changing before my very eyes.

"Seven kittens? Wow!"

"Yep. She had 'em the night of Labor Day. Kinda fits, don't it?" Mr. Lukens chuckled.

Callie lay on her side purring as the kittens, their eyes still firmly shut, squeaked and squirmed, trying to nurse. I petted Callie as her babies latched on, pushing with their itty-bitty paws, sucking blissfully on their mother's milk.

"Gonna be tough to give seven kittens away."

"Well, probably won't have to give away but six."

"You gonna keep one?"

"Nah. Got enough cats. Gonna spay Callie after this litter."

"Then . . ."

"Look," he said, indicating a tiny gray-striped kitten, mewling pitifully as he tried to wedge himself between two large calicos who kept shoving him back. "They're pushing out the runt."

"Why?"

"Callie's only got enough milk for six."

"Can't you make sure he gets in there?"

"I can, but they'll push him out again."

"But . . ."

"It's how it is, Lucy. Runt of the litter don't usually make it."

"What about feeding him yourself?"

"Ain't got time for that. I know it seems cruel, but it's nature's way. The smallest one dies so the others can live."

"Can I have him?"

"You talk to your mom yet?"

"Yeah," I lied.

Mr. Lukens eyed me warily. "I don't know, Lucy. It's a lot of work. We got to get a special bottle and formula from the vet, and you got to feed him often as he wants it, all day long. How you gonna do that when you're in school?"

"I'll figure it out. Please?"

Mr. Lukens took off his fedora, wiped his forehead with his sleeve, and looked at me thoughtfully. "Okay, Lucy. If

63

you're bound and determined to save that little guy, we'll get you what you need. Go on. Tuck that kitty inside your T-shirt. Keep him warm."

I picked up the little tiger-striped runt and tucked him right next to my skin, mewling away, his scratchy soft claws tickling my belly as Mr. Lukens and I walked toward his truck. Then he started to purr. I swear I wasn't even thinking of the fit that Mom was going to throw when I showed up at home with the kitten. For that moment, I was just plain happy.

"You can't name him Tiger," said Jake disdainfully.

"He's striped like one," I reasoned.

"Which is why you can't. You should name him Spot. That would be cool."

"I don't want to name him Spot. I want to name him Tiger."

"No, no, let me think about this."

Jake was spending the night. His mom had another date with Mr. Right, which wasn't really his name but that's what Jake was calling him. And after last weekend, she felt Jake was not to be trusted at home alone. So here he was, naming my kitten. *My* kitten. Did I mention he was mine?

Yep. Mom didn't have a fit at all when I showed up with him. Mr. Lukens and I had gone to the vet, who had given me formula and a bottle that looked like a toy. The vet told me to feed the kitten whenever he cried, to keep him in a box with a soft towel and a hot water bottle, and to rub his tummy so he'd poop and pee.

When we pulled up to my house, Mr. Lukens said he'd come to the door with me and explain all that to my mom, but I told him I could manage—I was afraid if he was there she'd make him take the kitten back. But after her talk with Dad, Mom seemed—I don't know—all out of argument.

She did say she didn't know what we were going to do during the week when she was at work and I was at school, but she said we'd figure it out. She even fed him the first time, snuggling him up against her body to keep him warm. She was cheering him on, saying stuff like, "Come on, little guy, there you go, there you go," and when he finally latched onto the bottle, she laughed, delighted, then smiled at me. She liked him too. I could tell.

"Mean Joe Greene," said Jake, completely satisfied with himself.

"What?" I said.

"That's his name. Mean Joe Greene."

"That's an awful name for such a sweet little thing," said Mom.

"No, no, it's perfect! You know who Mean Joe Greene is, right?"

It was impossible not to know—he was a humongous football player who played for the Pittsburgh Steelers. Even if you didn't watch football, which I didn't, you couldn't escape the name.

"Yeah," I said, waiting for the logic.

"Okay, this little guy here is a trooper. He's fighting for his life, right? So you gotta give him the toughest name in the world to help him out. You gotta do it. You gotta," said Jake intensely.

Then I understood. This tiny kitten, this little runt, meant more to Jake than he could possibly mean to me or Mom or anyone else. This kitten was an outcast, left to die just because he was the smallest one. Jake was pulling for him with every ounce of his being. Jake could relate.

"Mean Joe Greene, huh?" said Mom, mulling it over.

"You get it?" said Jake.

"I do," said Mom, smiling. And she did, absolutely.

"Lucy?" Jake looked at me hopefully. The final decision was mine.

I picked up the sleeping little runt and he squirmed and squeaked, settling into my cupped palms.

"Hey there, Mean Joe Greene," I said. "Hey there."

Mean Joe Greene yawned and slept on, a tough, tiny ball of fur nestled in my hands.

Chapter 8
The Truant

"Lucy. Lucy."

Fighting to stay asleep, I felt a hand on my shoulder, shaking me. "Stop," I whined, batting it away.

"Wake up. Mean Joe Greene's crying. We gotta feed him."

I opened my eyes to see Jake hovering over me in the dark. In the box next to my bed, the kitten squealed with hunger.

"Okay, okay." I sat up and focused my bleary eyes on Jake. He was fully clothed. "Where's your pajamas?"

"I had to get dressed. I snuck out," he said, picking up Mean Joe Greene and petting him gently, calming the hungry kitten.

"Jake!" I hissed in my best how-dare-you voice.

"I had to see."

"See what?"

"If Mom was home."

"Is she?"

"Not yet."

"She came home late last Saturday, remember?"

"It's two in the morning," he said, a worried tone creeping into his voice.

"You sure?"

"Yeah, I'm sure," he said, irritated. "I've been able to tell time since first grade. Come on. Let's go fix him a bottle." Jake padded off to the kitchen, leaving me to follow, completely unsure of what to say that might make him feel better about his mom and Mr. Right.

After the two a.m. feeding, Mean Joe Greene started squalling again at five. Since I sleep like the dead, Jake had taken the kitten into his room but felt a need to wake me up anyway and tell me he was feeding Mean Joe Greene. As I stood in the kitchen, with the sun barely beginning to brighten the sky, Jake told me that his mom had just gotten home. I didn't ask him how he knew—if he'd stayed up all night, watching and waiting, or had just stepped out to see her arrive when the hungry kitten woke him.

Mom took over the feedings at eight and finally got us up for good at ten. We were beat.

"You two look like a couple of raccoons," she said, whisking the eggs for French toast, eyeing the serious dark circles under our eyes. "If that kitten really does need to be fed every couple hours, I honestly don't know what we're going to do on Monday."

"Maybe my mom can take him," said Jake helpfully.

"To her office? I don't think so." Mrs. Little was an accountant, her office as tidy as her yard. "I could come home and feed him on my lunch breaks, but I know you two will worry about him all day and not pay any attention in school."

Which was true. So I waited for Mom to arrive at the one and only solution.

"I suppose I might be able to take him to work with me," she said, like she was trying out the idea for herself, "as long

68

as I clear it with Dr. Oartel." Mom had worked for Dr. Oartel since she'd gotten out of nursing school.

"I bet he says it's okay."

"Don't get your hopes up. He might not."

"I bet he does."

And he did. Mom called him when she was sure he was home from Mass, and though it took a tiny bit of convincing, he said that so long as none of the patients knew they were in the vet business too, it was fine with him.

"How much money you got?" asked Jake as we wandered through the graveyard on our way to the farmers' market.

"None."

"You sure?"

I double-checked the pockets of my cutoffs, my fingers touching lint, grit, and nothing else. "Nope. How 'bout you?"

"Thirty-five cents."

"We can get some penny candy." One of the booths had colorful jars of sour balls and jawbreakers and licorice whips and paper twists of taffy that sold for a penny a piece.

"Yeah. I guess."

Jake was quiet then as we walked past the little marble lamb that marked an infant's grave. He'd been quiet all morning and, until he asked me about my finances, had been downright mute since we'd stopped at his house to see his mother.

Mrs. Little, on the other hand, had been anything but quiet. In fact, she'd been absolutely chipper. I hadn't seen her that giddy since we'd had little-kid birthday parties and played musical chairs. I thought it was nice, but Jake clammed up and barely answered her questions about our overnight. That left it to me to tell her everything there was to know about Mean Joe Greene, and of course I did.

"Oh, I hope he makes it," she said.

"He's gonna," Jake growled.

"Honey, when they're that young, sometimes they don't do so well away from their mama," she explained gently.

"He'll do fine without her," he snapped angrily.

Mrs. Little's good mood evaporated instantly; the lightness in her was gone. She looked hard at Jake. He seemed furious, his fists clenched tight by his sides. "Well, I know you and Lucy will do everything you can." It wasn't a big vote of confidence, but it was the best she could do. "I'm cleaning house today. Could you pick up your room?"

It wasn't a question.

So after Jake had more or less picked up his room, we were crossing into Pennsylvania, past State Line Liquors, its parking lot empty on a Sunday morning, and on from there to the Talleyville Farmers' Market.

The Talleyville Farmers' Market is not exactly as charming as it sounds. It's in a huge old warehouse instead of in the open air, since the weather here isn't always summery, even in the summer. But once inside, the jumble of booths always makes it feel like an adventure.

Since it was Sunday, I was sure the Amish wouldn't be there. Deeply religious, they strictly observed the Sabbath, spending the day in church and prayer. But as we walked up to the building, outside stood a horse and wagon.

"Look," I said, thrilled by the sight.

"Uh-huh," grunted Jake, unimpressed.

"But it's Sunday."

"So?"

"The Amish are never here on Sunday."

Jake still seemed unimpressed as we walked into the hubbub of the market, but when his eyes landed on the unfamiliar Amish family selling their meats and cheeses, he froze, unable to believe his eyes. They had a girl, about our age, and she too was a dwarf.

It was stunning. I don't think Jake had ever met another dwarf his own age in his life. I sure hadn't.

A year ago, his mom's boss had introduced him to an elderly neighbor who was a dwarf, but Jake said it had been weird. All the old guy wanted to talk about was all the stuff he'd had specially built for him: lowered tables, chairs, and kitchen counter and elevated gas and brake pedals for his car. It was like he was telling Jake that, with a little ingenuity, his life could be just like everyone else's. Jake knew better. He knew his life would always be different. But here was Jake, facing a girl who was our age and his size. A girl who was just like him. Well, almost just like him. She was, after all, Amish.

Unfortunately, since she was Amish, it was going to be near impossible to talk to her. The Amish live like they're back in the 1800s, without cars, electricity, phones, or running water. They believe that owning modern stuff only makes people envy each other, and that the more simply they live, the closer they are to their families and to God. The Amish mistrust the modern world, so aside from what they have to say to sell their goods, they don't really talk much to the "English," as they call all non-Amish people. But that wasn't going to stop Jake. I could tell. He headed straight for that girl and planted himself smack-dab in front of her.

"Hi there. I'm Jake."

The girl, in her bonnet and plain blue dress, said nothing,

looking at him with that placid face the Amish always seem to wear when out in the big bad world.

"What's your name?"

Still she said nothing, though I could tell she was tempted. Jake didn't budge.

"You gotta have a name. Everyone does."

A tiny flicker of a smile crossed her face. Just as she was about to open her mouth, her father, a tall, gentle man with that funny chin beard the Amish men wear, stepped in front of her, calling her "Malinda" and saying something to her in German. Shyly, she retreated to the back of the booth as he addressed Jake.

"You want to buy some cheeses? Some Lebanon bologna?"

"No, sir," Jake said politely.

"You sure? Is good. The best."

"No. Thank you anyway." And with one last look at Malinda, who peered at Jake with curiosity from behind her father's back, we turned away and headed for the penny candy.

"I still don't get what they're doing here on a Sunday," I said as we stood in front of Madge, the penny candy lady. She was counting out sour balls, her crimson lips mouthing the numbers below her equally crimson hair.

"They're shunned," she said, like that explained everything.

"They're what?" said Jake.

"Shunned. Kicked out of the community. So long. Nice to know ya."

"Why? It's not because of their girl, is it?" asked Jake nervously.

"Good Lord, no, honey. Folks like you are a dime a dozen among them Amish."

"What?"

"Oh, sure. Runs in the families. Go on up to Lancaster County sometime. You'll see."

"I've been up there and I never saw any Amish people like Jake," I said, absolutely sure she was full of it.

"Okay, so don't believe me. But it's the God's honest truth. What else ya want?"

"A dozen red licorice whips, and ten—no—eleven pieces of Turkish taffy," said Jake, keeping count of his coins.

She closed the jar of sour balls and opened up a jar of licorice whips, coiling them into our paper bag. "Nah, them Amish there are shunned 'cause they got into some argument with the other Amish about whether the Sabbath was on Saturday or Sunday. They believe it's on Saturday— started having church all by themselves. The others couldn't stand for that, so out they went. Bye-bye."

"They actually talk to you?" I said in disbelief.

"Honey, everybody but everybody talks to me," she said, counting out the taffy, " 'cause everybody but everybody got a sweet tooth." She popped an extra piece of taffy in the bag. "Even dozen. Ya gotta come out even, now, dontcha?"

We smiled and Jake handed her his thirty-five cents. You could always count on Madge for a little something extra.

We sat in the graveyard tree, chewing on licorice and taffy. Jake was still pretty quiet, but it wasn't like earlier when he was mad at his mom. It was like he was working something out in his head, and I let him. I knew from past experience that when he was like that, you just left him alone. Finally, after handing me the last piece of taffy, he spoke.

"You think Madge is telling the truth?"

"About what."

"Lancaster County. I mean, you go there to visit your grandparents, right?"

"Right."

"And you've never seen anyone like me up there?"

"No," I said. I hated to disappoint him, but I hadn't.

"I'd like to go up there sometime. See for myself."

"Maybe next time I visit my grandparents, you can come."

"When's that?"

"I don't know." With Grandy still unwell, it didn't seem like they'd invite me any time soon.

"Maybe I could ask Malinda if it's true."

"Her father won't let you talk to her."

"Not today. But maybe next Sunday."

"Maybe. So, what if it's true?"

"I don't know. It'd just be nice to know that somewhere there's a place full of people like me. A place where I don't stick out like a sore thumb."

I sure couldn't argue with that.

Monday came, Jake and I went to school, and Mean Joe Greene went to work with Mom. Gary wasn't in school. He wasn't there on Tuesday either. Jake ran into Mark and Chaz in the hall and asked them if they knew if he was sick, but they just shrugged and said, "Dunno," and that was the end of it.

On Tuesday, though, for the first time, I saw Billy Stratton in the hallway, talking to a couple of cheerleaders.

I'd gone to elementary school with one of them, Debbie Flack. She'd been two years ahead of me and was a complete snob. She and the other girl looked up at Billy, clutching their books, laughing their heads off like he was the funniest guy ever. He glanced over their heads for just a second as I was looking right at him. I wasn't going to repeat the Wilmington Dry wave, but surprisingly, he gave me a little nod hello. I knew better than to go over and say hi, but at that point, I figured it was safe to wave back. As I did, Debbie turned around to see where Billy's attention had gone. She looked at me, gave me a big fake smile, then turned back to her friend, whispering loud enough for me to hear bits and pieces. What I heard was "dwarf" and "giant" and "total freak show." I kept moving in the sea of students, pretending like I didn't hear her, my face burning. Oh, I hated Debbie Flack, and that other girl, whoever she was. And Billy Stratton too, just because.

That night, as I gave Mean Joe Greene his bedtime bottle, I thought about what had happened in the hallway. Even though it wasn't anything I hadn't heard before, it still hurt. Up until then, I thought I was fitting in pretty well, and Jake was too. We were making new friends who didn't seem to think we were anything much out of the ordinary. Well, maybe because they were a little bit out of the ordinary themselves. Gary and Kwame weren't exactly what anyone would call normal. But at least if they thought Jake and I were even less normal, they kept it to themselves and didn't go blabbing it in the hall where everyone was meant to hear it. Over and over, I tried to think of what I should have said back to Debbie, but I couldn't come up with anything good.

Mean Joe Greene squeaked and pushed at the bottle

with his prickly claws, struggling to nurse. I looked at him, my sweet little runt, his eyes still tightly closed. On his forehead, he had a mark that looked like the letter M. As I traced it gently with my finger, I wondered what it must be like to be that tiny and helpless. He depended on me and Mom for everything, and it made me so happy to feed him and pet him and keep him safe. Just stroking his soft fur and tracing his markings took the sting of the day away. And even though it had hurt me, it didn't really matter what Debbie Flack had to say. I had my friends and I had my kitten and someday maybe I'd figure out how to answer back when someone was ugly to me.

By Wednesday, Gary still hadn't surfaced, and I was starting to worry. It seemed like, if he actually wanted to pass seventh grade, the least he could do was come to school.

"I know where his dad's garage is. Maybe we can walk by there after school," said Jake, eating a tuna sandwich he'd wisely brought from home. The school lunch was some kind of mystery meat.

"It's kind of far." We were both supposed to go straight home after school, no detours allowed.

"So? Your mom doesn't get home from work until five, and neither does mine. We can be there and back before they'd even know."

"What if he's just sick?" asked Kwame, munching his pimento cheese sandwich. He was now bringing an elaborate bag lunch every day. "Won't he think it's weird if we come by?"

"You wanna come too?" Jake asked him.

Kwame shrugged. "So long as I'm home in time to help Stephanie fix dinner, nobody's gonna mind."

"Lucy?" Jake looked at me expectantly.

"Oh, all right," I said, "but I've got to be home way before Mom."

"Don't sweat it. We're home before five, guaranteed."

We took the bus that Kwame usually rode home, telling the bus monitor we were going to do homework at Kwame's house. His bus dropped us off closer to the garage than our bus. We got off at Kwame's stop and made our way down the busy street, walking on the shoulder when we ran out of sidewalk. I know we were a sight: as if Jake and I weren't enough, Kwame had worn a painfully colorful African shirt he called a dashiki. I could feel traffic slow down to get a good look at the three of us. I just prayed that there was nobody gawking at us who knew me and could tell Mom I wasn't where I was supposed to be after school. Unlike Jake, I'm a nervous rule breaker.

"There it is," said Jake, pointing at a cinder-block garage with a row of motorcycles parked in front. The garage itself looked like a dump, the name "Geary's Garage" crookedly hand-painted on the front, but the motorcycles were as shiny as a brand-new dime. Behind the garage we could see the family house, completely covered with brick-patterned tar paper. The yard between the house and the garage was nothing but hard-packed dirt and rusting car parts. By the front stoop, two used tires had been made into planters and scraggly marigolds withered away inside them. It was depressing. There was no other word for it.

"I don't know about this," I said.

"What's your problem, Lucy? We're here," said Jake.

"I just think we should go home."

"Oh, come on, Miss Priss. It's not even three-thirty."

"I'm not afraid we'll get caught. It's just . . ." I didn't know quite how to put it, but I thought maybe Gary would be embarrassed.

Kwame knew what to say. "Hey, I know it's not nice like our houses, but everybody knows where he lives. His name's painted right on the side of the garage. It's no secret."

"You sure?"

"I'm sure."

"Okay, fine. Let's go."

We crossed half the street, getting stuck on the center line waiting for traffic to clear, and then we ran toward the garage. Even though the outside of the garage was a mess, the inside was completely organized, with spotless tools and small parts hanging in orderly rows. An old Mercedes was up on a lift, and a man in filthy coveralls was head and shoulders up under the chassis.

"Hello? Excuse me?" said Jake in his polite talking-to-grown-ups voice. "We're looking for Gary."

"What for?" said the man suspiciously.

"We're just friends of his from school."

"Oh yeah?" said the man, ducking out from the innards of the car. "Well, you found him." It was Gary himself, his face smudged with grease. "I thought you were the damn truant officer. What are you guys doing here?"

I couldn't tell if he was pleased or pissed off. Neither, apparently, could Jake, because he shut right up, looked at me, and left it to me to explain. "You haven't been in school and we were just worried, is all," I said. "And we wanted to make sure you were okay." That's something a girl can get away with saying and a guy can't.

"Oh," said Gary, surprised, I think, that anyone would worry about him. "Well, I'm fine."

"Well, okay, then," I said. And then an incredibly awkward silence fell, with all of us looking anywhere but at each other. It lasted forever and I started to say, "So, we'll just go," but Gary spoke up before I could get it all out.

"You wanna look at the motorcycles?"

"Yeah!" flew out of Jake's mouth so fast, his teeth nearly came with it.

"Sure!" Kwame chimed in eagerly.

The boys rushed over to the gleaming chrome machines, which looked fast even standing still. I lagged behind. To tell the truth, motorcycles kind of scared me. They were loud and mean-looking, and I'd heard all about the gangs who rode them. I couldn't imagine anyone like, say, my dad riding a motorcycle. They seemed like they were made only for outlaws, but as I joined the boys, I have to admit they kind of thrilled me too. They were both scary and thrilling, like Gary himself.

"That one's a rebuilt old Indian from the nineteen-forties. Really rare. That's a sixty-three Ducati—it's an Italian bike. It used to be a total junker. And this one"—Gary ran his hands lovingly across the handlebars—"is a 'sixty-nine Harley-Davidson Fat Boy."

"They're really bad," said Kwame admiringly, meaning, of course, that they were really cool.

"Super bad," said Jake, running his hand across the leather seat of the Harley. "Are they yours?"

"Yeah, I mean, sort of. They're my brother's bikes."

"Which brother?" I asked, hoping for some details about his great family drama.

"Luke," he said sadly. "They were Luke's bikes." The look on Gary's face was impossible to describe. It even stopped Jake in his tracks: he'd been inches from asking Gary if he could climb aboard the Harley, I could tell. Just as I was about to go one nosy step further and ask what had happened to Luke, a screen door slammed and a shrill voice called out from the house.

"Gary! What are you doing?" It was his mother, standing on the concrete stoop, hands on her hips, a cigarette smoldering between her fingers. She was a bony woman, wearing a pair of jeans, sneakers, and a worn plaid shirt with the sleeves rolled up. She was probably pretty once, but time and troubles had taken their toll—her skin was leathery, her hair was dull, and her teeth were stained by smoke. She drew on her cigarette one last time and ground it out underfoot. "I need you to finish Senator Hebner's Mercedes by four o'clock. He's coming to get it."

"I was just talking to some friends, is all," said Gary, instantly sullen.

"Yeah, well, do it on your own time."

"And when's that?" he said, challenging her.

"Look, mister, it ain't my fault your dad went on another bender and wound up in the damn drunk tank. Otherwise I'd be happy to give you all the time in the world to yap with your friends. But somebody's gotta fix what cars come in, and it sure as hell ain't me." She turned on her heel and went back in the house, the door banging shut behind her.

If the silence before was uncomfortable, this time it was absolute torture. Gary hadn't been grounded, wasn't sick, and wasn't playing hooky—he'd been forced to stay home and work. Finally, I said what I'd tried to say earlier. "Well, I guess we should go."

"Yeah," said Gary, looking into the dirt.

"See you in school," I said.

"Sure," said Gary, not sounding sure at all.

As we walked away, leaving Gary alone in the garage, none of us could imagine what his life was like, not even a little bit.

Chapter 9
The Littlest Trooper

He never saw the world around him; he never even saw me. He was not yet old enough to open his eyes, and Mean Joe Greene was gone. Mom came home on Friday with his tiny lifeless body wrapped up in flannel and tucked into a baby shoe box. He hadn't been eating much for the past two days and slipped away while he was at work with her, curled up on his hot water bottle. She was as upset as I was, crying with me as she told me the heroic lengths Dr. Oartel had gone to trying to save him. He'd even given the kitten mouth-to-mouth resuscitation, forcing his own breath into Mean Joe Greene's little snout. But none of it had worked—not Dr. Oartel's efforts, not our constant feedings, our care, our love. He'd needed his mama, plain and simple, and with six other kittens, Callie couldn't have saved him either. Mom promised me that as soon as Callie weaned them, I could have one of her other kittens, but at that moment, I couldn't really think about it. I wanted my tough little trooper. I wanted Mean Joe Greene, and he was gone.

"Do you want me to go tell Jake?" Mom asked gently.

"No. I need to do it."

"Okay, honey. You go on then."

"Can we bury him out back?"

"Of course we can."

I picked up the box with Mean Joe Greene inside. It was practically weightless. I don't know why I wanted to take him with me over to Jake's, but I did. I'd barely had him a week and I loved him so much it hurt, memorizing his every little stripe and cowlick when I'd run my finger along his fur. And now that he was gone, I guess I just wanted him with me for as long as possible. Mom didn't say a word—didn't ask me what I was doing, didn't tell me to leave him behind. She just wiped her eyes, smiled sadly, and let me go.

Jake was devastated. "But I just saw him yesterday. He was fine," he argued, fighting away the tears.

"He hadn't been eating."

"He ate when I fed him."

"Sometimes."

"Always." He looked at me fiercely, quickly losing his battle against tears as they spilled down his cheeks. "Dammit!" He impatiently wiped away the tears with the back of his hand. Dusk was falling fast, and he turned away so I couldn't see him cry, but I could hear him, his breath coming jagged and raw. It made me cry even more. Finally, he pulled himself together and started patting my back, trying his best to comfort me.

"Come on, Lucy, it's gonna be okay."

"I know. I just—I thought he'd make it. You know? I really thought he would."

"Me too."

"Mom feels awful. She said we can bury him in the backyard."

"No. Not there. Not at your house."

"Why not?"

"What if you move or something?"

"I'm not moving," I said defensively, wondering if he'd heard something about Dad that I hadn't.

"I'm not saying you are, but what if?"

"Well, what if *you* move?"

"I can't bury him here anyway. My mom would freak if I dug up her garden."

"Then . . . where?"

"Under the tree."

"*In the graveyard?*"

"Yes, in the graveyard. Then, no matter what, we can always go visit him."

I looked at Jake. He absolutely meant it, and when I thought about it, it made sense to me too. I mean, when we were all grown up, we probably wouldn't live here anymore. Someone else would be living in our houses, fencing off the yards, keeping us out. But the graveyard and our maple tree would always be where we could get to them. And so would Mean Joe Greene.

"Okay. Fine. But we have to do it right now. It's almost dark."

Jake knew how I felt about the graveyard at night. He nodded solemnly and went into the garage to get a shovel. Just as we were crossing the backyard, his mother pulled into the driveway, her lights barely missing us as we ran away from her and into the darkening rows of headstones.

Jake wanted to do the digging, and I let him, my back pressed up against the tree to stop the creepy crawlies I felt going up and down my spine. After all, if your back is covered, nothing can sneak up from behind and get you.

"Come on," I said, antsy as heck. "It's dark."

"I know it's dark. But I keep hitting tree roots."

"Maybe this wasn't such a good idea. We're not allowed to be digging here, you know."

"I know, I know."

"It's against the law."

"Lucy, will you just zip it?" He jammed the shovel into the ground and looked up at me, annoyed. Then the look on his face changed to one of absolute horror as a huge hand clamped down on my shoulder. I screamed, twisting away from its grasp.

"What the hell are you doing?" a gravelly voice growled.

"Lucy, run!" said Jake, dropping the shovel and scurrying away on his stunted legs. "Run!"

But I was way ahead of him already, my long legs carrying me swiftly away from danger, and as I looked back, I saw Otis grab Jake, who could not possibly outrun him. I hesitated as Jake tried to squirm away from Otis. It looked for a second like he might be able to break free. But then Otis had him for sure, tight in his clutches. There was nothing I could do to help him, so I kept running as fast as I could until I was safely home.

"Lucy? Where have you been?" Mom called out from the kitchen. "I've been worried."

Quickly, I caught my breath and started thinking up a whopper. "I've been with Jake."

"Where? His mother just called and he wasn't home when she got in."

"He was really upset about Mean Joe Greene."

"I'm sure he was," said Mom sadly. "He really loved that little guy." She noticed I no longer had the shoe box. "Did the two of you bury him already?"

"Yeah. We did."

"Where? You didn't come back here. I'd have helped you."

"We, uh, went to the woods."

"The woods?"

"Yeah. I mean, it's part of Mr. Lukens' farm, you know?"

"Oh, I see. You wanted to take him back where he was born?"

Mom was actually helping me fib. I truly didn't deserve it. "Yeah. And Jake wanted to hang out alone there for a while. I think he was crying."

"Oh, poor thing. That just breaks my heart. Well, I'll give Dotty a call and tell her where he is, and then I'll fix us some dinner. Go on and wash your face, sweetie. It's all streaked with tears."

Mom gave me a hug and a kiss and sent me off to wash up while she made her call. And as I rinsed my face, I looked at myself hard in the mirror. I'd just abandoned both Jake and Mean Joe Greene and lied to Mom as well. I'd never felt so rotten in all my life.

I was lying in bed, sleepless, when the phone rang. I could hear Mom talking and could hear the concern in her voice, but couldn't make out a word she was saying. Just as I was about to get up to tiptoe within earshot, she hung up and I heard her footsteps coming my way. I rolled over, shut my eyes, and pretended to be asleep.

"Lucy. Lucy." Mom gently prodded my shoulder. "Wake up."

"Hmmm?" I said sleepily. If you're pretending to be asleep, you'd better pretend to wake up too.

"That was Dotty. Jake's still not home."

"What?" I said, instantly alert, my mind racing with possibilities. Had he been arrested? Had Otis locked him in a mausoleum? Or might it be something much worse?

"It's nine-thirty and he's not come home yet. Is there anything else you need to tell me about tonight?"

I debated with myself for an instant, then answered, "No."

Mom looked at me, debating with herself too, I think, on whether to challenge me on my answer. Finally, she decided against it. "Okay. But if Jake comes by later to talk, you be sure and tell me, you hear?"

I looked at her in surprise. How did she know Jake made late-night visits through my bedroom window?

"I'm a light sleeper, remember? Have been ever since you were born," she said, smoothing my unruly hair. "Go on back to sleep, honey. I'm sure he'll be home soon."

She closed the door softly behind her and left me to toss and turn until I finally wore myself down and conked out, wrestling myself to sleep.

Morning came, and with it Mrs. Little, talking with Mom over coffee in the kitchen. I recognized her scratchy voice immediately. I quietly opened my bedroom door, straining to hear.

"After ten o'clock, blah, blah, blah, and not a peep out of him. I have half a mind to blah, blah, but his father, blah, blah, blah, blah, and you have no idea what a kettle of fish *that* is," said Mrs. Little.

I was relieved to hear that Jake had eventually come

home, but after *ten*? I had to know what had kept him so late, out there in the graveyard with Otis.

"Well, I do know this year is blah, blah, blah, what with the onset of puberty and blah, blah," said Mom, who was a big reader of childhood development books.

It was frustrating. I was missing all the good stuff, and I desperately had to pee, but the second I flushed the toilet, they'd know I was up. I thought about listening in for a bit, but my bladder won out, and the flushing toilet announced that I'd risen for the day.

"Anyway, since he clearly can't be left to his own devices, I'm having Frank over to dinner instead of going out tonight and was wondering if you and Lucy would like to join us. I think he'll be much better behaved if—"

I made my entrance into the kitchen, stopping all serious discussion.

" 'Morning, Miss Medusa," said Mom with amusement. Medusa was some lady in Greek myths who had snakes for hair, and in my hurry to get to the kitchen before they stopped talking, I'd skipped the morning ablutions. My hair was just wild.

"My goodness, Lucy. Did you comb your hair with an egg-beater?" said Mrs. Little.

She and Mom laughed and laughed.

I myself was not amused, as I headed for the fridge to get some orange juice. Lack of sleep had made me grumpy, and I didn't need to hear about my ratty hair first thing.

"Dotty's invited us over for dinner so we can meet her friend Mr. Grotowski," said Mom, even though she knew I'd overheard.

"Frank," said Mrs. Little, "please. It's what he's asked Jake to call him."

"Uh-huh," I grunted, swigging orange juice from the carton.

"Lucy," scolded Mom, "go get yourself a glass."

I didn't really like drinking from the carton. I was just doing it to bug her since they'd made fun of my hair and put me in a grouchy mood. I got a glass, poured some juice, and decided to try to be polite.

"That'll be nice," I said. "Whatcha having?"

"Lasagna."

Her lasagna was legendary, but she didn't make it often. I figured she must really like this Frank. "Yum," I said, and began searching for cereal. Maybe they'd think I'd disappeared and start talking again, but no such luck. I guess putting my head in the kitchen cabinets didn't make me invisible.

"Well, good then. Around six?"

"Perfect," said Mom. "Can I bring anything?"

"Just yourselves," said Mrs. Little, rinsing out her coffee cup and putting it in the dish drainer. "Lucy, I'm so sorry about your kitty. I know you must miss him."

My sadness had been dulled by a full night of sleep, but now that I was wide awake, it welled up inside me all over again. "Yeah," I said, "I do miss him."

"I knew it was going to be hard for him to make it. I don't know why old Mr. Lukens thought it was a good idea to put a couple of kids through that kind of grief."

"Lucy talked him into it. She's got a soft spot for lost causes. Plus, she's been wanting one of his kittens forever," said Mom, "but Richard is allergic."

Mrs. Little looked carefully at Mom, who rarely mentioned Dad anymore, but there was nothing on Mom's face that revealed her feelings. "Well, I know Mr. Lukens has no shortage of kittens. When this litter is ready, you can choose another."

"But I don't want any old kitten."

"Right now you don't. But give it time. Maybe you'll change your mind," she said, heading for the door. "See you two around six. This will be fun."

"Fun" wasn't exactly the word I'd use to describe it, but dinner was surely interesting. We were eating in the dining room instead of in the kitchen, so dinner was a little bit stuffy and formal. I wanted to get Jake aside to find out what happened after Otis had nabbed him, but I knew the grown-ups weren't going to cut us loose to watch TV until after dinner was over and they wanted to talk in peace and private. So I had to make do with meaningful looks and sharp secret kicks under the table.

Frank Grotowski seemed like an okay guy. He wasn't bad looking, except for the one big eyebrow that stretched across his forehead, and he was friendly in a goofy sort of way. I could tell he hadn't spent much time around kids, though. He treated us like we were much younger than twelve-going-on-thirteen, which, in fairness, might explain his patting Jake on the head. But then again, maybe he was just a jerk. Hard to say.

Clearly, though, he liked Mrs. Little a lot. His conversation was full of "Dotty, this" and "Dotty, that" and "When Dotty and I," until it made me dizzy. Mrs. Little was kind of girlish with him, which honestly embarrassed me a bit. And it embarrassed Jake a lot. But Mom laughed along with the both of them like it was nothing out of the ordinary, so I figured there was probably a side to Mrs. Little I just plain didn't know about.

The lasagna was incredible. I had two helpings and then immediately felt like I needed to go lie down, which Mrs. Little suggested as soon as she started clearing the plates.

"Why don't you kids go into the den and watch TV," she said, "and let us have some grown-up time?"

As we rose to leave, Frank did too, following us.

"Frank, where are you going?" said Mrs. Little.

"You said you wanted some grown-up time," he said jokingly.

"Oh, Frank," she said, swatting at him with a cloth napkin.

The grown-ups laughed like it was the funniest thing ever, when it was really just kind of dopey.

I sprawled on the couch and Jake turned on the TV. *The Bionic Woman* was on, which I thought was a silly show, but he thought it was cool because the Bionic Woman had special powers and got to run around and beat up bad guys in slow motion. That night, though, he was restless—almost annoyed, it seemed. I was stupid from all the food and couldn't tell if he wanted to talk or not, but I decided to give it a go since he wasn't paying total attention to the TV.

"So . . . what happened?" I asked, during a commercial, just to be safe.

"Last night?"

"No, dummy, last year. Of course last night."

"Well, after Otis scared the crap out of you—"

"He scared the crap out of you too," I said defensively.

"Did not."

"Then why'd you run?"

"Never mind." Jake wasn't going to admit that he'd run too. He shut right up and focused completely on some dumb toothpaste commercial.

"Oh, come *on*," I begged him. "Tell me."

"Okay, okay. So Otis grabbed me and hollered at me for a while and said he was going to have me arrested for—what was it? Oh yeah, 'desecrating' a graveyard. Which I didn't get at all. I mean, it's not like we were doing something gross like going to the bathroom out there or anything."

Jake's vocabulary isn't nearly as good as mine. "That's *'defecating,'* Jake. It's a different word."

"Oh. Well, anyway, after he'd yelled himself out, he finally asked me just what the hell we thought we were doing out there. And when I told him, he got all quiet. Then he walked over to the tree, picked up the shovel, and buried Mean Joe Greene himself."

"You're kidding."

"Nope. It's the truth. Then he said a little prayer and asked me to say a few words."

"Really? What did you say?"

"Oh, you know. How he was a good kitten and we loved him. That's all. Then we hung out for a while and talked."

"You and *Otis*?"

"No, me and President Carter. Duh. Of course me and Otis."

I know I was being kind of dumb, but, I'm sorry, I couldn't imagine sitting out there in the graveyard at night having a heart-to-heart with the grave digger. "What did you talk about?"

"Everything."

"Like *what*?"

"Just everything. Then when I got home, Mom grounded me again."

"For how long?"

"This weekend and next."

"Ouch."

"Her loss. She won't be able to go out with Mr. Right if she's stuck at home with me."

"You really don't like Frank, do you?"

"Do you?"

"I don't know. He seems all right."

"Shows how much *you* know."

"What's so bad about him?"

"I don't want to talk about it, okay? Shh. The show's back on."

With that, the discussion was over, and Jake's complete attention was given to the Bionic Woman and her super abilities.

As I wallowed on the couch like a beached whale, here's what I thought: if it was my mom dating some guy I didn't like, you better believe I'd want to talk about it. In fact, I probably wouldn't want to talk about anything else. And maybe it's because he's not a girl, but if something's really bothering Jake, he'll just stew about it until he's good and ready to talk. If I did that, I'd absolutely explode. But I guess that's the difference between me and Jake—aside from the obvious, of course.

Chapter 10
Settling In

Over the next few weeks, we all, for better or for worse, settled into school. After that first week Gary was out, he started coming to class again and got hit with even more after-school detention for all the days he'd missed. He was hopelessly behind, and though we'd all offered to help him out, he was stubborn about actually asking for help. I think, given what his home life was like, he never expected any help from anyone. Now here it was, almost midterms, and he was failing just about everything.

Even gym. I didn't think it was actually possible to fail gym, but Gary was. He and Kwame were in the same section for gym, and Kwame said that since Gary never brought his uniform and always wore his boots, he never participated in class. Honestly, it was hard to imagine Gary in gym shorts, white socks, and sneakers, kicking a soccer ball around. He just didn't seem the sporty type.

But one day, Mrs. Fogarassy, the girls' PE teacher, was out with the flu, so Mr. Bartell combined the classes. Since it was nice outside, he decided that instead of an indoor boys-against-the-girls game of dodgeball, he'd have us run some relays, with two boys and two girls on each team. One problem, though—there were thirty-five of us, unless you counted Gary. Mr. Bartell gave Gary a dirty look, like Gary was deliberately spoiling his plans. As usual, Gary was wearing his jeans, but instead of his boots he was wearing a pair of beat-up black high-tops.

"What, Geary, no motorcycle boots? You're going to blow your cool."

One of the jocks laughed, but Gary shot him a look that I definitely wouldn't have wanted to receive. "I wore 'em out," said Gary sullenly.

"Well, since it seems you do actually own a pair of sneakers, you'll be running in a relay today."

"I don't have my gym clothes, sir." Even Gary knew well enough to call Mr. Bartell "sir."

"And I don't care. You're running." Mr. Bartell looked at Mrs. Fogarassy's attendance sheet. "When I call your name, step forward." He called four girls and five boys and made them choose their relay teams.

I've always hated choosing up sides for sports. And I'm not sure which is more awful—having to choose or being the last one chosen. But I knew I wasn't going to be chosen last because Kwame was one of the five boys, and when it came his turn, he picked me first.

"So I think we oughta pick another girl next. Fewer fast girls than fast boys," said Kwame decisively.

"What—you're trying to win or something?" I teased.

"Come on. Help me out here. Who's fast?"

I looked at the girls. We hadn't really done much running. We'd spent most of our time in gym class batting a volleyball back and forth. But I remembered one girl was a swimmer, so I told Kwame to pick her.

"The chunky redhead?" he said doubtfully.

"She's not chunky. And if she can swim fast, maybe she can run fast too."

"Well, all right. What's her name?"

"Sandy."

"Sandy Swimmer? Cute."

Now we had to pick a boy, and though it was obvious to me who Kwame should pick, I wasn't going to say it. I didn't want Kwame to think I liked Gary or anything, even though he probably had figured that one out. Sandy was pushing for some guy she obviously had a crush on, but he got picked before it was Kwame's turn. Only three boys were left, and one of them was Gary. And even though I hated the thought of Gary being picked last, he looked so bored by it all he could hardly stand up straight.

"Gary," Kwame chose without hesitation.

Gary ambled over to us, taking his sweet time, looking like he could care less. But as he came close to Kwame, he leaned toward him and quietly said, "Thanks, man."

After the team selection, the race seemed kind of a letdown. Sandy ran first and did okay, putting us in fourth. Then it was Gary's leg, and he didn't exactly tear up the track. Gary had definitely smoked one too many cigarettes, and he lost some ground, dropping us down to fifth. As he crossed the line and slapped my outstretched hand to send me off, he immediately bent over, trying to catch his breath. I ran as hard as I could, moving us back into fourth place by the time my leg was over. Now it was Kwame's turn to run.

And run he did. I'd never seen anyone so fast. Kwame seemed to devour the track, each stride bringing him closer and closer to the leader, a stuck-up tennis player named Thad. Then, amazingly, Kwame was just half a stride behind.

"Come on, Kwame, go, go, go!" I yelled.

"Damn, he's fast," said Gary, finally catching his breath.

Kwame and Thad were now shoulder to shoulder, and Thad turned his head to sneak a look at Kwame. It seemed to infuriate him that Kwame had caught up, and he lowered his head, trying to bulldoze his way to the finish, his arms pumping wildly. But Kwame effortlessly accelerated, his legs a blur of speed, and he flew across the line in first place. Sandy was jumping up and down and screaming like a cheerleader and, okay, I was too. I had no idea Kwame could run like that.

Gary gave Kwame a high five. "That was unreal. Where'd you learn to run like that?"

Kwame shrugged. "Dunno, man. I've just always been fast."

Mr. Bartell came over to us, looking at Kwame in wonder. "Thompson?"

"Yes, sir?"

"Come track season, expect to hear from me. Okay, everyone. A lap around the track and then hit the showers."

On the day his detention ended, Gary came out of school and loped through the thick crowd of students waiting for buses. Some kids tried to ignore him, others looked at him like he was worse than dirt, but most seemed in awe of him, like he was some menacing wild animal with sharp teeth and claws. After school, I figured Gary would likely hang out with Chaz and Mark, but they were both in detention themselves. So instead he came up to me and Jake, his hands shoved in his pockets. He seemed unaware of the attention he'd just drawn.

"Hey. You waiting for the bus?" he asked, looking for something to say.

"Yeah," said Jake, trying to match Gary's cool. "You?"

"Nah. I walk."

"Cool." Jake crammed his own hands deep into his pockets, slouching as much as he could.

"So, you wanna wait, or you wanna walk?"

"It's kind of far," I said. "And it's drizzling."

"Well, you don't have to come," Jake challenged.

So of course I had to join them. As we were walking away from the row of arriving buses, we heard feet slapping the pavement with ridiculous speed, and then Kwame was beside us too.

"Hey, where you guys going?" he said, not even winded.

"We're walking home." Jake's legs churned to keep up with our longer strides.

"It's raining," Kwame observed.

"Afraid you'll melt?" asked Jake, already wet.

"Nah. But Lucy might, 'cause she's so sweet," joked Kwame.

The guys all laughed. I wasn't sure what was so darn funny about that, but then Gary looked over at me and gave me a little wink and a smile. And if I were in any danger of actually melting, that would have done me in.

We walked on for a while, Kwame kicking a rusty beer can ahead, when suddenly from behind us there was an ear-splitting roar. It gained on us quickly, the meanest-looking motorcycle I'd ever seen. The small front tire was pushed way out in front, the handlebars were way up high, and the whole thing was angled back, like it was heading into a howling wind.

"Look at that chopper!" hollered Kwame admiringly.

But I was too busy looking at what was riding it. The guy was enormous, with skin so white he might have been albino. His long blond hair and beard were both in braids. He wore a grimy denim vest over a ragged leather jacket, and sewn on the back of the vest was a ghoulish patch that read "Pagans Motorcycle Club." To top it all off, he sported mirrored shades and a greasy red bandanna on his head. He was the scariest-looking man I'd ever seen.

He turned his head, spotted us, and pulled his bike right over so he was rumbling alongside. I was ready to take off running when his face cracked into the biggest, widest, sunniest smile ever.

"Hey! Little Brother!" he yelled, cackling with glee.

"Big Bob," said Gary, smiling. "What are you up to?"

"No good, no doubt. Whatcha all up to, you and your freaky friends?"

"They're not freaks," warned Gary.

Big Bob just laughed. "Oh, Little Bro, you misunderstand the Big Man. I'm the original stone freak. I fly my freak flag high! It ain't no slam when I call y'all freaks. That's a compliment, that is."

"I like your bike," Jake blurted out, as if he couldn't hold it in a second longer.

I couldn't believe Jake had the guts to actually talk to Big Bob. Personally, I felt like I had a mouth full of dryer lint, the guy made me so nervous.

"Do you, baby? Well, I like it too. It's all that I have in this bad old world. So why you all walking in the rain?"

"Beats riding the bus," said Jake, now seemingly at ease.

"That it does, my friend, that it does. But nothing beats

riding a hog, and that's the God's honest truth. Hey—you want a ride, little man?"

"Me?" said Jake, swallowing hard.

"You. Yeah, you. Hop on. I'll take you for the ride of your life."

As quickly as he'd found it, Jake lost his nerve. "Yeah, thanks anyway, but I gotta get home."

"You sure, pal? Ain't every day you get to ride with Big Bob."

"No, thanks a lot, but I really gotta go."

"Suit yourself, then. And you, Little Bro—later." And with that, he rode off, swerving ahead of a slow-moving sedan before he revved his motor and let the bike fly, pulling up into a wheelie before roaring away.

Jake seemed to instantly regret his decision. "I would have taken a ride, but my mother will bust me if I'm not home soon."

Gary reassured him immediately. "I wouldn't ride with Big Bob if you paid me. Takes way too many chances. He's wiped out more times than anyone can count."

Then Kwame beat me to the punch, asking Gary what I'd been wondering myself. "Hey, man, how on earth do you know a guy like that?"

"Friend of my brother's."

"Damn. Your brother's in a motorcycle gang?"

"No," said Gary in a tight voice. "Luke used to ride with a couple of Pagans, work on their bikes, but he'd never have joined. Let's get going. I got a tune-up waiting at home."

As we walked on, I figured that Luke was the dead brother. The few times Gary had talked about Luke, he'd talked about him in the past tense and in a way that invited no questions. I also figured that Gary came by his tough reputation by association. If his brother had hung out with motorcycle gangs, then he must have been tough. And if he was tough, his little brother had to be tough too. Teachers, parents, kids, everyone expected it of him. It seemed unfair that people would judge Gary by the actions of his brother, but that's how it was, and I guess he was just used to it.

Jake soon used Gary's tough reputation to his advantage. Jake and I were both used to name-calling. I'd been called mostly string bean, stretch, and Long Tall Lucy. Oh, and of course the Jolly Green Giant. It could have been worse. Jake had been called everything under the sun: shrimp, midget, squirt, runt, sprout, half-pint, shorty, stumpy, and every one of Snow White's seven dwarves by name. But nobody, and I do mean nobody, threw any of those names his way if Gary was in earshot.

But one time after school in the parking lot of Wayside Deli, Chaz called Jake "runt" while Gary was around. He didn't really mean it in a nasty way. Since the fight in the woods, Jake had been hanging around some with Chaz and Mark, and and they called him "runt" kind of affectionately, even though it was still sort of mean. At least I thought so. But anyway, Chaz had somehow just bought a pack of Marlboros and asked Jake if he wanted a cigarette, saying, "Hey, runt, want a butt?" I've never seen anyone move so fast. Quick as a viper, Gary had Chaz up against a wall, his arm twisted behind his back, and said, "What did you just call him?" in a voice that scared me. Jake had to call Gary off, saying Chaz didn't mean anything by it, but I could tell he was thrilled. It was like he finally had his very own junkyard dog he could set on anyone. It gave him a swagger I'd never seen in him before. I didn't really like it.

Something else I didn't like was the way he started talking about things as though they didn't matter to him. Like the whole thing with Mean Joe Greene. Jake didn't talk to the guys about how much he'd loved that kitten. Not that I'd expected him to go on and on about how he'd cried and all. What he did tell them was that Otis busted him in the graveyard in the middle of the night while he was there to bury *my* kitten, like it was a big fat favor to me and wasn't in fact his idea. Then he told them he'd talked his way out of it and Otis felt so bad, he let Jake go and even buried the kitten for him, like Otis was some big sucker. As a whole, the story was true to a point, but told in a way that made him sound cool, made him sound like he didn't care. This wasn't the Jake I knew, but since his friendship with Gary, he was working on becoming a tougher version of himself.

I blamed his friendship with Gary for something else too: Jake was spending less and less time with me. Okay, it's not like he cut me out of his life completely. I mean, I still did stuff with him, but then Gary would come around and I'd be left behind. I spent whole stretches of the weekends alone while the two of them rode Gary's dirt bike, hung out with Chaz and Mark in the tree house, and generally bummed around together.

On Sundays, though, Jake sometimes still came looking for me if he wanted to walk to the farmers' market. Once or twice he'd been able to talk to Malinda before her father stepped in and stopped it. They hadn't really exchanged much more than "Nice day, huh?" or "How about that thunder last night" or that sort of thing. Since she was Amish, he couldn't really ask her where she went to school, what TV shows she liked, who her favorite band was. She was schooled at home and had probably never even seen a TV or listened to the radio. Aside from their height, they had nothing in common, but that wasn't stopping Jake. He was going to get to know her if it was the last darn thing he did. It wasn't every day he got to meet a girl like Malinda.

He was also spending time alone doing who-knows-what, but Mom said it was a typical phase for soon-to-be-teenaged boys, and since she had read heavily on the subject of soon-to-be-teenagers, I figured I'd take her word for it. He'd sit in the tree by himself for hours, and if I asked him if he wanted company, usually he'd say "Yeah, sure" but then wouldn't say much else once I'd climbed on up there. Mom said this too was typical, and suggested that I find some other friends to hang around with until he got over himself. Preferably girlfriends.

Not that Mom didn't like me hanging around with boys. She loved Jake like he was her own and took quite a shine to Kwame. But—according to her books, I'm sure—she said she thought it would be good for me to cultivate a girlfriend or two. The problem was, there were no girls in The Heights who were close to my age—unless you counted Cheryl Egby, and I didn't.

So that left me searching for girlfriends at school, and I found one in an unlikely place: home economics. Okay—maybe it wasn't so unlikely. I mean, home ec was full of nothing *but* girls. But in the first couple weeks of class, we had no interaction. In fact, the first couple weeks of class were spent in complete embarrassment trying *not* to make eye contact with each other as prim Miss Anderson, in her tidy, handmade clothing, spoke meaningfully to us about the beauty of "feminine hygiene and our monthly cycle" and "where babies come from." We'd all had a much briefer version of this in sixth grade. But now some girls were actually menstruating and acting wiser than thou, like they were members of some kind of secret club. Those of us who weren't yet having our period felt both left out and relieved.

Mercifully, there was only so much she could say on the subject, so after two weeks, the cooking began—or rather, the preparation for cooking began. The first part of learning how to cook was all about weights and measures and was about as dry as the flour we had to sift for practice. Some girls had obviously done a lot of baking-with-Mom. I was not one of them. Not that Mom didn't bake—at Christmas she baked up a storm. The rest of the year she just plain didn't have the time. Finally, after many pop quizzes on the proper abbreviation for teaspoon versus tablespoon and other dumb things, we were deemed ready to bake.

The home ec room held half a dozen kitchen stations, and we were divvied up into groups of four to begin work on our first assignment: buttermilk biscuits. My group had one unlikely experienced baker—Barb Roache, a short, scrappy, frizzy-haired girl who wore Levi's and T-shirts daily. Then there was Joanne DiMotta, who cracked her gum and had obviously combed peroxide through her hair all summer, and Charlene Puckett, who was almost my height and wore her short Afro in two pigtails that puffed up on top of her head like Mickey Mouse ears.

We set to work on those biscuits together, but soon, as it became clear that Barb knew what she was doing and the rest of us didn't, we just looked busy while she did all the work. So, as Barb baked, Charlene and Joanne and I spent our time washing dishes and talking. Joanne, it turns out, was as dumb as a post. Pretty, but dumb. Charlene, on the other hand, was smart and funny as all heck, and was someone I could potentially swap clothing with. It was a match made in heaven. Or home ec. Which is not the same thing at all.

"You're not going out?" asked Joanne in wonder.

"For cheerleading? Hell, no," said Charlene.

"Why not? It's the best way to meet boys," said Joanne.

"I know plenty of boys," I said.

"I know who you hang out with," said Joanne. "Everybody does. I mean *cute* boys."

She was not only an idiot, but she was rude to boot.

"I think Gary Geary's kinda cute," Barb piped up as she rolled out biscuit dough with a wooden pin.

"Oh my God, you do *not*," gasped Joanne. "I mean, the guy's a hood."

"He is not," I said defensively. "You just don't know him."

"And I don't care to. So if you're not going out for cheerleading, what *are* you gonna do? *Not* field hockey," said Joanne with distaste.

"I play field hockey," said Barb, grasping the rolling pin and taking a hard look at Joanne's noggin.

"Well, good for you. I wasn't asking you. I was asking Charlene."

Of course she wasn't asking *me*. A five-foot-ten cheerleader wasn't within the limits of her imagination, or, truthfully, mine. But Charlene, at five-eight, was an outside possibility.

"I think cheerleading is stupid," said Charlene.

"You do *not*."

"I just said I did. I mean, what's so great about bouncing around with pom-poms and hollering little rhymes while the guys play basketball?"

"It's more than that. I mean, you gotta be able to do cartwheels and jumps and formations and stuff."

"Goody for you."

"You're just saying you don't like it 'cause you don't think you'll make it," challenged Joanne.

"No. I'm saying I don't like it 'cause I don't. And you know what? I hope you make the squad. 'Cause I'm gonna *love* having you cheer for me when I make the basketball team."

"Cheerleaders don't cheer for girls' sports. Only for the boys."

"As of this year they do. New school rule. You don't believe me, ask Miss Anderson."

In addition to being the home ec teacher, Miss Anderson coached the cheerleaders, which made me like her even less. It was a double whammy against her, in my book.

"Well, I *will*. See what *you* know." And with that, Joanne flounced across the room to consult with Miss Anderson.

"She's a twit," said Barb amiably.

"Ain't *that* the truth." Charlene turned to me. "And how 'bout you?"

"I'm not a twit," I said defensively.

Charlene and Barb laughed.

"I know you're not a twit. I'm asking you about basketball."

"What about it?"

"You gonna play?"

"Mr. Bartell asked me to, but I think it's kinda boring."

"It's not boring. It's a blast. I play with my cousins all the time."

"Well, I'll think about it," I said without meaning it.

"If I was your height, I wouldn't need to give it any thought. Come on. Play. It'll be fun."

"If you're on a team, you get to skip gym," said Barb, trying to sweeten the deal.

"I know."

"And in the winter, when it's lousy outside, they do square dancing in gym class," she said.

"How do you know?" I asked suspiciously.

"My sister's in ninth grade. She told me it's really dorky. I might even try out for basketball myself to get out of that."

I'd done square dancing in Brownies when Mom had signed me up for a troop. I'd hated them both.

"Okay, okay. I'll talk to Bartell," I said.

"Oop. Here comes Joanne."

"Do cheerleaders really have to cheer for the girls too?" I asked.

"Look at that face," said Charlene, "and you tell me."

Joanne looked like she'd been sucking on lemons, her face was so sour. It was so positively perfect that Barb and Charlene and I just had to laugh.

Chapter 11
Picture Postcards

Coach Bartell was thrilled. While he didn't quite guarantee me a spot on the team without a tryout, he did say, "You're just what this team needs!" When I told him I wasn't exactly athletic, he kept saying, "You can't teach tall, Lucy, you can't teach tall!" Which I guess meant that it didn't really matter how athletic I was. If I couldn't actually learn the game, he was going to stick me under the basket with my arms up in the air, hoping that my looming presence would at least slow the other team down. Tryouts weren't for another few weeks, though, and until then he suggested I at least try to work on dribbling a ball without looking at it and shooting baskets in my spare time. I had no intention of doing either of these things, but then I remembered that if I didn't make the team, I'd have to square dance. So I figured as tryouts came near, I'd maybe ask Charlene if she'd help me, since this was really her idea anyhow.

It was now October, and the trees were changing color so fast every day looked different. I remember when I was in kindergarten, gathering the most colorful fall leaves—red maple, orange oak, golden birch—and bringing them home to Mom. She'd iron them between two sheets of waxed paper and we'd hang them in my bedroom window, where light would shine through them like stained glass. It was a little-kid thing to do, but sometimes still, I picked up the most perfect leaves and hung on to them for a while, pressing them between the pages of my heavy textbooks until they finally lost their color and crumbled to dust.

We were in the library, our American history class, doing research for reports we'd been assigned. Each of us had been given a different Revolutionary War figure to ensure we'd all do our own research and not crib off of anyone else. I'd been assigned Benedict Arnold, Kwame had John Adams, and Gary had been saddled with General Lafayette. Kwame and I were helping Gary as much as we possibly could, given the fact that Mr. Haley was hovering around checking up on all of us as we pored through encyclopedias and biographies. At this moment, though, we were safe to whisper. He'd just come by our table and, satisfied that we weren't goofing off, moved on to pester someone else.

"Kwame," I whispered, "go see if Joanne DiMotta is done with the *Encyclopedia Britannica* yet."

"Why don't you go?"

"She's got volume A. John Adams? You need the same one too."

"I'm busy."

"Come on. She hates me."

"She's not too fond of me either."

"Yeah, but Charlene and Barb make fun of her for cheer-leading." Of course, Joanne had made the cheerleading squad and was working hard on being insufferable.

"So what's that got to do with you?"

"I don't stick up for her."

109

"Why not?"

"Because she's a pill. Would you just go ask her for the book, please?"

"Okay, okay." Kwame hauled himself to his feet like it was some huge effort and slogged across the library to the table where Joanne sat with Becky York, who was a figure skater, and Kathie Chow, another cheerleader, who I swear wore a different perfect outfit every darn day.

I looked at Gary, who was slowly working his way through the *World Book* encyclopedia entry on General Lafayette, running his finger under each line of print as he silently mouthed the words. He'd told me that letters got all jumbled up whenever he tried to read. It was painful to watch. All of a sudden, he stopped, completely stymied by a word he'd never seen before. I tried to look over his shoulder to see what word he was stuck on but couldn't quite see past him. Just as I was craning to get a better view, he turned his head to ask for help and we were absolutely face to face. Once again, looking into his blue, blue eyes, I found myself unable to breathe.

"Lucy?"

"Yeah?"

"I don't know this word."

"Oh. Lemme see."

He pointed at the mystery word, and I was able to break away from his gaze.

"Marquis," I said, my breath returning to normal.

"What's that?"

"Some kind of royalty in France."

"Like a prince or something?"

"Not quite like a prince. More like a nobleman."

"So Lafayette was rich?"

"Yeah. He was rich."

"Why would someone like that come all the way across the ocean and fight in the army?"

"What do you mean?"

"Well, when my oldest brother Danny got drafted back in sixty-nine, I'd never seen my dad so pissed off. He went on and on about how all the guys who owned the fancy foreign cars he fixed got their sons into the National Guard, but because we weren't rich, his son was gonna have to go to Vietnam."

I figured I wasn't going to have a better chance to find out this part of Gary's family tragedy, so I just barged right in. "Did he?"

Gary's voice became hard, bitter. "Yeah. He went. Flipped out after six months in country and went AWOL on R&R in Saigon. Took the MPs thirteen weeks to find him. Now he's doing time in Leavenworth for desertion."

I wasn't sure what some of that jargon meant, but I got enough of it to figure out that Danny wasn't the Air Force brother: he was the brother who was in prison. I didn't know what to say, so I fidgeted with my books and, as I did, a blood-red maple leaf spilled out. Gary picked it up.

"What's this?"

"Oh, it's just a maple leaf. It's kinda dumb but I used to collect fall leaves when I was a kid."

"It's not dumb. It's real pretty. You are too."

I absolutely had no clue of how to answer him. At that very moment, though, Kwame bailed me out, dropping the heavy encyclopedia on the table right in front of me.

"There you go. *Encyclopedia Britannica.* Volume A."

"Thanks," I said, busily opening the book and flipping through it, my blushing face buried in the pages.

"And you're right. Joanne DiMotta is a pill."

Out of the corner of my eye, I saw Gary tuck the maple leaf between the pages of his own American history textbook. For the life of me, I could not figure him out. How could someone so tough be so sweet sometimes?

On Friday, the day the American history reports were due, I came to my locker between classes to find Gary waiting for me, a couple of rumpled pages of loose-leaf paper rolled in his hand. Since the day in the library when he'd said I was pretty, I'd steered clear of him, not knowing how to talk to him anymore. But now here he was, waiting, and I could hardly look him in the face without feeling my own grow hot and flushed.

"So, um, Lucy—I was wondering," he began, holding the tube of lined paper out to me, "if you could maybe look this over? Check my spelling? It's my paper on Lafayette."

I figured this was something I could do without eye contact, so I nodded and accepted the pages. In the roar of the hallway, I unrolled them and began to read. Word after word was hideously misspelled, his sentences running on or ending before they'd even begun. I looked at it, completely confused. I didn't know where to start.

"That bad, huh?"

"Well, it's just . . . I mean . . . if I had more time with it, but it's due in an hour and I've got biology and—"

Gary reached out and took the paper back from me. "It doesn't matter," he said defiantly. "Haley's gonna flunk me

112

no matter what I do." He turned and walked away from me, and as he did, I saw him wad the pages and toss them to the hallway floor, crushing them underfoot as he gained distance from me, certain of his fate. I wished there was something I could do to save him, but other than completely rewriting his paper during biology class, there was nothing for me to do but to let him fail.

The picture postcards were coming almost every day now as Dad made his way west, taking the scenic route. Driving Interstate 40 from Oklahoma, he was detouring north and south, visiting such places as Santa Fe, White Sands, and El Malpais in New Mexico. On the postcard of petroglyphs from Chaco Canyon, he'd said he'd crossed the continental divide, which made him feel very far away even though he was writing me all the time. Today's postcard was from Mesa Verde in Colorado. I knew from my Spanish class that meant "green table," but the picture on the front was of a small cavelike house made of reddish stone stuck way up high on a rocky canyon wall. It was called a pueblo dwelling, and the little description on the postcard said it was made by ancient people called the Anasazi who had mysteriously disappeared one day. Not unlike Dad.

But Dad said he was making this trip to check out all the places he was going to take me and Mom once we moved west with him. Whenever that was. Mom was still saying "the jury's out" on our joining him, which meant she was waiting to see if he stayed put in Pasadena. Now that I was hearing from him often, though, I missed him more than when I'd heard from him only once a week, which didn't make a lot of sense. But I guess it's just that with all his stories of the places he'd seen, I could clearly picture him in his car, his left elbow leaning out the window getting tanned as the wonders of the west rolled by, playing like a movie through his windshield. And I wanted to be there to see it with him. That's all.

He wrote that from Mesa Verde, he was driving on to Canyon de Chelly in the Navajo Nation and then to the Grand Canyon. From there he'd go through Las Vegas straight on to Pasadena and his new job, where he'd be working at the Jet Propulsion Laboratory. Dad said he'd been wanting a job there since forever, but first he would have to go through a trial period, which meant they were kind of testing him to see if he'd work out. I couldn't figure out why they felt like they needed to do that—Dad's the smartest person I know. But Mom said they do that to everyone they hire, and everyone there is as smart as anyone can possibly be. After all, they're a bunch of rocket scientists, right? So I suppose it's fair.

"How long is Dad's trial period?" I asked.

"A year," said Mom. She was wrapping a gift we'd bought Grandy for his seventy-seventh birthday, which we were celebrating with him on Sunday.

"A *year!*" It was forever.

"Yes, a year. We'll know definitely by the end of next September if they're going to keep him on."

"And then what?"

"And then we'll see."

I looked at her as she unspooled ribbon and began to twist it around the colorfully wrapped box. I saw that she wasn't wearing her wedding and engagement rings. She always took them off to wash the dishes, but the breakfast dishes were long done and the rings were still in the saucer on the windowsill. I couldn't really say if they'd been there for hours or for days. Until now, I hadn't noticed their absence.

"Finger, please," she requested.

I put my index finger on the crisscrossed ribbon on top of the gift to pin it down while Mom tied the knot. She looped the bow, tied it off, and then dragged the scissors' edge across the ribbon ends, curling them into ringlets. I couldn't let the moment pass without asking.

"Mom? Do you not want us to go live with Dad?"

She stopped what she was doing and looked at me. "Is that what you think?" she asked gently.

"I don't know. I guess."

"Oh, honey, that's not it at all. It's just . . ." She trailed off, searching for the words. "I know you think I'm mad at your father and I'm punishing him for leaving. Which I am and I'm not."

This was not exactly what I was thinking, but I figured I'd better keep my mouth shut and let her go on.

"I know your father has been wanting to do this, and I know that if it works out it will make him very happy. But he's made us very unhappy and, well, I know that if we're going to move west, I'm going to have to forgive him for that, but I'm just not quite ready to do it yet. You understand?"

I nodded, still keeping my lip zipped.

"And then there's the whole issue of packing up and moving when this job isn't a sure thing and me quitting my job and you changing schools and . . . it's just too much. Way too much."

She looked at me finally. It was the most I'd ever heard her say on the subject and I guess I looked like a deer caught in the headlights, because she immediately lightened up.

"I wasn't going to tell you this—we were going to surprise you—but your dad's coming for Thanksgiving."

"He is?"

"He is. He told me in his last letter. He misses you something awful."

"Wow!"

"You excited?"

"Yeah!"

"Good. Now, it's a beautiful day. Why don't you run on outside? See if you can find Jake. I need to clean the house today if we're going up for Grandy's birthday tomorrow."

"Okay. Bye, Mom," I said, giving her a quick hug that I know surprised her. I hadn't been very huggy in the past couple years since I'd shot up so much taller than she was, and it was an awkward hug, but I could tell that it pleased her. Sometimes it didn't take much to make her happy. I'd have to remember that.

I swung by Jake's house to find Mrs. Little and Frank out front gardening, each wearing one of her big straw gardening hats. I was surprised to see him, and it must have shown, because he said in his dopey, friendly way, "Hello there, Lucy. Ever seen a man in a hat like that?"

"Um, no, I mean, sure, I mean—is Jake home?"

"He is not," said Mrs. Little in a tight voice. "He's gone off with that . . . Gary person."

"Now, Dotty," said Frank, cajoling.

"Frank," she said irritably, "that kid is a disaster. You mark my words."

"Do you know where they went?" I almost hated to ask.

"A tree house somewhere. I'm sure it's a disaster too," she

116

said, taking out her frustrations on the hedge she was trimming.

"Okay, thanks. See you later." I moved along as fast as I could to put some distance between me and Mrs. Little's hedge trimmers.

As I came into the woods, I heard the whine of Gary's dirt bike. At least he'd been smart enough not to ride it by Mrs. Little's to pick up Jake. I was sure of that, or Mrs. Little absolutely would not have let Jake go. I figured both he and Jake were riding together, but as I came up on the tree house, I saw long legs dangling down. Definitely not Jake.

"Hey, Gary."

"Hey."

Like I said, I'd been shy around him since he'd said I was pretty, so except for the thing with his paper on Lafayette, I hadn't really spoken to him all week. Right now, though, he didn't seem much like he wanted to talk to me either because after we'd said hello, he didn't say anything else. He just sat there, swinging his feet, following the sound of the unseen dirt bike with his gaze.

"Is Jake around?" I asked, trying to get some conversation going.

"He's on the bike."

"Alone?"

"Yeah, alone."

And, once again, nothing. I thought maybe I'd done something to piss Gary off, but couldn't imagine what.

"Okay, well, could you tell him I was looking for him?"

Just then, the dirt bike made a horrible sound, the engine revving like a chain saw gone wild, and then there was a crunching noise and nothing else. Gary jumped down from the tree and ran toward the sound so fast, I was left behind in my surprise. After the split second it took me to recover, I ran after him.

"Jake!" I hollered.

"Over here!"

Gary was still ahead of me, obscuring my view. Then he started laughing.

"Jake?" I ran up, winded, to find Jake flat on his back, a scrape across his forehead beginning to ooze blood as he slapped the ground, roaring with laughter, the bike half buried in the leaves. "What's so funny?" I demanded.

"Oh, man," Gary said, "you got clotheslined, didn't you?"

"I got clotheslined *good*."

"What's *that* mean?" I asked.

"See that branch?" said Jake, pointing to a small horizontal tree branch at about chest level.

"Yeah?" I said.

"Well, I didn't!"

He and Gary started laughing again. I didn't see what was so funny. Jake could have really hurt himself getting knocked off the dirt bike like that. He had risen and was dusting crushed leaves from his clothing as Gary went over the dirt bike, looking for damage.

"You're bleeding."

Jake wiped his forehead. "Aw. It's nothing."

"You're gonna have a big bruise too. Your mother's gonna flip."

"Screw my mother. She's a witch."

Between Frank being around weekends and Jake getting

grounded a lot, I knew Jake wasn't thrilled with his mom, but he was being really nasty. I started to walk away.

"Hey, Lucy!"

I stopped and turned, looking at the two of them looking back at me in the now quiet woods.

"You won't tell her I was riding, will you?"

I couldn't believe he felt a need to ask me that. We'd sworn to each other before and he knew I'd never rat on him. I didn't have to answer. I just shook my head, turned, and kept on walking, toward Mr. Lukens' barn.

"Give 'em another week or so and they'll be ready," said Mr. Lukens. Callie was curled up on his lap as her kittens pounced on each other, playing in the loose hay. "They're mostly done with nursing now and they're eating some milk mush."

Callie looked exhausted and thin. She looked like she could use some milk mush herself.

"You decide which kitty you want yet?"

"No. I'm still not sure I really want one at all."

"I know that little guy dyin' made you sad, but these here are some fine kittens. Gonna be beautiful cats."

"They've got a beautiful mama," I said, knowing it would please him, and it did.

"Aw, she's the best cat ever, she is," he said, stroking her soft fur as Callie purred away. "Hey, Lucy, do you know what that sound is I keep hearing off in the woods on the weekends? Sounds like some motorbike to me."

I know Jake had asked me not to tell his mother, but he hadn't said anything about Mr. Lukens, and since it was his land they were riding on, I figured he had a right to know—but not necessarily everything.

"Yeah, it's some boys riding a dirt bike."

"You know these boys?"

"Sort of."

"Well, I can't never seem to catch up to them. I'd appreciate it if you'd tell 'em they can't be riding that thing in my woods. One of 'em hurts himself bad and his folks could sue me, take my farm, everything."

"If I see them, I will."

"Atta girl," he said, rising, Callie nestled in his arms. "I'm gonna take Callie inside and feed her. Only time of day she gets any peace. You stay as long as you want and play with those kitties. I just know one of 'em's gonna grab your heart."

It was Sunday morning, and Mom and I were heading up to Lancaster County, Grandy's gift and card sitting in the backseat of the car. We'd soon driven out of the range of the Wilmington rock station and I'd been spinning the radio dial for a while trying to tune in my Philadelphia station, getting static, news, and old-fogy music, and apparently driving Mom crazy.

"Lucy. Enough," she said, reaching over and punching the off button. "I can't even hear myself think."

As we drove on for a while in what Mom always called "blessed silence," I flipped through the stack of postcards Dad had sent to me. I knew he wrote to Grandy and Gamma and Aunt Jenny too, but I was sure they didn't get as much mail as I got from Dad and I knew they'd want to see the pictures of all the places he'd been.

"Lucy," said Mom in her serious voice as we rolled through Pennsylvania. "I need to talk with you about something."

This was never a great way to start a conversation. I stiffened up, wondering just what I'd done wrong.

"It's about Jake," she went on. "Dotty's very concerned about this boy, Gary, that he's been spending so much time with. Do you know him?"

"Yeah," I said, relieved we weren't talking about me, but wondering what I was going to be asked to tell.

"Dotty says he seems, well, a little rough."

"He's nice. Really. He's in my history class and he eats lunch with us sometimes."

"I know his family owns Geary's Garage on Naaman's Road. The one with all the motorcycles. Your Dad used to take the car there for tune-ups."

"Uh-huh."

"Jake doesn't ride motorcycles with Gary, does he?"

Okay. Here was my problem—Jake and Gary rode a dirt bike, which was kind of like a motorcycle but not exactly, so . . .

"No, Mom, they don't ride the motorcycles."

"Good. Dotty was terrified. One of the Geary boys died a few years ago in a motorcycle accident."

Just like that, there it was—the rest of Gary's family tragedy. Luke had died riding one of his motorcycles.

"Promise me you'll never get on the back of a motorcycle, Lucy. They're dangerous things."

"Yeah, Mom. I promise."

We drove on, the fall trees bursting with color along the side of the road, a blur of red, orange, and gold.

Grandy sat in his favorite armchair, wearing the slate blue cardigan Mom and I had given him and a shiny foil party hat shaped like a crown. He was flipping through the picture postcards I'd brought while we talked about Dad's travels. As I knelt beside him, I could see that Grandy did not look well.

"Canyon de Chelly?" he said, pronouncing it wrong. "Never heard of it."

"They say it like 'Canyon de Shay,' " I corrected.

"Then how come they spell it C-h-e-l-l-y?"

"It's a Spanish word, but I don't know what it means."

"Sounds kinda French to me. You say it's in the Navajo Nation?"

"Right smack in the middle."

"You'd think it would have a Navajo name then. But whatever they want to call it, it sure is beautiful. Looks a lot like the Grand Canyon," he said, comparing postcards of the two.

"Dad said the same thing, except the Grand Canyon's bigger."

"That's why they call it grand, right, Lucy Goosey?"

"Right."

Only Dad and Grandy called me Lucy Goosey, and it made me miss Dad even more. Grandy was a tall man too, though over the years he'd shrunk some, as arthritis had bent his back. But he was still head and shoulders above Gamma, who was tiny.

Grandy had always loved to measure me, recording my growth since I was old enough to stand with pencil lines drawn and dated inside the kitchen doorway. Dad's growth lines were directly across the doorway from mine, and I prayed I'd never catch up to them.

"You know, Lucy, I'm seventy-seven today," he said. "I'm as old as the gosh-darned century."

Grandy had been born in 1900 and carried a silver dollar from that year in his pocket, worn smooth from his fingertips. He'd pull it out and roll it over and over in his hand when he was thinking hard about something. Like now.

"In my lifetime, I've seen a lot of things. I started out riding in horse-drawn buggies and have seen a man land on the moon. But I've never seen the Grand Canyon, and I always wanted to," he said wistfully.

"You can still go see it, Grandy," I said encouragingly. "It's not going anywhere."

"Oh, I know that, Lucy. But neither am I. I'm not going anywhere."

"What are you going on about, old man?" said Gamma, coming in from the kitchen, wiping her hands on her apron. She always called Grandy "old man," even though he wasn't that much older than she was.

"The Grand Canyon."

"What about the Grand Canyon?"

"I'd like to see it, is all."

"Well, no one's stopping you. Go on. Jump in the car and head on west like Richard. Send us a nice picture postcard every now and then."

"Now, Mother," said Aunt Jenny, trying to slow down Gamma's coming tirade.

"Don't 'Now, Mother' me, Jenny," Gamma began, but she actually stopped herself there in the interest of keeping

Grandy's birthday happy. Gamma, in her own words, took a "dim view" of what Dad had done, leaving us the way he did. "I got a pot roast and potatoes getting dry in the oven. Who's hungry?"

Even though dry pot roast and potatoes didn't sound very appetizing, we knew better. Gamma was a terrific cook, and we all headed for the table like we hadn't had a good meal in years.

It wasn't too late as we pulled into the driveway, but the days were getting shorter and darkness had fallen. As our headlights swept across the house and landed on the garage door, I got out to lift it and saw Jake leave his house and trot toward ours. He must have been sitting in his front window, waiting for us to come home. I rolled the garage door open and Mom pulled the car in as Jake reached our front yard.

"Hey, Lucy."

"Hey," I said, looking at the bump on his forehead. "Nice bruise."

"It's a good one."

"What did you tell your mother?"

"I fell out of a tree. So, where ya been?"

"Lancaster County. It was Grandy's birthday," I said, feeling a little guilty. I'd promised to take him the next time we went.

Mom had turned off the car and was closing the garage door. She looked out to see Jake and me in the yard. "Hey, Jake. Come on in for some ice cream." Without waiting for an answer, Mom shut herself in, entering the house through the garage. I started heading for the front door, but Jake stopped me.

"Wait. I gotta tell you something."

I waited, thinking maybe he was finally apologizing for being so scarce over the past few weeks but no, it was something else.

"I talked to her," he said excitedly.

"Who?"

"Malinda," he said, looking at me like I was hopeless.

"Really? How?"

"Her dad wasn't there today. It was just her and her mom and sisters."

"So?"

"So, what?"

Now it was my turn to look at him like he was hopeless. "So what did you talk about, Jake?"

"Oh, stuff."

"Stuff?" He was being as vague as he'd been when he'd talked with Otis. It was maddening.

"You know. What her life is like. What mine's like. What it's like to be . . . you know . . ."

Jake never called himself a dwarf, so I never called him that either.

"Short?" I said.

"Yeah," he said. "And she said what Madge told us is true—that there's a bunch of people like her and me up where she lives in Lancaster County and that it's not weird at all."

If you ask me, it was weird enough just being Amish, and anything beyond that wouldn't really matter, but I didn't want to burst Jake's bubble, he was so happy that there was a place where he felt like he sort of belonged.

"Must take them forever to drive their horse and buggy down from Lancaster County every Sunday."

"They don't anymore. She said they catch a ride with a Mennonite farmer who's got a truck. You know, I'd like to go up there and visit her sometime."

"Did she ask you?"

"Kind of."

"Well, what did she say?"

"Just that it was pretty up there and I'd like it."

"That's not an invitation."

"I don't care," he said stubbornly. "I'm going."

"Oh yeah? How?"

"I'll figure it out, okay?"

"Fine."

We both stewed for a second, unsure of how our conversation had become kind of an argument. But it had. Then I had to push it further.

"By the way, Mr. Lukens doesn't want you and Gary riding dirt bikes in his woods anymore."

"What did you tell him?" Jake asked angrily.

"Nothing. He already knew. He could hear the bike. But I didn't tell him it was you."

"I don't believe you."

Now it was my turn to be angry. "Well, I don't believe you either. You've been such a jerk lately."

"*I've* been a jerk?"

"Yeah, you have."

"Well, you've been a jerk too."

"I have not," I said, wounded by his accusation.

"You have," he insisted.

"How?" I was puzzled. He'd been the one acting strange lately, not me.

"You just don't understand anything anymore. You just don't," he said with finality.

Mom turned on the front light and then opened the door, sticking her head outside.

"You two coming in for ice cream, or you gonna stand out front yakking all night?"

"I'm sorry, Mrs. Small, I gotta go."

"You sure? I've got chocolate syrup. We can make sundaes."

"Thanks anyway. I've still got a ton of homework to do."

"Okay, honey. Next time."

Jake turned and walked away, leaving the pool of light in front of our house and entering the darkness of the yard, heading for his own lighted home.

"Is everything all right, Lucy?" Mom asked, concerned. "I thought I heard the two of you arguing."

"Nah. We're fine, Mom, honest," I lied. But nothing was fine between me and Jake, and I didn't have a clue as to why.

Chapter 12
Tricks and Treats

Now that I was in junior high, I was officially too old to trick-or-treat. Even in the past few years, when Jake and I would go out on Halloween, I'd often hear, "You're mighty big to be trick-or-treating," or even worse, "Isn't it sweet of you to take your little brother trick-or-treating?" Though I'd miss all the chocolate, I definitely couldn't face another year of that. Mom said she'd buy extra treats and I could have what we didn't hand out, but it wasn't the same. There was something magical about wandering the streets in the dark, filling our bags from door to door. Eating leftovers wouldn't be nearly as fun, and Mom definitely got a little wistful about not sewing a costume for me. But it was time for trick-or-treat to come to an end.

Anyway, Jake was now far too cool to have anything to do with Halloween, so I had no partner in crime. Of course, we'd seen each other since we'd squabbled after Grandy's birthday, but we hadn't hung around any. He'd been moodier than usual, spending more time alone than he spent with Gary, Chaz, and Mark. Apparently Mrs. Little was worried, because I heard her talking to Mom one afternoon about his general "malaise," which was a word I actually had to look up. It basically meant Jake seemed uneasy and weird. Mom agreed with her that Jake was not his usual self and gave Mrs. Little a book on teenagers to read. Then they started to talk about Frank.

Okay, yes—I was eavesdropping again. I know I've said before that it's something I do only when I really need to hear something or I can't help myself, but that's not true. I do it all the time. So arrest me or something.

"The Bahamas?" said Mom.

"He goes every Thanksgiving for a week. Fishing."

"Well, what do you think?"

"I don't know. I just don't know. He offered to pay for us both, but I don't really feel right about that. Plus, Jake would have to take a few extra days off of school and, truth be told, he's not doing all that well."

"He's always done well in school."

"Well, not recently. I think it's that new kid he's been hanging around with. Gary."

"Lucy said he's a nice boy."

"Oh, he's plenty polite to me, but let's face it, given the family business, and the fact that he's been held back twice, he's destined to be a grease monkey. Jake needs to be around people who challenge him. Like Lucy."

"They had a tiff the other day."

"Did they?"

"Oh, not that I'm worried about it. They're just at the age where they really need to have peers of their own sex. It's all in that book."

"I'll be sure to read it. So, you think we should go?"

"If I had the choice between an all-expenses-paid vacation to the Bahamas or cooking a turkey, I know what I'd choose. But if you're uncomfortable about accepting the trip as a gift . . ."

"You know, honestly, I don't think I would be except for the fact that Jake is so surly toward Frank."

"Still?"

"Still. And I wish he'd get over it. I think Frank is going to pop the question."

"Really?"

"I get that feeling."

"Oh, Dotty, that's wonderful."

As they went on and on in excited voices about why Mrs. Little suspected and what she was going to say if Frank proposed and all that, I had to stop listening. It was too big a secret and I couldn't breathe a word of it to Jake. I just couldn't. In the past, I'd told him everything, but I knew this was not for me to tell. It was a terrible secret to keep, but it would have been worse for me to blab. If it was true—if Frank was really going to ask Mrs. Little to marry him— guaranteed it was going to flip Jake out. For once in my life, I absolutely had to keep it to myself.

The kittens were ready. Mom had said again and again that if I wanted one, I could have one. I was still feeling tender about Mean Joe Greene, but Mom said the only way to be sure if I wanted a kitten or not was to go and look at the litter one last time before Mr. Lukens gave them all away. So the Saturday before Halloween, I headed off through the woods toward the farm. I knew I wasn't going to run into Jake in the woods. From my backyard I could see him wedged in the branches of the graveyard maple, a solitary, sulking little lump. I thought about asking him to join me, but since he hadn't asked me to do anything with him recently—not even to go to the farmers' market—I decided to just go alone. If I was coming home with a kitten, I'd choose it myself, thank you. Besides, if he came with me he'd want to name it and I figured since he'd named Mean Joe Greene, it was my darn turn.

So as I headed off through the woods, I sure didn't expect to come up on Gary, sitting in the tree house all by his lonesome. His dirt bike was nowhere to be seen.

"Hey, Lucy."

"Hey, Gary."

"What you doing?"

"I'm just gonna go to the farm. Look at the kittens."

"There's kittens there?" he said, sounding interested.

"Remember I had that little kitty who died?"

"Oh yeah."

"I got him from the farm."

"You gonna get yourself another one?"

"I dunno. Maybe." I still wasn't really sure.

I stood there for a minute like a dope, looking up at him in the tree house, before I realized he was waiting for an invitation.

"You wanna come with me? Help me pick it out?"

"If you want." Gary sounded bored, almost.

"I mean, sure. If *you* want," I said, flustered.

"Yeah. Sure."

He leapt down from the tree house, landing like a panther at my feet. I hadn't realized how graceful he was, but as we walked through the woods toward the farm, he moved like an athlete, sure of his every step. It made me feel even more awkward than usual, especially when I whacked myself across the face with a small tree branch that slipped from my grasp as I held it out of the way.

"Ow!" I said, covering my eye.

"You okay?"

"I think I got something in my eye."

"Lemme see."

Gary tilted my head back, moved my hands aside, and gently pulled up my eyelid with his fingertips.

"Ah. There it is."

He blew softly into my eye, dislodging whatever was stuck in there, then lightly brushed it off my cheekbone.

"Better?" he asked, looking at me with those arresting eyes.

"Uh-huh," I gasped, unable to say anything else.

"Good," he said, striding on. "Let's go get you a kitten."

All I could do was follow.

Three kittens were left: a calico with yellow eyes, a tiger stripe with green eyes, and a solid black with orange eyes.

"That little calico is the spitting image of Callie here," said Mr. Lukens, Callie draped across his shoulders like a mink stole.

"She's a really pretty kitty," I said, watching Gary as he played with the black kitten, making it leap and box at his wiggling fingers.

"And that stripy one reminds me of your own little guy."

"Me too."

"I don't know about you, but since Rex passed I can't even think of having a dog looks anything like him."

"Yeah. I don't think I want the tiger stripe."

"How about this one?" asked Gary, snagging the jet-black kitten by the scruff of his neck and holding him up for us to see.

"Oh, that little guy," sighed Mr. Lukens. "I'm having a heck of a time giving him away. Don't anybody want a black cat, especially coming up on Halloween."

"I do. I want him," I blurted out.

"You sure?" Gary asked, handing the kitten to me. "I was only asking. I don't mean for you to take him if you think you want the other one."

"Someone else will take that pretty calico home. But no one wants this little guy, so he's coming home with me."

"Atta girl. Folks are too darned superstitious about black cats if you ask me. I've always thought they were good luck myself."

"How's that?" asked Gary.

"Well, one night some years back I was driving home late, coming up on the railroad tracks. I was sleepy, but I swear to Pete there wasn't any signal. All of a sudden, this black cat goes streaking across the road right in front of my truck. I slam on the brakes so I don't run him over, and damned if right then, a train don't come barreling down them tracks. I'd have been smashed to smithereens for sure."

"For real?" said Gary in amazement.

"It's the God's honest truth. That black cat saved my life."

I held the black kitten in front of my face, looking him straight in his pumpkin orange eyes. And then I knew for sure.

"Lucky," I said. "You're my kitten, and that's your name."

"A black cat named Lucky," said Gary, smiling. "That's way cool."

Way cool. Gary Geary actually said that something I did was way cool. It was dumb, but I felt like I'd won a grand prize or something. Lucky purred away, looking up at me with his jack-o'-lantern eyes, his tickly tail swishing back and forth against my bare arm. Lucky was the way coolest cat ever.

Monday was Halloween, and most of the teachers actually wore costumes to school. Miss Anderson, of course, wore her old college cheerleading outfit from Penn State; Señorita De Leon came dressed as some old Mexican artist named Frida Kahlo, in a long embroidered dress and tons of silver jewelry; Coach Bartell came dressed as Dr. J., in a Philadelphia 76ers basketball jersey and a huge Afro; and the principal, Mr. Offenbach, came as the Grim Reaper. One of the few teachers who didn't dress up was Mr. Haley. He was in a foul mood. His car had been egged, his windows soaped, his trees TP'ed, and his mailbox cherry bombed on Mischief Night.

Mischief Night was the night before Halloween, and it was the one night when kids got to wreak some havoc on neighbors who'd been nasty or teachers who'd been mean. It was kind of a bad-boy thing to do, and Chaz and Mark were the usual suspects in our neighborhood. Mrs. Egby caught them red-handed one year, tossing rolls of toilet paper up into her trees.

You'd think, because he was so strict and unpopular, that Mr. Haley would expect a yearly slime of eggs and toilet paper and soap, and I guess that part of it didn't surprise him. But word was that he felt this year's mischief makers had gone a step too far by blowing up his mailbox with a cherry bomb. He was determined to get to the bottom of it and punish those responsible.

Throughout the day, names were announced over the school's PA system—boys called into the principal's office for questioning. Even though they'd be sitting across the desk from the Grim Reaper, I couldn't imagine that anyone would actually rat himself out. But if the kids who did it had been stupid enough to brag, someone who heard something might be persuaded to squeal. As the day went on, the predictable jocks and delinquents were called—including Billy Stratton, Gary, Chaz, and Mark. All of a sudden, while I was in English class, a name I hadn't expected to hear came squawking from the tinny speaker:

"Jake Little, please report to the principal's office. Jake Little, please report to the principal's office."

I looked over at Kwame and he looked at me, raising his eyebrows and shrugging his shoulders in a sort of "who knows?" gesture.

In the break between classes, we didn't see him in the hallway. Nor did we see Gary as we sat through seething Mr. Haley's history class. Before the class ended, Mr. Haley felt a need to embarrass himself further by staring us down and saying: "I assume you all have heard by now of the damage done to my car and property. I know many of you may find this amusing, but I don't. My son, who was so excited about Halloween, is now too frightened to leave the house. However you all may feel about me, I'd like to think that sort of venom doesn't extend to a five-year-old boy who has been looking forward to going trick-or-treating for weeks. Now it's been ruined for him. If any of you know anything about the boys who did this, I hope you'll do the right thing and see that they are punished."

We were all squirming in our seats, trying hard not to look at him. And then, mercifully, the bell rang. I've never seen a classroom empty so fast. As we fled the room, I looked back at Mr. Haley, who was just sitting at his desk, his head in his hands. And I saw him not as the mean American history teacher, but as a dad who was worried about his little boy. I actually felt bad for him.

Jake wasn't in the lunchroom. Gary wasn't either. I had no idea of what to think, except, maybe, the worst.

"You think they did it?" said Kwame, chewing thoughtfully on his meat loaf sandwich.

"I don't want to, but they're both still in the principal's office. It's so unfair. Everybody always thinks if something bad happens, Gary did it."

"It's not like he's so innocent, Lucy."

"What do you mean?"

"Well, he does have a juvenile record."

"He *what*?"

"Has a juvenile record."

"For what?"

"I don't know."

"I don't believe you."

"Okay, fine, don't."

"So why isn't he in reform school if he's got a record?"

"They don't always send kids to reform school. You gotta

do something really bad or get caught over and over doing a lot of little stuff to get sent there."

"So whatever he did wasn't so bad?"

"Probably just shoplifting or something."

"That's pretty bad."

"Everyone does it."

"I don't."

"Come on. You've never even boosted a piece of bubble gum?"

"Never."

"Wow. How come?"

" 'Cause it's *stealing*, Kwame. And, even worse, you might get caught."

"Yeah. Getting caught is definitely worse," he said sarcastically.

"That's not what I meant. Since you have to steal to get caught, stealing's worse."

"I shoplifted once on a dare. I knew it was stealing and I felt really bad but mostly I was scared to death of getting caught."

"So I guess you all heard."

We looked up to see Charlene standing there, holding her lunch bag and milk. She sat down with us, looking relieved to not have to be the one to tell us the bad news.

"Heard what?" I asked.

"About Gary and Jake getting caught."

"What? No!"

She looked dismayed. "Oh. Well, you were talking about getting caught, and I just figured . . . well, sorry." She dug into her lunch bag, pulling out her sandwich and unwrapping it. "Yeah. They got caught and they got suspended. Both of them."

"Whoa, whoa, whoa, back up," said Kwame, who lived for the details. "What exactly did you hear?"

"Well, I was in the office," she said between bites. "I had my teeth cleaned this morning so I was coming in late with a note from the dentist. Anyway, Jake and Gary were sitting outside the principal's office. Then the door opened and their mothers came out with the principal, still talking. What I heard was that there were a few kids who went over to TP Haley's trees and all, but that the cherry bomb was Jake and Gary's fault, so they're out for a full week. Oooo, their mothers were *pissed off*."

I could clearly picture Mrs. Little and Mrs. Geary, an unlikely pair, unified in their anger. I would have hated to have been either Jake or Gary, sitting outside the principal's office, waiting for that door to open. But something about it all bugged me.

"What kids?"

"Huh?"

"You said a few kids went to TP Mr. Haley's house. Who else?"

"I don't know. I only know what I heard."

"Jake and Gary would never tell on themselves. Someone else must have gotten snagged and ratted on them."

"What does it matter? They still blew up Mr. Haley's mailbox, whether someone ratted on them or not," said Charlene, voicing the obvious.

"You don't rat on someone for doing something you're doing yourself," said Kwame. "It's a rotten thing to do."

"No, blowing up a mailbox and scaring a little kid is a rotten thing to do," I said, my voice rising.

"Who are you mad at, Lucy? Jake and Gary or the guys who told on them?"

"Well, everyone."

"Can't be mad at the whole wide world," said Kwame.

"Look, Jake knows better and Gary . . . well, Gary *should* know better. He's been in trouble all year, then he goes and does something dumb like this. And it's mean. It's just mean."

"It's mean to rat on someone too," said Kwame defensively.

"Maybe whoever ratted got offered something in return." I tried to puzzle it all out.

"Like what?" asked Charlene.

"No suspension."

"I'd love to get suspended. Stay home, watch old movies on TV, sew," said Kwame wistfully.

"Sew?" said Charlene, looking at Kwame, astonished. "You sew?"

"Yeah, I do." Kwame looked like he was bracing himself for ridicule.

"How do you know how to sew?"

"My granddad is a tailor."

"You any good?"

"I'm *real* good," he said with pride.

"Well, when we get to sewing in home ec, I know who's making my darn dress," said Charlene, not missing a beat. "Deal?"

"Deal," said Kwame, smiling.

I was still thinking, though, about Jake and Gary and

what the next week would bring. Gary, I figured, would be working in the garage. But Jake? I hated to think of what a week's suspension with a furious Mrs. Little would be like. I felt bad for him, but I was also mad at him. It was terrible, blowing up the mailbox and scaring that little kid, and it's something he never would have done—before Gary, that is. If I had to be honest, that's who I was really mad at. I was furious at Gary for getting Jake in trouble. And as much as I hated to admit it, and as mad as he'd made me for what he'd done, I still couldn't help liking him. But I could steer clear of Gary, or at least I could try.

Chapter 13
Basketball Jones

Pick and roll, give and go, posting up, boxing out: I had no idea what any of these things meant, but I was learning fast. Basketball tryouts had begun. Coach Bartell was disappointed that I hadn't been working on my skills, but he had the perfect solution to the problem. Billy Stratton had broken his leg and was out for the season. Some friends had built a huge dirt ramp and he'd wiped out badly jumping his bicycle over a row of metal trash cans. Coach was furious that Billy had been so stupid—with Billy went his hopes for a championship season. So, as penance, Billy Stratton had to work with me one-on-one at the far end of the gym while Coach Bartell worked with the rest of the girls at the other end. Billy Stratton was to be my own personal guide through the wonderful world of basketball. Part of me was thrilled. The other part? Well, I was clumsy enough without an audience. With everyone watching, and Billy hovering over me, I became Lucy Small, Super Klutz.

"One, two, three, and shoot," said Billy, demonstrating the layup as best he could with cast and crutches.

I took three steps and banged the ball off the backboard. Sheepishly, I chased it down and came back with it. "Sorry."

Billy sighed and rolled his eyes. "See that box up there right above the basket?"

"Yeah."

"Put the ball in the box, it'll drop in the hoop."

"Okay." I stood on the foul line, holding the ball, and began to move toward the basket.

"Whoa! Stop!" said Billy, exasperated. "You gotta dribble the ball. Remember? If you don't, it's a travel."

"Oh. Yeah. Sorry."

I began to bounce the ball by my side, trying hard not to focus on it. I'd already been told and told and told I wasn't supposed to look at it while I dribbled, but as soon as I took my eyes off it, I bounced it right off my foot and had to go chase it down, all the way to the other end of the gym.

"How's it going, Lucy?" asked Coach Bartell, picking up the ball and tossing it to me.

"Um. Okay, I guess."

"Good. Good. Okay, girls. In and out of the cones. Fast, fast, fast. Let's go," he hollered, blowing his whistle. Three lines of girls dribbled, weaving between orange cones set up in a row. I was relieved to see some of them were as bad as I was, but happy to see that Charlene was the best ball handler of them all. When I trotted back to the far end of the floor, I saw Debbie Flack standing there, pom-poms in hand, talking with Billy as the other cheerleaders ran for the water fountain, hopping and jumping like a bunch of deranged bunnies.

"It's not like I was dying to do this," he said. "Coach made me."

"Well . . . just quit."

"I can't. He stuck his neck out for me."

"Oh, please. Haley got what he wanted. I just figured since you weren't playing, we'd have more time now."

"For what? We broke up, remember?"

"We did *not*. We had an argument, is all." Debbie looked up, saw me, and gave me her big sunny smile. "Well, hi there, Lucy. I guess you're gonna be Caesar Rodney's very own Wilt the Stilt, huh?"

"Knock it off, Debbie," said Billy, irritated.

"Ooooh. Sorry. Didn't know you cared. See you after practice, Coach Stratton," she said, flouncing off, swinging her pom-poms by her side.

Not only did that little conversation confuse me, but it put Billy in a crankier mood than before. For the rest of practice, he worked me relentlessly. By four-thirty, when it was over, I felt as if I'd been bounced off the floor like the ball itself. Though now that I was getting a grasp on the game, I kind of got Charlene's attraction to it and I found I liked it too—just a little. But my tiny new affection was nothing like her love for it. She said she had a basketball jones. I hoped, in time, I too would feel that way.

"Lucy? Is that you?" Mom called out from the kitchen when I got home from practice. Whatever she was cooking smelled wonderful. I followed my nose to find her basting a roast chicken. I could have eaten the whole darn thing, I was so hungry.

"Oh, sweetie, you look like something the cat dragged in. Why didn't you shower after practice?"

"The showers at school are gross," I said, picking up Lucky, who was winding between my ankles. Truth was, I wasn't too comfortable getting naked in front of the other girls. They all looked somehow smaller without their clothes, and it made me feel even more huge. "Anyway, Stephanie was in a hurry and we had to go." Kwame's sister, Stephanie, had given us a ride home in her cherry red VW Bug. Kwame had stayed after school to do some extra-credit project in wood shop. He turned out to be really good at woodworking and was making his mother an inlaid jewelry box for Christmas.

"Well, dinner's going to be ready in about half an hour. Why don't you run over and give Jake his homework and then hurry home and clean up, okay?"

"Okay." I set Lucky down and went to get Jake's assignments from my notebook. Since his suspension, I had to bring his homework home for him every night and get what he'd done that day to hand in the next morning. Given the rotten mood both he and his mom were in, it wasn't the happiest task in the world.

I headed across our yard in the early November dark, wet leaves slippery underfoot. Mom and I tried to keep up with the raking and we weren't doing so well. But as I crossed the next-door neighbor's yard and the yard after that, I noticed we weren't the only ones behind on fall cleanup. Then I entered Mrs. Little's yard. It was, of course, clean as a clock.

I rang the bell and was surprised to find Frank answering the door.

"Well, hello there, Lucy," he said cheerily. "I bet you're here to see Jake."

I sure as heck wasn't there to see him or Mrs. Little, but I smiled and nodded and said yes anyway. The man meant well.

"He's back in his room. His mother went to the store and left me in charge. Tell you the truth, though, I think they both just needed a break. The two of them are at each other's throats, and it was the least I could do to help keep the peace."

For the first time, Frank wasn't goofy or dorky. He looked like any guy concerned about the people he cared for, and really, he just seemed kind of sad.

"Go on, Lucy. He'll be real glad to see you."

As I headed for Jake's room, I heard the radio playing at a volume so loud it was distorting the sound. Tentatively, I knocked. I heard feet stomping toward the door, and then it flung wide open.

"What?" demanded a furious Jake. Then he saw it was me and softened a bit. "Oh. Lucy. Sorry. Come on in."

The room was a total mess. Clearly, Jake was working overtime to piss his mother off. There were piles of dirty clothes on the floor, half-full glasses of soda on the desk and bedside table, wadded paper surrounding the trash can, and books open everywhere. His bed looked like it hadn't been made in days. I figured Mrs. Little had wisely decided not to go to war with Jake over this, but I was wrong.

"Wow. Who died in here?"

"Thanks. That's what Mom says too, every damn day," he said angrily, turning down the radio so we didn't have to shout.

"She actually comes in here?" I was amazed.

"Oh, sure. She tails me around from room to room harping at me, then, when I try to get away from her, follows me right on in here and keeps on bitching. I swear to God, I'm losing my mind."

"Well, at least she's at work all day."

"No, she's not. She's been home."

"How?"

"She took vacation time. And you better believe I'm hearing all about that too."

"So I guess you're not going—" I stopped myself. I couldn't say anything about what I'd heard about the Bahamas or the proposal. Especially now.

"Not going where?"

"Nothing."

"What, Lucy? What do you know?"

"Nothing."

"You're lying."

"I'm not."

"You are. You're a lousy liar and you're lying. I can tell."

I weighed the consequences. If I told him everything, he would go through the roof. But if I just told him about the trip . . .

"I heard your mom talking to my mom and she said Frank had invited the two of you to go with him to the Bahamas over Thanksgiving."

"You're kidding."

"I'm not."

"He invited us both? Why would he do that? He hates me."

"He doesn't hate you. He likes you."

"Come on. He's just nice to me so she'll like him more. I bet he wants to marry her or something gross like that."

The radio played a song by Fleetwood Mac about going your own way. I'd really liked the song, but now it was ruined for me. Now I'd always associate it with this night and this moment, when I didn't tell my best friend the whole truth.

"I don't know anything about that. All I know is that I heard your mom say he'd invited you both to the Bahamas."

"Great. Well, there's another thing for her to blame me for. Ruining her romantic vacation with Frank."

I know it was chicken of me, but I couldn't take anymore. I wanted out of that room and away from Jake's anger. "Listen, Jake, I gotta go. Mom's fixing dinner and told me to hurry back."

"Fine. Go on."

"Here's your homework." I handed him the stack of assignments.

"Screw it," he said, dropping it on the floor.

"You got yesterday's for me to hand in?"

"Nope."

"If you don't keep up—"

"I don't care. I just don't."

"You gotta care."

"Do I? Why?"

"Because this week will be over and you'll be back in school and everything will go back to normal."

"Normal?" he said, laughing humorlessly. "What's that?"

There was no talking to him tonight, that was certain. "I'll see you tomorrow, Jake, okay?"

"You know what? Don't bother."

He turned his back on me and cranked up the volume on the radio. I left the room to the fuzzed-out sound of ABBA singing "Fernando," which, luckily, I hated anyway. Otherwise, another perfectly good song would have been ruined for me forever.

The next morning, as I was getting stuff out of my locker for my first class, Joanne DiMotta came up to me with Kathie

147

Chow in tow. They were actually being pleasant. I wasn't sure I should trust them.

"So, Lucy, you're really playing basketball, huh?" said Joanne brightly.

"I really am."

"That's so great! And I see Billy Stratton's spending a lot of time with you at practice."

"Yeah, well, he kind of has to."

"Oh no, I'm sure he likes doing it. Coaching and all."

"I don't think so."

"I bet he does, or he wouldn't do it. Hey, you know who Debbie Flack is?"

"Yeah. She went to my elementary."

"You know Billy used to go out with Debbie?"

"I kind of figured. They were talking yesterday."

"You heard them?"

"A little." I felt peppered by all her questions,

"Does he ever say anything about her?"

"About Debbie?"

"Duh. Yes, about Debbie," Kathie piped up, annoyed with me.

"Kathie! Be *nice,*" said Joanne, playfully swatting her.

I was starting to figure out where this was heading. I'm a little slow about these things.

"All we talk about is basketball."

"Well, if he *does* say anything about Debbie, you'd let us know, right?"

"Swear to God. We only talk basketball."

"Come on. I mean, Debbie still *really* likes him and all."

"Okay. Fine. Why not?" I figured I was safe—I'd never

have to report to them. Billy Stratton had nothing to say to me that wasn't basketball related.

"Great! Thanks," said Joanne with a big smile. "I knew I could count on you. Hey—how come you don't spend time with your friend anymore? That little guy?"

I knew when she called him "that little guy," it wasn't because she remembered his last name. "You mean Jake."

"Yeah. Him."

"Duh. He was *suspended,* Joanne," said Kathie, giving her a giggly little shove.

"Oh yeah. Duh. I forgot. Well, maybe he'll figure it out, you know? I mean, you were both hanging out with Gary Geary and Mark Morelli and all them, and those kind of guys get you nowhere and everybody has something to say about it. You know what I mean? I mean, if your friend wants to still hang out with those kind of guys who got him in trouble and all, let him. You're hanging out with much cooler people now. Right?"

The way Joanne babbled, I had a tough time following her, but she was saying I had been judged by the company I'd kept. Now that I *wasn't* spending time with Jake and Gary but *was* spending time with Billy, I wasn't social poison anymore. As rotten as Jake had been the night before, I still felt a need to defend him.

"I've known Jake since kindergarten."

"Oh. So you're really old friends and all."

"Yep."

"And you're still gonna hang out?"

"Yep."

"Well, whatever," she said dismissively. "See you in home ec!"

149

"See you."

Joanne and Kathie bounced down the hall, gossiping, their heads leaned toward each other, their ponytails swinging behind them. I closed my locker and headed off for Spanish class. As I turned the corner, I was amazed to see Gary, with Mr. Offenbach looming nearby. Since Gary had been suspended, the last place I figured I'd see him was in school, but there he was, emptying out his locker. Mr. Offenbach was deep in conversation with Mrs. Myers, one of the English teachers, so I figured it was safe to go up to Gary and see what was happening.

"Gary?" I said tentatively.

"Hey."

"What are you doing here? What's going on?"

"I'm cleaning out my locker."

"Why?"

"Why do you think?"

"They didn't kick you out, did they?" It was terrible to have to say it, but it was the only possible reason he'd be there, clearing his locker.

"Yeah, they did," said Gary, glumly shoving notebooks and sneakers and papers and things into an army surplus duffel bag.

"They can't do that."

"They can do anything they want."

"But you gotta go to school. I mean, don't you?"

" 'Til I'm sixteen."

"So what are you gonna do?"

"I'm being sent to trade school."

I looked at him. Trade school was for boys who were failing everything, who were disciplinary problems, and who were destined to become mechanics and plumbers and welders. And I hate to say, I'd always looked down on trade school boys, but here I was, having to think twice about that. For the first time, I actually knew this trade school boy, and even though I'd been mad at him for what he'd done, I liked him more than I cared to admit.

"Just as well," he went on. "I can't pass a spelling test, but I can fix just about anything."

"I could help you with spelling."

"Look, Lucy, it doesn't matter. Regular school is for people like you. People who are smart."

"You're not stupid."

"Then how come I can't read?"

At that moment, Mr. Offenbach looked up from his conversation with Mrs. Myers and glared at me.

"Lucy. Isn't there somewhere else you're supposed to be?"

I was surprised he knew my name. I thought he only knew the names of kids who got in trouble a lot and got sent to his office. "Yes, Mr. Offenbach."

"Well. Move along then."

I looked at Gary, who shrugged and went back to cleaning out his locker.

"See you, Gary."

"Yeah. See you."

He'd said the words, but he didn't mean them. I was sure I wouldn't see Gary Geary ever again.

Chapter 14
Team Spirit

"Yep. You were right. Frank wants us to go to the Bahamas with him," said Jake while we were waiting for the bus, his first day back to school in a week. Sleet was falling, and we wore hats, scarves, and mittens, stomping our chilly feet to keep them warm.

"See? What did I say? You going?"

"Nope. I told you. Mom blew her vacation days playing prison warden."

"How pissed is she?"

"Really pissed. She made a huge deal of telling me all about it and how it was gonna be a big surprise for me and all the cool stuff we were gonna do and how I ruined everything with a stupid cherry bomb. Thanksgiving's gonna be a joy."

"Maybe you guys can come to dinner at Aunt Jenny's with us."

"No such luck. Since we can't go to the Bahamas, Frank decided to stay in town too, so Mom's in a total frenzy planning a big turkey dinner for him and his folks and my grandparents. It'll be hell on earth, guaranteed."

"It might not be so bad."

Jake looked at me like I was nuts.

"Okay, you're right. It's gonna be awful."

We stood there, hunched over in the icy wetness, trying to keep our books dry. Of course neither of us carried an umbrella. That would have been dorky, and we were both working hard to rise above dorkiness. Between my basketball and Jake's famous bad behavior, we were sort of succeeding in our own different ways.

For example, in the hallway, after his suspension was handed out, I'd seen some of the jocks high-fiving Jake. Neither he nor Gary had named any names in the Mischief Night fiasco and these guys obviously thought that was cool.

I, on the other hand, had been invited one day at lunch to sit with girls who, before my association with Billy Stratton, hadn't given me the time of day. It made me uncomfortable, though, their sudden friendliness. That plus the fact that I would have had to eat a salami sandwich in front of girls who always looked perfectly put together and probably never ate stinky food. So I had begged off, hoping they wouldn't think I was stuck-up.

Jake shook the rain out of his hair and stomped his frozen feet. "So when's your dad coming?"

"Day before Thanksgiving, but he's got to go back on Sunday."

"That's not very long."

"Well, he's got this new job and all and . . ." I trailed off. Honestly, I couldn't understand myself why he wouldn't stay any longer, and it bummed me out.

"Is he coming for Christmas?"

"I don't know yet. I hope so."

"I wish I could spend Thanksgiving with my dad," said Jake wistfully.

"Why don't you?"

"Like Mom's gonna send me down to see him after screwing up her trip to the Bahamas? Not a chance."

"Couldn't your dad ask?"

"He could. But he won't."

"How do you know?"

"Because he hasn't. That's why. Look, Dad's got a whole other family and all their crap to deal with. The last thing he wants is me there too."

"That's not true."

"Yes, it is."

"You don't know that."

"Yes, I do."

"How? Have you ever asked?"

"Lucy, just leave it alone."

"Oh, come on, Jake. Have you ever asked your dad if you can go see him whenever you want?"

"No," he snapped. "Have you ever asked *your* dad?"

It was like Jake had socked me in the gut. It was a mean thing to say, but he was right on target. I never had asked Dad if I could go see him. Whenever we'd talked, Dad always said things like "Wish you were here" or "It's so beautiful out here, I can't wait for you to see it," but had never made any plans to bring me to him, to let me see what he was seeing, go where he was going. And I guess I figured he must like it that way. He liked his adventures, and he liked telling me about them, but I'm not so sure he'd have liked having me along for the ride.

We stood there, the two of us, in wet and sullen silence until finally the school bus came.

Billy Stratton wouldn't let up. We were standing down close to the basket. He was right behind me with his arms up in the air. My back was to him, the ball was in my hands, and with Billy up against me like that, I had not a clue what to do. I was more than a little flustered.

"Come on," he said, exasperated. "Where's the basket?"

"Behind us."

"Can you shoot with your back to the basket?" he asked wearily. "No, you can't. Face up to it!"

I took a big step away from him, established my pivot foot, spun around on it, faced the basket, and shot the ball, miraculously banking it right off the backboard and into the hoop.

"Okay. Atta girl. That's how it's done," he said, tossing the ball from hand to hand. He was hopping around now without his crutches, even though he wasn't supposed to. "Do it again."

I did, with less spectacular results, running down the loose ball before it got to midcourt.

"Again."

I faced up, shot, and sent the ball careening off the rim and into the bleachers. It was going to be a long afternoon.

Coach had made first cuts and narrowed the tryouts down to twenty girls. He'd ultimately carry a team of twelve, and even though Charlene said I was a shoo-in, I had my doubts. I was improving, no question, but was I improving fast enough? It was surprising to me, but I was starting to like the game and the idea of being part of a team. But just because I was the tallest girl in school, was I going to make the squad? And, tall as I was, I thought how embarrassed I'd feel if I *didn't* make it. Charlene was the real shoo-in, though, and oddly enough Barb too, who though barely five foot three was speedy as all heck. Final cuts were to be posted right before Thanksgiving break, two days away, and my skills left a lot to be desired.

"One more time," said Billy, "and this time, make it count!"

I backed up to Billy, then, in perfect rhythm, bounce, catch, step, pivot, shoot. The ball went zinging across the court again. I was hopeless.

"Okay, Lucy, let's just stop. Go get a drink of water." He was clearly disappointed in me.

"No. I can do this. I can," I said insistently.

"You don't want a break before scrimmage?"

"This is driving me crazy."

"You too, huh?" said Billy, smiling. "Okay. Let's do it 'til we drop."

And we went at it hard, until Coach blew the whistle for scrimmage.

After practice, I waited for Mom out front of school, my sweaty gym clothes steaming under my winter coat, my legs bare. Everyone else had showered, changed, and been picked up already, and for the first time, I regretted not showering— I was goose-bumpy and chilled. After school hours, though, once you were out of the building, you couldn't get back in. The doors locked behind you and, unless someone let you in, you were stuck outside. I went up to the front doors to see if anyone was inside the entryway and saw Billy in conversation with Debbie. He seemed uncomfortable, looking down and away from her, but she was all agitated, like there was some big point she had to make. I didn't want to knock and interrupt, but I was freezing to death. I stood there, hopping from foot to foot, trying to stay warm and debating what to do. Billy looked up, saw me, and opened the door. The expression on his face was one of sheer relief.

"Lucy. You must be freezing."

"Yeah. Sorry. My mom's late."

"My goodness, Lucy," said Debbie, sounding way too concerned. "You're gonna catch your death of cold."

"No. I'm fine. Sorry. I'm usually picked up by now."

"Oh well," said Debbie with forced cheeriness. "No such luck today, huh?"

A car horn blew. We all looked down the front steps of the school to see a buttery yellow Cadillac with a well-dressed woman at the wheel.

"Ooop. There's my mom. Gotta go. See you both later," said Debbie breezily.

We both watched her skip lightly down the steps, her pom-poms swinging, and as she opened the passenger door, she turned and waved at us before getting in the car. Out of politeness, I gave a little wave back, but Billy didn't. He looked miserable.

I didn't say anything. I didn't know what to say to Billy Stratton off the basketball court, and anyway, it seemed like he didn't really want to talk. But I was wrong.

"You ever like somebody a lot, then just all of a sudden stop liking them?" he said, looking out the safety glass at the heavy gray sky.

I thought about Gary. I'd tried to stop liking him all of a sudden, but when I saw him cleaning out his locker, I realized it hadn't really worked. He'd looked so forlorn and vulnerable. "Sort of, yeah, I guess."

"I mean, I like Debbie and all, but not like that anymore, you know?"

"Uh-huh."

"And, really, I like someone else now and she just doesn't get it."

"Have you told her?" I asked tentatively.

"The girl I like?"

"No. Debbie."

For the first time since I'd met him, Billy seemed unsure of himself.

"Not yet. I haven't even told the girl I like that I like her."

"How come?"

"Can't tell if she likes me," he said, turning away from the window finally and looking me right in the eyes.

My heart started beating really fast. He couldn't be talking about me. Or could he? I couldn't hold his gaze, and as I looked away, I saw my mom pull up in our station wagon.

"There's my mom," I said, relieved. "See you at practice tomorrow!"

I dashed out the door and down the steps to the safety of the idling car.

"Hey, Lucy! Come here!"

It was the next day and I was in the lunchroom, making my way toward the table where Jake and Kwame and I always sat, when Joanne and Kathie flagged me down.

"Come sit with us!"

They were sitting with Becky York and Bebe Anders, a willowy blond ballerina who was dancing in *The Nutcracker* suite in Philadelphia at Christmastime.

I couldn't say no again without looking like a snob, so I came over to them, carrying my rumpled lunch bag. All of them had lunches that looked like they'd been packed by a professional. Their carrot and celery sticks were perfectly symmetrical, their tiny sandwiches had the crusts cut off, their fruit looked shiny and unreal. Their lunches also looked like they wouldn't fill a rabbit. I sat and unpacked my lunch—bologna and mustard on a kaiser roll, Fritos, Oreos, and an apple—trying to draw as little attention to it as possible, but Kathie zeroed right in on the cookies.

"Ooooh. Oreos."

"Um . . . yeah. You want one?"

Kathie looked sorely tempted.

"Uh-uh-uh, Kathie, you know what Miss Anderson said," scolded Joanne.

"Like one little cookie's gonna make me fat?"

"I'm just telling you for your own good."

"My ballet master makes us get on the scale every week at rehearsal," said Bebe, "and if we've gained even half a pound, he's, like, completely furious."

"Me too," said Becky. "When I switched over to skating pairs, my coach started weighing me every week. She said my partner shouldn't have to haul around a hog on the ice."

The girls all giggled. I felt like a blimp.

"But you're so tall, Lucy, you can carry more weight," said Bebe, trying, I think, to be kind.

All of a sudden, my lunch tasted like gravel. I set my sandwich down and took a swig of milk.

"So, Debbie says you and Billy were here late yesterday," said Joanne significantly. "Alone."

"Uh-huh." I finally realized why I'd been invited to join them for lunch, and it had nothing to do with a rise in my popularity.

"So, what? Did he say anything about her? She said they were talking, but then they had to stop because her mom came and all."

I didn't want to tell them what Billy had said to me—it had seemed like a private thing. But they were being nice, or as nice as they could be, so I decided to say enough just to be polite. "Well, we did talk some, but—"

"But *what?*" said Joanne impatiently.

"I don't know," I said, stalling.

"Come on. Debbie *really* needs to know. I mean, she doesn't want to be looking like a jerk, trying to get back together with him and all if he's not interested. Put yourself in her shoes."

Since I thought Debbie was a jerk anyway, I didn't see why I should keep her from looking like one. But then again, putting myself in her shoes, I could see how awful it would be to think she had a chance with Billy when clearly he'd moved on. So I gave in. "Yeah. Okay. He said he doesn't like her anymore."

"He *didn't!*" said Joanne.

"He did."

"That's it? That's all he said?"

"No."

"Well. Come *on,* Lucy. What else did he say?"

"He said he liked her but not like that anymore because now he liked someone else."

"Oh my God!" said Kathie. *"Who?"*

"He didn't say."

"I know who it is," said Becky, in a teasing, singsongy way.

"You do not," said Kathie.

"I do too. Who's he been spending all his time with? Who do we see him with every darn day?"

All eyes were on me, waiting, expectant. There was only one possible answer.

"Me?" I said, questioning it even as it came out of my mouth.

All eyes opened wide, then Becky and Joanne and Kathie erupted in gales of laughter. Bebe, however, didn't laugh. She just looked embarrassed too, like me.

"Oh my God!" said Becky. "You can't possibly think—well, I guess you do. I mean, *you?*"

"Well, you said—"

"No, Lucy, it's not you. It would never be you. It's gotta be Joanne who Billy likes. That's who he's been spending all his time with," said Kathie.

"Joanne?" I said, puzzled.

"You don't know? Billy's just with you every day because he has to be. It was his cherry bomb that your friends set off. Coach found out from some other guys that Billy had brought the cherry bomb and made Billy tell on Jake and Gary so he wouldn't get suspended and he could still play ball. When Billy broke his leg, Coach made him work with the girls' team as punishment. I can't believe you didn't know all that. I mean, don't your friends tell you *anything?*" said Kathie, happy as a clam to fill me in on all the details.

Joanne sat there looking smug. I'd been had. She didn't want me to report on what Billy said for Debbie's sake. She

161

wanted to know for herself. And Billy—after spending all that time with him on the basketball court, I had started to think he was a good guy. Now it turned out he was at fault for Jake being suspended and Gary getting kicked out. He had brought the cherry bomb they blew up and then he'd ratted on them. I felt sick, like I was going to throw up or, even worse, cry. I got up from the table, leaving my lunch behind.

"Lucy? Are you okay?" said Bebe, who was the only one of them who actually had anything like a soul.

"Oh, just let her go," said Joanne, who was done with me.

But I was already gone, stumbling down the aisles of lunchroom tables and heading for the hall, blinded by the tears I now could not stop. I ran straight into the bathroom, where Monica Tweed, the female version of Chaz and Mark, was standing in an open stall, smoking. She froze, ready to ditch her cigarette in the toilet, but then saw it was me and went right back to puffing away. I shut myself in the stall next to her and sobbed as quietly as I could, but the smoke made me cough and snort.

"Hey."

I looked up. Monica was standing on the toilet, peering over the stall, looking down at me.

"You okay?"

"Yeah."

"You sure?" Monica said with concern.

"Yeah. Thanks."

"Hey, you're that friend of Gary's, right?"

"Yeah. I guess."

"He really liked you, you know?"

"Did he?"

"Yeah. A lot. He said."

The bathroom door opened. Monica looked up and immediately ducked down.

"Oh, shit."

The toilet flushed.

"Monica Tweed, I saw you smoking. I want you out of there right this second."

It was Mrs. Myers, on cigarette patrol. Monica came out of the stall to face her captor.

"Who's in the other stall?"

"I don't know. She just came in."

"Mr. Offenbach's office. Now. Let's go."

As they exited the bathroom, I wiped my nose and my eyes and thought about what had just happened. In the eyes of most people, a girl like Joanne DiMotta was a dream: a pretty, peppy cheerleader. A girl like Monica, on the other hand, was a nightmare. But I wasn't most people, and I knew better.

I also finally knew for sure that Gary liked me as much as I liked him, and even though Joanne had just tricked me, knowing that took some of the sting away.

In no time at all, the gossip was all over school of how I'd thought Billy Stratton liked me. Joanne and Kathie made sure of that. Basketball practice was horrible that afternoon. I was so uncomfortable around Billy, I couldn't do a single thing right. All I really wanted to do was to hurl the ball at him and scream, but instead I spent the entire practice swallowing my anger and shame and tripping over myself. It was the very last practice before final cuts, and Coach watched me, shaking his head and making notes on his clipboard as I flailed away, sending the ball into the bleachers more often than I put it in the basket.

By the time I set off for school on Wednesday morning, even Jake knew about the Billy rumor, and he wasn't ever interested in knowing who liked who and who was dating who since it had never concerned him. No one had ever had a crush on Jake. Or me, for that matter. But I'd always kept up with the gossip of who liked who. Don't ask me why.

"You really thought he liked you?"

It was a crisp, cold day, and for the first time there was frost on the ground. Our feet crunched through it with a satisfying sound as we walked to the bus stop.

"No. I mean, they kind of made me think that, but I never thought it myself," I lied.

"How did they *make* you think that?"

"Oh, I don't know. You had to be there."

"Wish I had been. I'd have popped her one. That Joanne DiMotta is a cow."

Even though I knew he wouldn't have, it made me smile to imagine the scene.

"Hey," I said, "how come you never told me about Billy Stratton?"

"I don't know."

"I mean, he was there that night. It was his cherry bomb, right?"

"Yeah. He kind of put us up to it."

"How?"

"He dared us."

"That's *it*? He *dared* you?" I hadn't heard anything so stupid in my life.

164

"Yeah, okay, it was dumb and mean, and I do feel bad about scaring Haley's kid, but like you just said, you kinda had to be there."

"I'm glad I wasn't."

Jake sighed. "You just don't get it. I mean, there we were with all these jocks egging us on, and Haley was failing Gary again, and I was there with Gary, and it was us against them, so we did it."

"So why didn't you say anything about Billy and the other guys?"

" 'Cause you just don't *do* that, Lucy. You just don't rat."

"Billy did."

"Gary and I blew up the mailbox. Billy didn't."

"But you wouldn't have if you didn't have a cherry bomb."

"Look. Guys like Billy Stratton, no matter what, they're always gonna get a break. Didn't matter what Gary or I said, guys like him are never going to get in the same kind of trouble anyone else would. So why go on and on about it, you know? He's the captain of the basketball team, and we're . . . well, we're not."

"But Gary got kicked out."

"Gary was going to get kicked out sooner or later. He was failing everything."

"You still see him?"

"My mom said if I ever see Gary again, she'll send me to military school or something." Jake always said I was a lousy liar, but he was definitely acting cagey.

"Not even at the tree house?"

"Keep a secret?"

"Oh, please, Jake. I can't believe you're asking me." Sometimes he was just exasperating.

"I'm meeting him there Saturday. If the weather's okay, we're gonna ride his dirt bike."

"Mr. Lukens said—"

"Oh, jeez, Lucy, will you put a sock in it?" he barked. "We're not gonna ride in Lukens' woods, okay?"

"Okay. Fine," I said, all huffy.

We stood there in wounded silence for a second, waiting for the bus.

"Sorry," Jake said, so quietly I could hardly hear. "I've been in a really crappy mood lately, with Mom and all."

"Uh-huh."

"And, well, sorry I yelled at you."

I couldn't believe that Jake was apologizing. He was, for a moment, his old sweet self again.

"It's okay. I kinda snapped at you too."

"So, you gonna be all right at school today?"

"Yeah, I mean, at some point everyone's gotta stop talking about me, right?"

"I guess." Jake didn't sound very convincing.

"And then there's the long weekend and all," I said, hoping for the best.

"Hey—your dad's coming home today, right?"

"Yeah."

"That'll be cool."

"Yeah," I said casually. Inside, I was all wound up. I could hardly wait, but was also pretty nervous. Dad had been gone since January.

"Well, if anyone gives you any crap today, just do what my dad always told me to do."

"What's that?"

"Imagine them sitting on the john."

I snorted with laughter.

"Really. Pants down around their ankles. It helps."

"I'll do that," I said, still laughing. "Thanks."

In that moment, between Jake and me, it was just like old times.

Somehow I made it through school that day without having to imagine anyone on the john. Every time I walked through the halls, I felt like all eyes were on me, all whispering was about me, and all laughter was at me. Jake and Kwame stayed close by, though, so I was rarely alone. I thought home ec would be especially tough, but for some reason, Joanne DiMotta was strangely quiet. She never once teased me or gloated.

Finally, the end of the day arrived, and with it, the posting of the basketball team list. As everyone else burst from the school, free for a whole four days, Charlene and Barb and I headed back toward the gym to see if we'd made the team. There it was, The List, posted on Coach Bartell's office door. My heart started to race. I couldn't believe I cared so much, but I really wanted to make the team, to belong somewhere. A tight group of girls surrounded the list, some squealing with joy, others turning away in despair. Barb hopped up and down, trying to see over their heads.

"Lucy, come on, can't you see?" she said, bouncing like a jumping bean.

I was scared to look, but I forced myself. There was Charlene's name. "You made it, Charlene." I looked further. "You too, Barb." But as I scanned down to the bottom of the list, I didn't see my name. I looked again. Nothing. I felt my throat close up and my eyes fill with tears. My name was just not there.

Charlene and Barb were hugging each other, screaming, and jumping up and down when they noticed my face.

"You're not on the list?" asked Charlene.

"I don't see my name."

"Oh, come on, you gotta be there," said Barb. "Lemme see!" And like a little linebacker, she bulldozed her way through the crowd, getting right smack up to the list. She ran her finger down it, checking each name individually. Triumphantly, she stabbed her finger way down at the bottom of the list where I couldn't see. "There you are, Lucy. Right there!"

"Yay, Lucy! You made it! You made it!" hollered Charlene, grabbing me and giving me a squeeze.

I don't know how I'd missed it—my very own name—but I had, and it had totally devastated me. Now my tears turned to pure happiness. I had made the team! I jumped up and down with Charlene, hollering like a fool.

"Whoa! Check this out," said Barb, still hogging the list. "Up here at the top. It says Billy Stratton is going to be assistant coach."

All of a sudden, my joy was replaced by nausea; all of my team spirit was gone. Charlene noticed immediately.

"Hey. He's gonna be coaching *all* of us. Not just you. Don't worry about it. I swear you won't have to spend any time alone with him, okay?"

I nodded but still felt a little queasy.

"Hey! You wanna go get a Coke or something? Celebrate?"

"Nah. I gotta get home."

"Come on!" said Barb. "I've got a couple of bucks. We could go to the Charcoal Pit. They've got a jukebox in every booth."

"I can't. My dad's coming home today."

"He's been away?" asked Charlene.

"Yeah," I said, "for a while." I didn't want to go into any more detail, and Charlene somehow sensed it.

"Oh, well, some other time, okay?"

"Yeah. Absolutely."

As we turned to go, I almost ran smack into Billy Stratton. We both moved aside to get out of each other's way, Billy swinging on his crutches, and ended up right in front of each other. We moved aside again. Same thing. Barb giggled. It *was* pretty silly.

"Sorry," he said.

" 'S okay."

"Hey, Lucy, can I . . . I gotta tell you something."

"Um, yeah. Okay. We'll just go. Bye now," said Charlene, tugging Barb along with her and leaving me alone with Billy, right after she'd sworn I'd never be alone with him again.

At least Billy looked like he felt guilty. That made me feel better.

"So, um, I know you heard about the cherry bomb and all and, well, I'm sorry about that, but I told Coach about it and . . . well, he really didn't want me to get suspended."

I was honestly so surprised and relieved he didn't say anything about the whole Joanne nightmare that I almost forgot to be mad at him. But not quite. "So instead you lied and let Jake and Gary get suspended."

"Coach said they were probably just gonna get detention or something. But if you'd tell them I'm sorry—"

"Gary got kicked out. I don't see him anymore."

"Well, what about Jake?" Billy looked crestfallen.

"I don't think he'll forgive you. His Thanksgiving is screwed because of you."

"I feel bad."

"You should."

"You know what, though? One good thing happened. I ended up working with you. I mean, I was pissed that I broke my leg and couldn't play and all, but I really like this coaching thing. Guess you know I'll be working with the team all season."

"Yeah."

I crossed my arms and looked at him hard. After what I'd been through, I really didn't want to give him an inch, but it wasn't working. It's not so easy staying mad at someone who actually says he's sorry.

Billy could see my struggle, and he smiled. "Well, okay, then. I guess I'll see you at practice on Monday, huh?"

"I guess," I said, still trying to be stern.

"Oh. And by the way, I wouldn't go out with Joanne DiMotta if you paid me."

"What?"

"Can't stand her. She comes off like she's nice, but really she's just plain mean."

"But—" I was completely confused.

"I was hanging around her to spend time with Bebe Anders. That's who I really like. Bebe. And since you seem to be good at telling people what I say, feel free to spread that one around, okay? See you Monday, Lucy."

I stood there, my mouth wide open like a big dumb fish, as Billy spun around on his crutches and swung away from me. I tried to work it all out in my head, but it just kept circling around. Billy hung out with Joanne to get to Bebe, and was happy to have me spread the word for him, and Gary told Monica he liked me a lot, but never had the gumption to tell me himself. Boys made no sense. No sense at all. They were worse than a bunch of gossipy girls. I was sure I would never in my entire lifetime figure them out.

Chapter 15
Snow Beanie

"Daddy!"

"Hey, Lucy Goosey! How's my girl?"

Dad stood there smiling, arms spread wide like a big bird, and closed me into a hug right as I came in the door from school that day. I fit perfectly up against his chest without having to stoop. He about squeezed the ever-living life out of me.

"Dad. You're suffocating me."

"Aw, honey, I've missed you so much," he said, squeezing even harder and rocking me side to side. "You don't know how much."

"Me . . . too . . . can't . . . breathe."

"Okay, okay. Lemme look at you." He let go of his bear hug and held me at arm's length. "Oh my good Lord, you've grown."

"I have not!"

"You have."

"No! Please, no."

"Okay. Fine. You haven't grown. You've shrunk."

"Dad," I said, rolling my eyes.

"You've shrunk and now scientists all over the world want to study you. So tell me what else is new."

"I made the basketball team."

"You did!"

"Uh-huh. I'm the center."

"Well, then it's a terrible shame you've shrunk, isn't it?"

Dad gave me his crooked smile. For the first time, I took a good look at him. He looked the same, but different. His skin was tan, his dark brown hair was a bit more gray, and he'd lost the little potbelly he'd started to grow—the one Mom teased him about. But there was something else.

"You've got new glasses!"

"I do. You like?" he said, angling his head slightly from side to side so I could admire them. Dad had always worn heavy framed glasses that made him look, well, square. These were old-timey-looking wire rims and they actually kind of disappeared on his face. It was definitely an improvement.

"I like," I said. "What happened to your old ones?"

"Got smacked across the face with a chain working on an oil rig. Snapped those old glasses right in two but didn't even scratch my face. How 'bout that luck?"

"Wow. Hey, where's Mom?"

"Went to the store. She's making pumpkin pies for dinner tomorrow and forgot to buy the darn pumpkin."

Mom had been distracted lately. I think she too had been both excited and nervous to see Dad again. Right then, Lucky came zooming into the house on a romp, chasing absolutely nothing. He saw us, puffed up, walked sideways on tippy-toe, all fierce and growly, then dashed out of the house again.

"What the heck was that?" said Dad.

"Oh, that's Lucky. He's just doing his Zap Cat thing. He does that sometimes, but I don't know why."

"You have a kitten?" Dad asked, puzzled.

"Um . . . yeah." I hesitated, remembering Dad's allergies.

"Since when do you have a kitten?"

"Since Halloween."

"Huh. Well, I hope your mom's got some antihistamines then, 'cause I'm gonna be sneezing up a storm. Come on, honey, why don't you introduce me to the wild beast."

We headed off together in search of Lucky.

Dad sat on the sofa watching TV as Mom baked her pumpkin pies, the homey smell of cinnamon and nutmeg filling the house. I was lying on the floor, stuffed from dinner. Mom had made meat loaf, mashed potatoes, and butter beans, which doesn't sound very fancy, but it was our favorite meal. Dad was stuffed too.

"Lucy? Will you change the channel? There's a basketball game on."

"But *Charlie's Angels* is next," I said. Mom didn't much like *Charlie's Angels,* but she let me watch it if I'd done all my homework, and since there wasn't any school tomorrow, I figured I was in the clear.

"Well, now that you're on the basketball team, don't you think you should actually watch some basketball?"

"I guess." Sort of sulky, I hauled myself up off the floor to change the channel.

"Come on." He patted the sofa beside him. "Sit here with me."

I changed the channel, then schlumped over to the sofa and settled in next to Dad. He put his arm over my shoulders and drew me close to him. He smelled the way he'd always smelled, like the bay rum aftershave he wore, tobacco smoke, and the little dab of Brylcreem he put in his hair to keep it from falling into his eyes. The familiar smell of him immediately made me feel all woolly and cozy.

"Okay. Somebody needs to tell me when a half hour is up," said Mom, wiping her hands on a dish towel as she came into the den.

"Is the oven timer broken?" asked Dad, checking his wristwatch.

"Has been for months."

"Well, I'll fix it tomorrow. Come here, Joy." He patted the sofa on his other side.

"There's no room." Mom had been a little tentative around him since she'd gotten back from the grocery store.

"Sure there is. Scoot over, Lucy."

"Mmmph," I said, drowsily scooching over to make room for Mom.

"Oh, all right." Mom perched herself on the edge of the sofa next to Dad, setting her dish towel on the coffee table.

"A little closer," urged Dad, throwing his other arm around Mom.

"Richard—"

"Relax, Joy. I won't let your pies burn up."

Mom stiffly settled next to him, and there we were, the three of us on the couch, watching the 76ers play.

"What could be better?" said Dad contentedly. "Warm house, pies in the oven, snuggled up with my girls."

Just then, Lucky tore into the room, took a flying leap, claws outstretched, and landed smack-dab in the middle of Dad's lap.

"Yow!"

"Lucky!" said Mom, sitting up quickly and plucking the small cat from Dad's lap.

"It's okay, Joy. I guess he's just trying to tell me who's the man of the house, right, big fella?" Dad gently scratched Lucky between the ears as he curled onto Mom's lap, balling up like a little black sock.

"Richard—don't touch him or you're gonna be sneezing all night."

"Don't worry, honey. I found the antihistamines in the medicine chest. Lucky and me—we're gonna work it all out. Aren't we, boy?"

Lucky purred agreeably, closing his big orange eyes and giving in to the pleasure of being petted by Dad.

Aunt Jenny's Thanksgiving table was perfection itself. She had her best tablecloth down, the fine china out, the sterling silver, the linen napkins, the stemmed crystal glasses, and a centerpiece of dried flowers, gourds, and candlesticks. It made me nervous to think I was actually going to have to eat and drink with these delicate things. It made me even more nervous to think Beanie was anywhere near this table, but he was. In a moment of weakness, Aunt Jenny had invited Ira, Rebekah, and Beanie to join us for Thanksgiving since they had no family of their own nearby. Rebekah, however, remembering Labor Day, never let Beanie stray more than a foot away from her clutches. It was exhausting to watch her chase that child around while Ira, Dad, Uncle Pete, and Grandy watched football and Gamma, Aunt Jenny, and Mom fussed in the kitchen.

I was bored. I've always thought Thanksgiving was boring. I mean, after the Macy's Parade is over, it's all downhill. It's football, football, and more football, way too much food, and other than me, no kids. Except for Beanie, who didn't really count. But as I looked outside, it had started to snow hard, which definitely improved the situation. It was piling up already, and I looked forward to a weekend full of snow-fort building and snowball fights with Jake and Dad.

"Oh, look," said Rebekah, who had snagged Beanie just as he was about to tug on the tablecloth. "Look at the pretty snow!"

Beanie stopped struggling in his mother's grip and looked out the window at the wonder of it all. "No! No!" he crowed, trying to actually say the word.

"Yes, pretty snow," she repeated.

"Me no!"

"You want to go play in the snow?" said Rebekah wearily.

"No! No!" said Beanie, reaching toward the window.

My mother had joined us, looking out at the fast growing whiteness. "Oh, I don't remember the last time we had a good snow at Thanksgiving," she said happily. "Really makes it feel all Christmassy, doesn't it?"

"I guess. We don't celebrate Christmas," said Rebekah, wrestling with monkey Beanie.

"Oops, that's right. Well, makes it feel all Hanukkah-y, then, huh?" Mom had had a couple glasses of wine and was just a tiny bit slaphappy. Which is the only reason she came up with the next suggestion, I think. "Lucy, why don't you take Beanie outside to play in the snow. Give his mother a little break."

"Oh, she doesn't have to," said Rebekah, but I could tell she was hoping I would.

"No. It's okay. I will." I wanted to get outside myself, and if it meant I had to keep an eye on the trouble child, so be it.

So Rebekah bundled Beanie in countless layers of clothing until the kid could hardly move, which is really something she should have thought of doing sooner. I stood there sweating in my jacket, hat, scarf, and mittens until she was finally done, and then Beanie and I tore out of that house jumping and squawking like a couple of chickens flying the coop.

There's a lovely hush with a snow like that, as it drapes over everything, muffling all sound. Beanie ran and ran and laughed and laughed, so happy to be free. I followed him, trotting at times to keep up, the dry snow squeaking under the soles of my shoes. Finally, Beanie squatted down and ran his mittens through the powder, gathering it up and tossing it into the air like confetti. Then he shrieked with laughter and did it again. And again, and again, and again. His laughter was so loud and so joyful, I found myself laughing too, and joining him in his celebration, the two of us giving thanks in the snow.

"No! No!" yelled Beanie gleefully.

"No! No!" I agreed, as the snow drifted down on our heads.

When we came in from the cold, our cheeks red and our noses running, Aunt Jenny's perfect Thanksgiving table sagged with the weight of all the food. There was stuffing and mashed potatoes and candied yams and buttered baby peas and green bean casserole and gravy and a relish tray and cranberry sauce and popovers and icky creamed pearl onions. The turkey hadn't even made it to the table, and I had no idea where she was going to put it until she took away the centerpiece and Uncle Pete plunked it down in the middle of everything. It was almost as big as Beanie.

Rebekah stripped off Beanie's wet outerwear and crammed the hungry little guy into his high chair, which Aunt Jenny had wisely set on top of a drop cloth. Uncle Pete sharpened his carving knife with a *zing-zing* sound as the rest of us gathered around the table. We each stood behind our chairs, waiting for Grandy to say the grace before we sat down. Aunt Jenny looked at Grandy sideways. He was known at times to give what she considered "inappropriate" blessings, but I liked the one that went, "Good bread, good meat, good God, let's eat!" Short, sweet, to the point. We waited. And waited.

"Dad?" chided Jenny. "Remember? Grace?"

But Grandy had nothing to say. He gasped for air, clutched his chest, and crumpled to the floor.

Chapter 16
Everything but the Oink

Everyone was there in the emergency waiting room, waiting. Everyone but Rebekah and Beanie, that is. When Grandy collapsed, Dad quickly called for an ambulance, and Ira took care of Grandy, ignoring suggestions like "Raise up his feet" and "Look down his windpipe." Turns out Ira was an intern, which is almost a doctor but not quite.

"He overdoes it. He does. I've been trying to get them to move in with us for ages, but Mother just won't hear of it," said Aunt Jenny, who hadn't stopped pacing since we'd arrived. "I wish you'd try to talk some sense into her so long as you're home, Richard."

"I can talk to Mom 'til I'm blue in the face, Jenny, but you know she'll never move in with you. She likes her own place, her own things, her own kitchen," said Dad reasonably.

"We can bring their things, set them up in the downstairs bedroom. Lord knows we've got the room. And as far as the kitchen goes, she's welcome to it whenever she wants."

"It's not the same," said Mom, speaking up for the first time.

"What's not?" asked Aunt Jenny.

"It wouldn't be *her* kitchen, it would be *your* kitchen, and you know how Gladys is. All the years I've been going to their house, she's never once let me help out in her kitchen, and it's not because she thinks I can't cook. It's because that kitchen's *hers*."

"Well, hell, I can build them an addition. Separate entrance, separate bath, separate kitchen. The works," said Uncle Pete amiably.

"That's a fine idea, honey. I mean, once we sell their house, we can afford to build them a really nice place," said Aunt Jenny, instantly warming to the notion.

"You know, why don't we just wait and see how he is first before we go selling off their house and building additions for them," said Dad, starting to get irritated. "I swear, Jenny, sometimes you treat them like they're children who need to be cared for."

"I do *not*. And besides, they *do* need care. They *do* need help. If you were ever around to see that, Richard, you'd know."

That shut everybody up.

Aunt Jenny continued to pace. Dad and Uncle Pete went outside in the snow to smoke. Mom flipped through old magazines. And I hate to say it at a time like that, but all I could think of was the fact that I was starving. We'd left Thanksgiving dinner sitting on the table and none of us had had a bite.

"Mom?"

"What, sweetie?" said Mom, looking up from an ancient *National Geographic*.

"Can I have some change for the vending machine?"

"Oh, honey, you must be famished. You haven't had any-thing to eat since breakfast," she said, digging through her purse for loose coins.

"Oh my God! There's Ira," said Aunt Jenny, dashing toward him as he approached the waiting area. "Ira! Ira!"

Dad and Uncle Pete had seen him too, and came right in from their smoke. Mom immediately stopped hunting for change to hear the news.

"So? What is it? Is he okay? What's wrong?" said Aunt Jenny, not pausing long enough for Ira to answer.

"Everything's fine. It was an acute attack of indigestion. That's all. He's resting comfortably now."

"Indigestion?" said Aunt Jenny, truly puzzled. "Indigestion? I mean, it seemed like a heart attack. You're sure it wasn't a heart attack?"

"We're sure it wasn't a heart attack," said Ira, smiling. "He's in exam room three. Come on. Let's go see him."

We trudged down the shiny gray hallway, following Ira like an obedient little herd, and entered an exam room where Grandy sat propped up in a bed, sipping on a cup of flat ginger ale through a bendy straw. He looked fine, Gamma by his side, holding his paw. As soon as he saw us all, his face about cracked in two, he smiled so wide.

"Hey, look at you all. Gave you quite a scare, didn't I?" he said, clearly pleased with himself.

"Oh, good Lord, Dad," said Aunt Jenny. "You scared us half to death."

She leaned over and gave him a little peck on the cheek. Dad, on the other hand, gave Grandy a good big hug and a kiss. Dad's the touchy-feely sort.

"So I guess Ira here told you what the big medical emergency was, huh?"

"Yes, but we hadn't even eaten yet," said Aunt Jenny. "How on earth could you have had indigestion that severe?"

"Gladys?" said Ira, raising his eyebrows at Gamma.

"What?" said Gamma innocently.

"Don't you have something to say?" he asked.

"Oh, all right," said Gamma, all prickly all of a sudden. "I fed him some scrapple this morning."

"Scrapple? You fed him scrapple?" Aunt Jenny was aghast.

"That's right. I fed him scrapple. You know how he loves it," said Gamma defensively.

"Unfortunately, scrapple doesn't love him," said Ira.

Scrapple is a Pennsylvania Dutch breakfast meat that contains every part of a pig but the oink. Even if you're raised with it, you either love it or you don't. I don't.

"So no more scrapple, right, Ed?" said Ira, gently scolding Grandy.

"Oh, if you insist. I guess life is still worth living without scrapple, right, Lucy Goosey?" said Grandy, winking at me.

"Right," I said.

"We're gonna keep Ed overnight. His blood pressure was a little elevated when he came in," said Ira, all business.

"Yours would have been too," said Grandy.

"It was," said Ira, laughing. "You didn't just scare your family to death. You scared me too. Remember, Ed, I'm new at all this doctor stuff."

"Oh, great. My doctor's a beginner? Now you tell me," said Grandy.

Everyone got a good laugh out of that. Yep, Grandy was definitely himself again. We could all breathe easy.

When we got back to Aunt Jenny's, the snow was coming down thick as a curtain. Rebekah had thoughtfully wrapped the entire dinner in aluminum foil to try to keep it warm, but it was stone-cold anyway. Aunt Jenny and Mom set to heating it all back up again, fixing containers full of everything for Ira to take home. Everyone was in a festive mood, since we were now sure that all was right with Grandy.

Gamma, against everyone's urging, had decided to stay the night in the hospital with Grandy. At first she said it was because, if left alone, Grandy wouldn't ask the doctors the right questions when they checked up on him in the morning. But when Aunt Jenny told Gamma she'd drive her back to the hospital first thing, Gamma finally confessed that she couldn't sleep without the old man. Her bony little backside got too cold. That made everyone whoop with laughter, and we all headed out of the hospital promising to bring them back a full turkey dinner that very night.

We feasted on reheated everything, and honestly, it tasted just as good as it would have the first time around. Better, in fact, since, as Aunt Jenny was fond of saying, "a good appetite is the best sauce," and we were all plenty hungry. It was almost eight-thirty when Dad announced it was time for us to drive home and we'd take Grandy and Gamma their dinner on our way.

Aunt Jenny wouldn't hear of it.

"Richard, it's snowing like Siberia out there. You are *not* driving back home in this. You're going to stay the night."

"After we take dinner to the hospital, we might as well keep on driving."

"No, Jenny's right, Richard," said Mom. "It's late, we're all exhausted, it's snowing hard, let's just stay."

"Well, what about Lucky?" asked Dad. In the one full day he'd known Lucky, Dad was attached.

"Lucky's got food and water and a houseful of beds to sleep on. He'll be fine."

"You sure?"

"I'm beat. Please? Let's stay."

"Okay," Dad conceded. "But I'm still gonna take dinner to Mom and Dad. Anyone want to ride with me?"

We all sat there, full of food and comfy cozy. No one budged.

"Lucy?" Dad asked, inviting me along.

"Oh, Richard, look at her. She's whupped," said Mom, noticing my droopy eyes.

"No, no, I wanna go." I was almost slurring my words, I was so drowsy.

"Lucy, you're dog tired," said Mom.

" 'S only eight-thirty," I argued. " 'S not my bedtime."

Mom looked at me. I was curled up on the sofa, a crocheted afghan tucked over me, snug as a bug in a rug.

"Okay, fine. If you're not asleep by the time your dad is ready to leave, you can go with him," she said. "But I think you're about down for the count."

Mom was wrong. By the time Aunt Jenny had fixed the heaping containers and closed them up tight, I was on my feet and out the door with Dad. We drove slowly through the thick downfall, practically the only car out on the road. I could hear our tires scrunch through the packed snow and once felt us skid sideways before Dad steered us straight again, grinning away like he was having the time of his life.

"It's like riding a bike," he said.

"Huh?"

"Driving in the snow. It's like riding a bike. Once you

know how, you never forget. You know, it's seventy degrees in Pasadena today."

"It is?"

"Yep. Seventy. Never snows."

"Never?"

"Nope. But you can stand in your yard right next to a palm tree and see snow on top of the mountains. And if you want, you can even drive up there and go skiing."

"That's weird."

"Good weird, or bad weird?"

"Just weird."

"You're going to love California, Lucy. I promise."

"I don't know."

"What don't you know?"

"Well, Mom said it wasn't a sure thing, your job, and, you know, it's just . . . I like it *here*. Jake is *here*. All my friends are *here*. All our family is *here*."

"I know, honey."

"I mean, don't you like it here?"

"I do."

"Then why do we have to go?"

"We don't. I just thought . . ." Dad grew silent for a moment, like he was somewhere deep inside his head. "I know you want me to come back, Lucy. I know you're unhappy, your mother's unhappy, and I'm unhappy too. It's something I think about every day. Especially today."

"So why don't you come back? Why don't you?"

"Maybe I should."

We'd arrived at the hospital, following a snowplow into the parking lot.

"Let's get this dinner up to Gamma and Grandy before it's as cold as a Popsicle," he said, smiling, even though I could tell he didn't feel like smiling.

I didn't either.

Grandy was sitting up awake in a reclining chair, watching TV with the sound down low and the lights off. Gamma was snoozing in his bed, snoring lightly, her longish gray hair down out of its French twist and spread across the pillow. When we came into the room, Grandy put his finger to his lips, warning us to hush. He rose and came to us, clutching his hospital gown shut behind him.

"Lemme get some clothes on and I'll meet you down in the smoking lounge. Don't wanna wake the old gal up," he whispered.

Dad and I took dinner to the smoking lounge down the hall. It still smelled kind of ashy, but it was clean and empty now at nine o'clock, the visitors gone home for the night.

Grandy came in moments later, wearing pants, his hospital gown, slippers, and his cardigan. It wasn't the most stylish outfit in the world, but he looked great, rubbing his hands together in anticipation of his Thanksgiving feast. He opened container after container, dipping his fork into each and sampling the food, a look of pure bliss on his face.

"Ah, I do love a good turkey dinner with all the trimmings," he said, coming up for air briefly before diving in to truly eat. "So, Lucy—how do you like having your dad back again?"

"It's nice."

"Yeah, it sure is. I bet you miss him like all heck. I bet you want him home."

"Dad—"

"I'm talking to Lucy here, Richard. Lucy?"

"We were talking about that in the car, me and Dad," I said tentatively.

"Were you? And what did you decide?"

"Nothing," I said. "At least I don't think so."

"Huh. Well, you want to know what I think?"

"Dad, I know what you think," said Dad sharply.

"No, Richard, I don't think you do."

"Lucy. Maybe you ought to wait outside while your Grandy and I have a talk."

"This is about her too. I think she ought to hear it."

Dad looked at me, then at his own father. He shrugged. "Fine, Dad. Go ahead. You might as well."

"You're thinking about coming back, Richard, aren't you? You're thinking how much you miss your little girl and Joy and how your mom and I aren't getting any younger and I'm sure Jenny's given you an earful about how we can't take care of ourselves anymore."

"How'd you know?"

"About Jenny, or about all of it?"

"All of it."

"I'm your damn father, son. If I don't know you, who does? So, what's it gonna be? You staying put, or you coming back?"

"I don't know."

"Well, I do. You're not coming back. You've put Joy and Lucy through holy hell this past year, chasing down yourself and chasing down this job. Now that you've finally got it all figured, you're not gonna cut bait and head on home 'cause you've just all of a sudden realized how very much you left behind. You're gonna stick it out, son. You're gonna see it through. 'Cause if you don't, you're always gonna wonder. You're always gonna look at Joy and Lucy and blame them for letting go of your dream."

"They're part of my dream. The biggest part."

"I know that. They know it too. But that doesn't mean squat. You're gonna have some serious making up to do and you can't blame them if they decide not to accept your apologies. That could happen. But I guarantee you if you don't see this thing to the end, you'll come back home, end up resenting them for it, and you'll just leave again."

"How do you know?"

"I just do."

Dad thought for a bit. It was a lot to take in. Then he looked at Grandy, suddenly seeing him like he was someone new.

"Did you ever want to go, Dad? You ever want to leave us?"

"At least once a day, son."

"Be serious."

"I am. There was plenty I wanted to do, but I never did go do it. Don't ask me why not—maybe it was the times. Or maybe it was Gladys. If I left, she'd never let me set foot inside the door again and I couldn't bear the thought of that. But you've gone and done it. You up and left and put your whole family through one god-awful year. The only way to make all that pain worth it is to at least finish what you started. Right, Lucy?"

"I don't know, Grandy. I just don't know." I couldn't help myself. I was crying.

Grandy looked at me and opened his arms. "Come here, sweetheart."

I went over to him, and he drew me down onto his lap like he used to do back when my feet didn't reach the floor.

"I know all of this is really hard for you to understand, so don't even try," he said, wiping my tears and smoothing my hair. "When you're older, you will."

I always hated when people said I'd understand stuff when I got older, but this time I was willing to accept it. It was true, I didn't understand why Grandy was telling Dad he shouldn't come home when it was what everybody wanted.

"Anyway, son, if you leave the west, I won't have a good excuse to drag the old girl out to see the Grand Canyon. And I don't want to die without seeing that sight."

"It is truly something to see, Dad."

"Of course it is. It's the damn Grand Canyon, isn't it?" said Grandy, holding me to him as I sat there. I was way too big for his lap anymore, but somehow, right then, I fit there just right.

Overnight, so much snow came down that when we got up in the morning, it had drifted as high as the windowsills. Aunt Jenny fixed eggs and sausage and hash browns, and then we all went outside to dig out the cars, the driveway, and the front walk. After that, we went over to Ira and Rebekah's house and helped them dig out too. Beanie was having the time of his life, staggering through snow up to his waist, then throwing himself in when it got too deep. He'd come up out of the drifts, completely caked in white and giggling like a maniac, which made everyone else laugh too. His joy was infectious.

Gamma called us hourly, wondering when we would be there to take them home. Being stuck in a building full of sick people made her antsy, she said. Besides, she was good and ready for a hot turkey sandwich, and she suspected we were going to eat up all the leftovers before she could get her mitts on them.

It wasn't until well after lunchtime, though, that the plows came through and anyone could drive over to the hospital. We had to head on home, so Uncle Pete went to pick up Gamma and Grandy.

"So, Richard, when are we going to see you again? Christmas?" Aunt Jenny asked, standing with Dad by our idling car, her heavy sweater clutched around her.

"I don't know, Jenny. Maybe."

Mom looked at Dad sharply from the front seat, then looked away. I sat in the backseat, bundled up in the blanket Mom always kept in the car.

"Well, whenever it is you come home, we'll be happy to see you. It was a good treat to have you all for as long as we did," she said, and she meant it.

"Happy Thanksgiving, Jenny," said Dad, as he gave Aunt Jenny a big hug and a kiss.

"Happy Thanksgiving," she said, hugging Dad back just as hard.

Dad climbed into the car and we pulled out of the driveway as Aunt Jenny ran toward the house, waving goodbye until she was through the front door and closed within the warmth of her home.

It was a quiet drive. Mom and Dad didn't talk much and I was drowsy again from all the shoveling and the turkey sandwiches. I stretched out on the backseat, still cocooned in the blanket, and drifted in and out, waking once to hear a small bit of argument.

"Okay, fine, Richard. That's what your father thinks. What do *you* think?"

"I wish like hell I knew."

"I wish like hell you did too. He's right about one thing, though. This year has been god-awful. It absolutely has."

Then silence fell between them again as I drifted off to sleep.

Even though Chadds Ford wasn't far away, the roads were so bad it took us quite a while to get home, so by the time we arrived it was good and dark. I woke to the sound of the garage door rolling open as Dad pulled the car in and Mom closed the door behind us. I sat up, all rumpled and drooly from my long nap in the backseat.

"Well, hello there, Sleeping Beauty," said Dad, looking back at me and smiling.

"Humph," I said. Like I've mentioned before, I don't like being teased when I wake up. It makes me grumpy.

"You coming in, or are you spending the night in the backseat?"

"I'm coming, I'm coming," I said irritably, untangling myself from the blanket.

Dad went on into the house, following Mom. I could hear him calling for Lucky as I stiffly climbed out of the backseat, which is not the most comfortable place to sleep when you're five-ten.

As I came in the house, Dad was walking around with Lucky cuddled up against him. He was already starting to sniffle.

"Hey there, little buddy. How's my little buddy?"

"Richard, you really should take an antihistamine *before* you pick that cat up," said Mom, also clearly irritated with Dad.

"I'm trying to build up an immunity to him."

"Doesn't work that way. Anyhow, I don't know why you would bother."

"What does that mean?"

"Well, clearly, you're leaving again just as soon as you can pack your bags."

"Joy—"

"So why bother? Really. Why?"

"Joy, I want you to understand why I'm doing this."

"No, you don't. You don't want me to understand. You just want me to accept whatever it is you choose to do. And you know what? I can't anymore. I just can't."

"Stop it! Please, just *stop!*" I yelled without thinking.

I couldn't take it. Since I'd left school on Wednesday, I'd been up and down and up and down—mortified about the whole Billy thing, sad when I thought I hadn't made the basketball team, happy when I did, confused about Gary, thrilled to see Dad, frightened about Grandy, and turned completely inside out with all the arguing.

Mom and Dad looked at me in stunned silence. I marched right up to Dad, snatched Lucky from his arms, and stomped off to my room for a good cry, slamming the door behind me. As I curled up on my bed and buried my face in Lucky's warm black fur, I could hear Mom and Dad talking, but I didn't even try to hear what they were saying. I'd had it. I really had.

I woke to a dark and silent house. I was lying on my bed, fully clothed except for my shoes, which someone had removed. Someone had also covered me with a quilt. Lucky was still curled up with me, though, and I was happy to see his sweet little self, sleeping peacefully without a worry in the world.

My mouth felt like I'd been chewing on dirty socks and I

193

had to pee, so I got up, went to the bathroom, and brushed my teeth. I was hungry but didn't really know if I wanted to eat once I saw that it was midnight. I poked quietly around the kitchen, though, deciding finally on a bowl of cornflakes and milk. As soon as I finished eating, I padded back to my bedroom and about jumped out of my skin to find Jake sitting on my bed with Lucky in his lap.

"Jeez, Jake, scare me to death, why dontcha?"

"Sorry. Where ya been?"

"Aunt Jenny's. I told you we were going there."

"Oh yeah. You said. So, guess what? I was right. I knew it was gonna happen. I just knew it. There we all were, sitting at the damn Thanksgiving table, and Frank makes this huge deal about saying grace and he goes on and on about all the many things he's thankful for but mostly for having us in his life now, and he was planning to do this in the Bahamas, and then he gets down on his knees and goes, 'Dotty, I love you, will you marry me?' I mean, can you believe it? He's got some stupid diamond ring and everything and Mom's going 'yes, yes, yes!' and she's crying and Grandmom's crying and Mrs. Grotowski's crying and I feel like I'm gonna puke."

Jake spit out that whole story in practically one breath, he was so anxious to tell it. He didn't spare a bit of breath to ask me how I was, or why we were back a day late, or how it was having Dad home, or why I was still fully dressed, or anything. No. He was just going on and on about the horror of his mom marrying Frank while it looked like my dad might be walking out the door again. And I know it wasn't fair, but in that instant, I just added Jake to the long list of things that had me so upset. I thought he was being a big selfish pig, and so I let him have it.

"Guess what? Big deal. I've known for weeks now that Frank was going to ask your mother to marry him."

"What?"

"Yeah. That's right. I knew."

"Wait—you *knew* Frank was going to ask Mom and you didn't even tell me?"

"Yeah, and you know what? It's not some big damn tragedy. Your mom's getting married. So what?"

"What do you mean, so what? If it was your mom getting married, you sure as hell wouldn't say 'so what.' "

"Well, it won't be my mom 'cause my dad came back."

"He's not staying."

"Yes, he is."

"No, he's not. I heard your mom say so."

"You did not."

"Why? Because I heard something and didn't tell you?"

"You're just trying to get back at me for not telling you about your mom and Frank."

"Am I?" said Jake, toying with me meanly.

Immediately I was furious. "My dad's staying. He is."

"No, he's not. And you know it."

In the space of less than a minute, Jake and I had hurt each other deeply, and there was no backing down.

"Screw you, Jake!"

"Yeah? Well, screw you too!" he said, dumping Lucky from his lap, getting up off the bed, and heading for the window. Jake climbed out into the bitter cold. I shut the window behind him, scooped Lucky up, and held him to me. For the first time ever in my life, I was way too upset to cry.

Chapter 17
To the Rescue

Waking to the glow of bright, bright daylight bouncing off all that fallen snow, I could hear the scrape of Dad's shovel clearing the front walk. I thought he could probably use some help, but I was so warm and cozy that I hunkered down and pulled the blankets up over my head. Just about to drift back to sleep, I heard the unmistakable sound of Mrs. Little yammering with Dad out front. She was upset—I could tell from the sound of her voice. It could only be about Jake. Nobody else could make her so crazy. Reluctantly awake, I threw the covers off of me, stepped into my fuzzy slippers, and shuffled off to the bathroom, still wearing my wrinkled clothes from the night before.

When I came out, Dad had brought Mrs. Little inside and Mom was talking with her in the kitchen in that soothing voice people use to calm down barking dogs. I tried to hear what they were saying, but Mom was talking way too low for even my big ears. Probably Mrs. Little had caught Jake sneaking back in last night and had grounded him again, but somehow I couldn't muster up any feeling about it. Jake, Mom, Dad, Grandy, Billy, Gary—everyone had just worn me right out.

I considered going back to bed, but my stomach was growling and there was only one thing to do about that. So I took a deep breath and headed on into the kitchen.

"Lucy," said Mom, "I was just going to wake you."

Mrs. Little paced the kitchen, back and forth and back and forth, wringing her hands. Dad sat on the counter by the sink, which was high enough so his legs could dangle. Mom was fixing a pot of coffee.

"Jake's missing," Mrs. Little blurted out, clearly too agitated to break the news gently.

"Missing?" I gasped.

"This morning, it was late, so I went to wake him and he wasn't there. He was gone."

"Maybe he just got up early," I said, knowing that was unlikely.

"Jake? Get up early? No," she said, still pacing. "I don't think he got up early. I think he was out all night. And it's freezing. Absolutely freezing."

As numb as I felt about everything and everyone, the thought of Jake spending the night alone outside in the cold jolted me right out of it. I felt instantly responsible. He'd come to me for sympathy and all I'd given him was a fight. I wrestled with myself for a second, wondering whether I should confess about his late-night visit, but then decided against it. Clearly, Mom had not heard us talking or she'd have said something, so I was going to do him a huge favor and keep my mouth shut. I knew exactly where Jake was. He was up in the tree house, waiting for Gary, and if I told Mrs. Little he was off meeting Gary, he was worse than grounded.

"Don't you think we should call the police?" asked Mom.

"I did. The police won't do anything about a missing person

until they're gone for twenty-four hours," said Mrs. Little. "He's just a kid, he's been gone all night, and they won't do a thing!"

"Most kids don't run too far away from home and they come right back once they get over whatever it was that upset them," said Dad reassuringly.

"I don't think he's going to get over this. I don't."

"Get over what?" asked Mom, plugging in the percolator.

Mrs. Little stopped wringing her hands and looked down at her left hand almost like it was alien to her. Then she held it out for all of us to see. There it was—the diamond ring, sparkling away on her finger.

"You're engaged?" gasped Mom. "Oh, Dotty, that's . . . well, it's wonderful. You think that's why Jake took off?"

"I know it. He hates Frank. He does."

"He doesn't *hate* Frank."

"Well, he doesn't like him either."

"Who's Frank?" asked Dad, completely out of the loop.

"Frank Grotowski. You haven't met him, but I know you'll like him. Everybody does. Everybody but Jake, that is."

I was poking around in the kitchen as they talked on, looking for something to eat. I had already tuned them out. I knew exactly what I was going to do once I'd had my breakfast. I took the milk out of the fridge and poured myself a glass.

"Oh, Lucy, you didn't have any dinner last night, did you?"

"She had some cornflakes in the middle of the night," said Dad, looking straight at me.

"Cornflakes?" said Mom.

I shrugged, looking back at Dad, who winked at me. He'd heard me and Jake. He knew.

"Well, we'll have to do better than that for your break-fast, won't we?" said Mom, opening the fridge and getting out some eggs to scramble.

There was a box of fresh doughnuts on the kitchen table. Dad must have gone to his favorite doughnut shop when he got up. I couldn't wait for the eggs. I started munching on a warm cruller right away.

"How about I drive you around the neighborhood, Dotty? We'll go looking for Jake," offered Dad.

"Frank and I already did that, first thing."

"Well, like I said, he'll be home soon. Soon as he's good and hungry, I'll bet. Right, Lucy?"

I nodded, chewing on my cruller and drinking my milk, the very picture of innocence.

The woods were beautiful, with thin ridges of snow balanced perfectly on barren tree branches and pillowy drifts under-foot. I trudged through the snow, following a foot trail that led me to believe I'd find Jake shivering away up in the tree house, but I was wrong. Gary was there, alone, wearing a down vest under a black leather motorcycle jacket that was way too big for him.

"Hey, Lucy," he said, jumping down, snow raining from the tree branches onto his bare head. He actually looked happy to see me.

"Hey. You seen Jake?"

"Nah. I'm waiting for him. I told him we'd ride my dirt bike, but with all this snow, there's no way. I guess he figured that one out himself, huh?"

"Oh no!" I said, worried now. "I was sure he'd be with you. He's gone."

"Gone?"

"Yeah. He came by at midnight to talk—sometimes he comes in through my window, you know—and he was really upset about his mom getting married and we had a big fight and now he's gone and I feel like it's all my fault."

"No. It's not your fault, Lucy."

"It is. It is my fault. I knew all about his mom getting married and I didn't tell him and it made him really mad and we said awful stuff to each other and then he left and he never went home and it's freezing out and his mother called the cops, and—"

"Whoa, whoa, whoa. Slow down. He's been out all night?"

"Yeah," I said, teetering on tears.

"Well, I think I know where he is."

"You do?"

"Yeah. I do."

"Where?"

"Come on. I'll show you."

The graveyard looked like something out of an old-timey storybook. The older, tilted gravestones wore crooked caps of snow, and the newer gravestones wore their snowy hats straight and tall. Already, the wrought-iron fences surrounding family plots were decorated with Christmas wreaths and evergreen garlands. The only thing spoiling the storybook picture was Otis, pushing a noisy snowblower, clearing the roads so people could come jolly up the graves of their dear departed with potted poinsettias and holly.

Otis saw us coming, shut off the snowblower, and waved us over, which wasn't at all like him. He wore his usual red cowboy hat, but underneath he wore furry white earmuffs, a thick red snowsuit, and heavy black boots. Surrounded by all that snow, he looked like some Wild West version of Santa Claus.

"What are we doing here?" I asked Gary as we trudged through unplowed drifts toward Otis. "Did Jake spend the night in the tree?"

"Nah," said Gary, smiling. "He's got a better place to stay."

I had snow jammed down the tops of my boots as we stepped into the clear space that Otis had just plowed. I leaned over and started digging it out with my gloved hands before it shook down to the bottom of my boots and froze my toes.

"Hey, Mr. Otis," said Gary.

"Morning, Gary. How ya doin'?"

"Just fine. How's your truck running?"

"It ain't. It don't seem to much like the cold. But funny you should ask about my truck. It had itself a little stowaway this morning. Came to the garage to get the snowblower and your buddy Jake was snoozing away, all curled up in the cab."

"Is he still there?" I asked, hopeful.

"Nah. Offered him some breakfast, but he said he wanted to go off to the farmers' market. Them Mennonites got those nice fresh-baked cinnamon rolls with the icing on top. Makes me hungry all over again just thinking about 'em."

As relieved as I was to know Jake wasn't frozen stiff, I was a bit miffed at the fact he had this secret place to stay. Secret to me, that is. Gary was in on it, and Jake had pointedly left me out. Still, Jake was alive and well and probably chatting away with Malinda. "We need to go there. To the farmers' market," I told Gary.

"Okay," said Gary. "We'll bring you a cinnamon roll on our way back, Mr. Otis."

"That's a deal."

"And you bring your truck back in. It shouldn't be stalling in the cold like that."

"Hate to say it, son, but your daddy's work ain't what it used to be since, well, you know, since all your troubles. I'm sorry to tell you this, but I need to find me a new mechanic."

"Please, don't do that. Okay? Bring your truck in and I'll work on it myself." Gary sounded almost desperate.

Otis looked at Gary, his face full of sympathy. I'm sure Gary's life had been better once, before his brothers' tragedies likely drove his father to drink. But now his life was harder than I could imagine. Obviously it was now up to him to keep whatever business the garage had going. Thinking about his troubles put my own troubles into perspective and made them feel just a little less large.

"Your daddy gonna be okay with that?" said Otis gently.

"My dad isn't around much anymore. Bring it in. I'll take care of it."

"All right. I will, soon as I can get it down there. And don't you two forget about my cinnamon roll, you hear?"

We were almost to the farmers' market when it occurred to me to ask Gary why Jake would even think to spend the night in Otis's truck.

"Mr. Otis offered it to him."

"When?"

"You remember the night he caught Jake trying to bury your kitten?"

"How could I forget? He scared me to death."

"Well, I know they talked about the problems Jake was having at home and all. Then one night after that, late, Mr. Otis found Jake up in the tree. He told Jake if he ever needed a place to spend the night, he could stay in the truck in the garage. Mr. Otis even left a blanket in there for him."

"Wow. That's really sweet," I said. Clearly, Otis was really a big softie. "Hey, how come you call him Mr. Otis?"

"It's his name."

"Not his last name. His last name is Lincoln."

"No, it's Otis. Lincoln Otis."

"You sure?"

"Yeah, I'm sure. His name's printed on the checks he writes the garage."

"It must be funny, you know? Having your last name first and your first name last."

"Tell me about it."

I looked at Gary Geary and he shrugged—the boy with the same name twice.

Jake wasn't at the farmers' market. Neither was Malinda. She and her family were gone. Madge, as always, was the source of all information.

"They found out about some group of Amish over in Indiana who think the same as they do—that the Sabbath is supposed to be on Saturday and all—so they up and decided to go off and join 'em," said Madge, counting out sticks of horehound candy for a customer.

"When?" I asked.

"They told me last week. Said they was gonna pack up and

203

go, soon as they could. I don't imagine, with the weather and all, that they're on the road, though. No. My bet is they stay put 'til the weather clears and then they'll head off west."

"You told Jake?"

"Sure I did. He asked me, same as you." She turned to her customer. "There you go, dear. A dozen sticks of the best horehound you'll ever have. Now what else can I get for you?"

The woman ordered a bag of lemon drops and Madge scooped them up and weighed them as I tried to think the same way Jake would think. I didn't like what I came up with.

"You know where they live in Lancaster County?" I asked Madge.

"I sure don't. But you ask them Mennonites over that-away. They're the one's who bring 'em down here in their truck. They'll know for sure."

The Mennonites gave us a rural route number in Lancaster County and told us Jake had asked them the same question that very morning. I didn't really know what good it was going to do us, knowing their address. Because they had no phone, we couldn't look up their number, call Malinda's family, and tell them what I suspected—that Jake was on his way up there to join them. The whole idea seemed completely ridiculous.

"You really think that's what he's doing?" asked Gary, buying the cinnamon roll for Otis. "You really think he's heading up there to join the Amish?"

"No, he's not trying to join the Amish. Just *those* Amish. And not really join them anyway, like they're some kind of club. He's just—" I stopped, realizing all of a sudden that even though Jake had told Gary all sorts of things, only I knew about Malinda. "Jake never told you about Malinda, did he?"

"No."

"Well, Malinda's like he is. A dwarf. And she's our age and she's pretty, even though she wears those dumpy, plain Amish clothes. And he's been coming to visit her since just before school started."

"You're kidding."

"I'm not."

"Jake's got an Amish girlfriend?"

"She's not his girlfriend. They just talk. But he found out there's lots of Amish people like him. He told me one time he wanted to go to Lancaster County. To be somewhere for once where he didn't stand out."

Gary thought for a moment. As much attention as he drew himself, looking as tough as he did, it was nothing compared to the kind of attention Jake got for just being who he was. I wasn't sure if that had ever occurred to him, but apparently it had.

"When I first met him, he definitely stood out," Gary said, smiling at the memory. "But it didn't take long before I forgot about that part and he was just Jake. You know?"

I did know. Jake was Jake, and the fact that he was a dwarf was just Jake too. It wasn't everything, unless you didn't know him. For people who didn't know him, his dwarfness defined him. But if you knew him, it went away. It was just him, our friend, Jake.

"If he's hitchhiking to Lancaster County, I bet he hasn't gotten too far yet," said Gary.

"Hitchhiking?" I said, horrified. "Jake would never hitchhike."

"He did once with me."

"You and Jake went hitchhiking?"

"Yeah. To the river. People won't usually stop for me. I guess I look like I might hurt 'em or something. But they'd stop for Jake—maybe because he's so little. He was good at it."

"Oh my God! I didn't dare tell his mother he was heading off to meet you 'cause she'd kill him. Now I've got to tell her he's hitchhiking?"

"You don't have to tell her."

"I do. I mean, it's dangerous. What if some lunatic picks him up or something?"

"No lunatic's gonna pick him up."

"It could happen."

"No. 'Cause we're gonna go get him."

"What are you talking about?"

"We're gonna go get Jake."

"You're crazy, Gary. How are we gonna go get Jake? How?"

I stood there inside Geary's Garage, the three gleaming motorcycles lined up in front of the big garage door. I looked at them with a lump in my throat. Gary was rummaging around in the drawer of a huge red tool case, looking for the key to the Harley. I didn't know how I was going to do it, how I was going to swallow my fear and climb aboard one of those scary things to go searching for Jake, but it was what I had agreed to do. I remembered my promise to Mom and felt absolutely ill. There was no way I could ride on a motorcycle.

Then I thought of Jake, cold, alone, standing on the side of a road, his thumb out, waiting for a ride, hoping that whoever picked him up wasn't a maniac or a murderer, and I swallowed my fear. Mostly.

"Here it is," said Gary, holding up a key. "I knew Dad kept a spare in there."

He went over to the motorcycle, stuck the key in the ignition, took hold of the handlebars, kicked up the kickstand, and straddled the bike. In his motorcycle jacket, the Harley balanced between his legs, on a mission to rescue Jake, he seemed cooler than ever, and I felt like I was way in over my head.

Not because of the motorcycles, though that was part of it, but because of Gary himself. He seemed epic, like he was born to ride a Harley, so perfectly at ease with that massive machine. I wondered how I could ever reconcile that ultracool image with the Gary I knew. Then I thought about what he'd said—how once he'd gotten to know Jake, Jake's differences disappeared. I tried to do the same—ignore the image and think about the sweetness of Gary and what he was willing to do for a friend. I desperately wanted to climb up, wrap my arms around his waist, and ride. But then my fear started to get in the way. So I stood there gaping at him like a dope. He looked at me expectantly, waiting for me to climb onto the Harley.

"Lucy? Any time now."

"Um, Gary, do you have a helmet or anything?"

"I don't usually wear one."

"Well, I do," I said, like I rode a motorcycle every day, "and I bet Jake will want one too."

Gary looked up in the air, rolled his eyes, threw his leg back over the bike, and kicked the kickstand down. "What am I thinking?" he said in a disgusted tone of voice.

"But it's okay, really, I mean, if you don't have any helmets," I said, instantly backpedaling.

"I'm not using my head. I didn't even think about how three of us were gonna fit on the bike once we found Jake."

"Oh. Right," I said, finding it hard to hide my relief. "Well, I guess you'll have to go without me then."

"No. You gotta come. You're his best friend."

At the same time, we both looked over at the lone car sitting in the garage for repairs. It was Stephanie's VW Bug.

"Does it work?" I asked.

"It works great. I just did a tune-up."

"Stephanie won't mind."

"I don't know about that."

"Honest, she won't." I talked faster and faster, trying to convince myself as well as Gary. "Sometimes when she gives me and Kwame a ride home, she lets him drive it around the parking lot and he can't drive at all. He almost hit a lamppost once and she was laughing her head off. She won't mind if you drive it."

"Really?"

"You've been driving forever, right?"

"Since I was ten."

"I swear she won't care."

Gary looked at the car, the keys dangling from the ignition.

"Okay, Lucy. Climb on in. Let's go."

I've said before that I'm a nervous rule breaker. And taking Stephanie's car wasn't exactly a good thing to do. But strangely enough, as I got into the passenger seat, I was as calm as a pond on a still, still day.

We drove down the road, Gary shifting gears like a pro as I searched ahead, looking for any sign of Jake. The engine sounded like my mother's sewing machine, tinny and loud, as we puttered through Pennsylvania. It was still daytime, but the sky had become dark and heavy and looked as though it threatened snow.

I knew this road well. It was the same road we took to go to Grandy and Gamma's house, and I guided Gary through the twists and turns of it. Just as we went up a small rise, we had to veer to the right to descend. It was what Dad had always called a blind curve, which made it sound dangerous to me. As we came around it and could once again see ahead of ourselves, there he was, Jake, his collar turned up against the cold, his thumb forlornly extended, begging for a ride. If we'd have been going any faster, we'd have run him right down.

"Pull over! Pull over! There he is! There's Jake!" I yelled, but Gary was already pulling over in front of Jake onto the narrow shoulder of the road.

Jake trotted up to the VW, expecting it to be no more than just a lift, when Gary and I opened the doors and unfolded ourselves from the cramped front seats. That stopped Jake right in his tracks.

"Lucy? Gary? What the hell are you doing here?"

"What do you *think* we're doing? Looking for you, you dope," Gary said.

I mean, really, what *did* he think—we were out for a sunny Saturday drive or something?

"Well, good for you. You found me. Now, you gonna help me or what?"

"Help you?" I said, confused. "We *are* helping you."

"No, you're not. You're not gonna take me up to Lancaster County, are you? You're here to take me back."

"Of course we're here to take you back."

209

"Then you're wasting your time. Go on home. I'll find a ride."

"Don't be ridiculous," I said, my teeth chattering.

"*I'm* being ridiculous? Whose car is that?"

"Stephanie's," I said, as innocently as I could manage. "She said we could take it."

"She did not. I can always tell when you're lying, Lucy. You're a rotten liar. You stole that car."

Here we were on the shoulder of the road on the back side of a blind curve in the bitter cold, arguing. I was completely exasperated. "Oh, what does it matter whose car it is or how we got it, Jake? It's about to snow any second now, we're all freezing to death, and everyone's worried about you like you don't know, so why don't you just climb in and we'll all go home."

"I'm not going home."

"You have to."

"Why? Give me one good reason why."

"Your mom's really upset."

"Tough. She's got what she wants. She's got Frank. She doesn't need me."

"Well, I do. I need you."

It came out of my mouth with such complete ease. I did need Jake. Over these past weeks as we'd grown apart, I'd been truly miserable without him.

I hopped from foot to foot, trying to keep warm. Jake looked a little limp, like I'd just knocked the stuffing out of him. He stepped toward the car, hesitated, stopped.

"Here's the thing, Lucy. I know you mean that right now. I really do. But this is what you don't get—soon enough you

210

won't need me. It's already happening. You're gonna have your basketball buddies, and you and Gary, well, you like each other, I can tell. My mom's got someone, my dad's got someone. I swear, even Kwame is gonna find someone one of these days. But who's gonna ever want to be with me, huh? Who's gonna want that? Sometimes I feel so all alone I can't even see straight. And I know maybe it's crazy to think I could go up to Lancaster County and fit right in. But why not? I don't fit in where I am right now. Why not there?"

Standing on the shoulder of the road, he did look all alone, I couldn't deny it. I didn't know what else to say to him but what I'd already said—that I needed him. I thought that should be enough, but clearly, it was not.

"You know what, Jake," said Gary, finally weighing in. "I can't think of a time in my life when I didn't feel alone. Especially after Luke died. He was the only person I ever felt close to. Yeah, I hang around with Chaz and Mark and guys like that, but they don't get me, not at all. And then I started hanging out with you, and you totally got me. And I thought it went both ways. But if you can stand there and say that you're still all alone when you've got two people here telling you you're not, well, fine, I'll drive you up to Lancaster County. I will."

Snow was beginning to fall, the gray sky finally producing the fat flakes it had been hoarding away. They swirled around us, dusting our shoulders, our hair, but not one of us moved, waiting on that peculiar breathless edge for Jake's decision.

His decision never came. Instead, a rumbling police car appeared from out of the blind curve, gliding slowly onto the shoulder behind us like a great big shark. A police officer got out and walked toward us in the thickening snow. The other officer hung back, talking on their squawking radio, the voice on the other end as distant as the moon. There was no doubt about it: we were in deep, deep trouble.

Chapter 18
In the Slammer

If you've never been in any trouble with the law, here's something you wouldn't know: there are no inside door handles in the backseat of a police car. So once you're in, you can't get out unless someone lets you out. When you think about that, it makes perfect sense, but like I said, if you'd never been there, you wouldn't know.

When the cops pulled up behind us, my first instinct was to run—where to, I don't know. We were in the middle of nowhere. But I could hear Gary say under his breath, "Be cool, Lucy, just be cool." And so I was.

The officer who came up to us politely asked if we were having car trouble, and Gary, in his deepest voice, said, "No, sir, we're fine." The officer tried to get a good look at Gary, but Gary's face was obscured by the snow. He seemed just about ready to walk away and let us go when the other officer came up and said something to him. He nodded, looked at Gary, planted his hands on his hips, and shook his head.

"Son, how old are you?"

"Sixteen, sir," said Gary, calm and polite.

My heart was pounding so fast I thought it was going to fly right out of my chest. Jake tried to look casual, but I could tell he was scared to death too; his breath was short and shallow.

"Uh-huh. Can I see your driver's license?"

"Umm, you could, but I don't have it with me, sir. It's in my other jacket."

"I see. How about your registration?"

"Registration?"

"For the car. Your registration. Or is that in your other jacket too?"

"No, sir. It's in the glove box. But my name's not on the registration because it's not my car. I borrowed it."

"You want to rephrase that, son?"

"Excuse me?"

"You didn't 'borrow' that car, son. You stole it. It was reported stolen from a garage in Wilmington half an hour ago."

"No, sir. It's my garage. I mean, it's my family's garage. Geary's Garage, right? On Naaman's Road? The car belongs to a friend, and she said—"

"Doesn't matter what she said. You're driving without a license, probably underage, and the garage reported the car stolen, so guess what—you're coming with us. All of you."

And that's how I found myself in the backseat of a police car for the very first and, hopefully, very last time.

We sat there in the police station, drinking instant hot cocoa from thick paper cups as the bustle of cops, criminals, and ringing phones buzzed around us. Our parents had been called and were on their way. That made swallowing the lumpy cocoa difficult, I can absolutely tell you that.

None of us had been very talky since we'd been nabbed on the roadside. I guess each of us was thinking about what

214

our parents would say when they arrived, and none of it was good. I'd never dreaded seeing anyone so much in my entire memory as Mom and Dad. I'd also never wanted to see anyone more. I just wanted to go home, crawl into bed, pull the covers over my head, and make this whole lousy day disappear.

"This cocoa sucks," said Jake, trying to smooth out the lumps by stirring it with his finger. "And I'm starving. You think maybe they might give us something to eat?"

"You can think about eating?" I said. "I'm so darned nervous I feel like I'm gonna lose my breakfast."

"Well, at least you had breakfast. I haven't eaten since last night."

Gary silently reached into his jacket pocket, pulled out the smushed cinnamon roll, and handed it to Jake. In our hurry to ride to the rescue, we'd never given it to Otis.

"Wow, thanks!" Jake peeled off the bakery paper stuck to the icing and started to devour the roll ravenously, like some wild beastie.

I couldn't watch. I truly did feel ill. And Gary looked about as ill as I felt. Since we'd been put in the police car, he hadn't said a single word. He'd just glumly hung his head, isolated in his despair.

"You okay?" I asked him, concerned.

He shook his head, looking down at his sneakers.

"What's wrong?"

"Lucy, we're sitting in a police station," said Jake, his mouth full of sticky cinnamon roll. "What do you think is wrong?"

"Duh, Jake, I know that. And I wasn't talking to you anyway."

I looked at Gary, who seemed weighed down by sadness.

He looked up and met my eyes and once again made me catch my breath, but not in the way he'd made me feel breathless before. His eyes just looked so raw and open, like a completely empty sky. This was not like me at all, but without hesitating, I reached over and took his hand in mine, and he let me. Even in this awful place in this rotten situation, I felt like my heart was going to explode with happiness. I was holding Gary's hand.

He looked at me, then over at Jake, and he smiled. "You two are the best friends I've ever had. Whatever happens to me, this was all worth it."

"What do you mean, 'whatever happens to you'?" asked Jake suspiciously.

"Nothing. I don't mean anything."

"Yes, you do. What's going to happen to you, Gary?"

"I can't say."

"You can't say 'cause you don't want to or 'cause you don't know?"

" 'Cause it doesn't really matter."

"Yes, it does! You're in trouble because of me—both of you. It does matter. It does! You gotta tell me!"

Jake was on his feet, pleading with Gary, when the doors to the police station flew open and an army of people came rushing in. Mrs. Little was leading the charge, her arms flung open as she ran toward Jake, crushing him in an embrace.

"Jake! Oh my God, Jake, Jake, Jake! I've never been so worried in all of my life!" Tears were streaming down her face. I'd never seen Mrs. Little all emotional like that, but it didn't seem a bit strange. On the other hand, Jake hugging his mother back as hard as she hugged him? Now *that* was strange.

Right behind Mrs. Little were Frank, my mom and dad, and Kwame and Stephanie.

"Lucy," said Mom, embracing me, her head resting on my shoulder. "I am so glad you're safe. You don't know. You just don't know."

Dad kissed me on top of the head and stroked Mom's back. As Jake and I were wrapped up in the warmth of our mothers' arms, I looked over at Gary sitting all by himself. Mrs. Geary was nowhere to be seen.

Dad, who could see over everyone, noticed Gary too.

"So," he said a bit sternly, "you must be Gary."

"Yes, sir," said Gary, still at his most polite.

"Well, son, there's some good news and some bad news. The good news is we've spoken to your mother and she admits she panicked when she saw the car was gone and called the police prematurely. It appears Stephanie here did give you permission to use her car."

I looked over at Kwame and Stephanie. Kwame gave me a big wink and Stephanie smiled.

"But there's that little detail about driving without a license, which is kind of a problem. And then there's the issue of your prior juvenile record, which is definitely a problem. I'm afraid there's nothing much we can do about either until your hearing. So the bad news is, you'll be spending the weekend in juvenile hall."

"What?" I said, completely confused.

"Juvenile hall?" said Jake, looking totally stricken.

Gary looked at us both and shrugged. "Like I said, whatever happens, it's okay."

"No! He can come home with us, right, Mom? Right?" Jake pleaded with his mother.

"Honey, even though driving a borrowed car without a license in a blizzard was not the brightest thing to do, I'm sure Gary's intentions were good. I'd take him home, but the police won't let us. There's nothing we can do."

"It's not right! He's in trouble because of me! It's my fault. It's all my fault!"

"And the judge will take all that into account," said Frank. "But in the meantime, Gary, you and I have a few things to discuss. I'll be representing you in court. I pulled some strings to get you on the docket so you won't spend any more time in juvie than you have to. Your hearing's Monday morning."

Frank was a lawyer? This was news.

"Why don't the rest of you go on home while I get Stephanie her car back and clear up a few things with the police and the juvenile authorities," he said.

"I won't go home without Gary," said Jake stubbornly.

"Honey," said his mother gently, "you're going to have to."

"I won't," said Jake, verging on tears.

"Go on, Jake," said Gary.

"No."

Jake looked at Gary fiercely, willing with every bit of his being that all would be well. Gary gave him a small smile, trying to reassure Jake and maybe himself too that everything would turn out fine, but it seemed like he knew differently. He knew from experience that just wishing for things to be better wouldn't make them so.

"I'll be okay," Gary said finally, with every bit of conviction he could muster.

"You sure?"

"Yeah," he said, looking around at all of us. "I'm sure."

Maybe his mother wasn't there, but for what it was worth, at least Gary had all of us firmly on his side.

On the ride home, Mom and Dad didn't say a word. I did all the talking. I told them absolutely everything there was to tell about Jake, Gary, Malinda, Otis, Billy, basketball, Charlene and Barb, Chaz and Mark, the cherry bomb, burying Mean Joe Greene, awful Joanne DiMotta, the dirt bike, the Geary family tragedies, and on and on. Everything, everything, everything. I talked so much I was almost too tired to eat when I got home, but not quite. The meat loaf sandwiches Mom fixed for us really hit the spot. If there's one thing Dad and I like more than meat loaf, butter beans, and mashed potatoes, it's cold meat loaf sandwiches with spicy brown mustard and lettuce and a big pile of potato chips on the side.

I was cozy in bed, my stomach full, the house warm and toasty, just drifting off to sleep, when a vision of Gary popped into my head, hungry and alone on a cold, hard bunk in juvenile hall. That woke me right up. I tossed and turned, trying to get to sleep, but couldn't get the picture out of my mind. It was so unfair. Gary took the car because I'd talked him into it and because Jake had run away. None of it was really his fault. None of it.

Then I heard Mom and Dad talking in their room. Their door was cracked and so was mine and, well, I don't have to tell you that I absolutely needed to hear what they had to say. So I got out of bed and stuck my ear out my open door, tuning them in, their voices wafting faintly across the hall.

"I think she's been through enough without having to go through this too," said Mom decisively.

"Why? What do you think is going to happen?"

"I don't know, but I don't have a good feeling about it."

"Well, since she's been a participant in this whole thing so far, don't you think she should be there in court? See for herself how it all turns out?"

"So you think Lucy needs a bigger dose of reality than the one she's had for the past year?"

"Don't make this about me and you, Joy," said Dad sharply. "This is about Lucy and Jake and their friend, and this is about growing up. I know neither of us likes to think about Lucy growing up and confronting the big bad world, but whatever happens in court on Monday, we'll be there to help her make sense of it all."

"And then what? Will you be here after that, or will she have to make sense out of that too?"

"Joy—one thing at a time," said Dad calmly. "Let's get through Monday and then we'll see what comes next, okay?"

Dad left their bedroom and his footsteps headed right toward me. I leapt into bed and pulled up my tangled covers just as my bedroom door opened wide and Dad came softly into the room to smooth my blankets and tuck me in. The rumpled covers wouldn't give me away—like I said, I tend to thrash around in my sleep. But I didn't even bother to pretend. I rolled over and looked right at him.

"Still awake, honey?"

"Yeah."

"Any reason?"

"Just thinking."

"I'll bet you are," he said, sitting on the edge of my bed. "You've had a big day, you and your friends."

"I feel so bad for Gary. He's all alone. His mom didn't even come to the police station."

"She had things to do."

"Like what? I mean, she's his mom. It's like she doesn't even care about him."

"She does care."

"Then why wasn't she there?"

"She had good reason. She's working on something that just might get Gary out of the jam he's in."

"What?"

"I don't really want to say, Lucy. It's a long shot and I don't want to get your hopes up."

"I still think she should have been there. I mean, you were there and Mom and Mrs. Little and Frank. Gary had no one."

"Really?" said Dad, smiling. "No one?"

"Well, okay, we were all there for him. But we're not his family. I mean, maybe they care, but it sure doesn't seem like that to me."

Dad thought for a second before he spoke. " 'All's well that ends well.' You've heard people say that, right?"

I nodded.

"And you understand what it means?"

"I think."

"Well, today, you kids driving off in the snow—it was a bad idea and a lot of terrible things could have happened, but, thank God, it all ended well."

"No, it didn't. Gary's practically in jail."

"It did end well, Lucy. You're all safe, and that's what really matters. And Monday, when everything's said and done, I want you to think about that saying, and even if things don't end well, I want you to tell me if you still think Mrs. Geary doesn't care. Okay? Because that's what really matters."

"Okay," I agreed. Then I remembered something that had puzzled me. "Hey, Dad—how did you know to call Stephanie about the car?"

"We didn't. She and Kwame came by the garage to pick up her car right when Mrs. Geary got the call that the police had found her VW with you all in it. Mrs. Geary asked her not to press charges, and Stephanie was happy to oblige."

Lucky came bounding into the room and leapt up onto the bed, turning around a couple of times before settling into the crook of my arm.

"Well, you got your little bed buddy—you think you're going to be able to sleep now?"

"I guess."

"I'm sure you will," Dad said, kissing me on the forehead and smoothing my hair. "Love you."

"Love you too, Dad."

He stood up, left the room, and closed the door softly behind him. I knew he'd be back later to cover me up again once I'd fallen asleep, and that comforting thought stayed with me as I finally drifted off to the land of the sandman.

Chapter 19
Grounded

For the first time in my life, I was grounded. In a way, I didn't mind—after the Thanksgiving holiday I'd had, my head was in a whirl. Grandy's collapse, Jake's disappearance, driving off with Stephanie's VW, and getting arrested had already made for a very full weekend. A quiet Sunday at home, talking to Jake on the phone and watching TV, was not such a bad idea. Trouble was, I was forbidden to do either of these things. I was to do my homework, help Mom if she needed help, and contemplate what Gary and I had done and why it had been such a tremendously bad idea.

I didn't really need that last assignment. I knew I was going to think about Gary all day long, and I was sure Jake would be doing the same. It seemed silly to me that we couldn't talk about it. But Jake was grounded too, with no phone privileges either.

"And don't even *think* about sneaking out to see him," warned Mom.

"Lucy's been sneaking out to see Jake?" Dad asked.

"No, the other way around. But since Dotty's got Jake nailed down, I thought Lucy might be tempted to try it herself."

Honestly, it hadn't occurred to me until Mom had said something about it. And now that she had, I sure as heck wasn't going to try. I'd had enough trouble for one weekend, thank you, and I didn't relish the thought of any more.

But whenever the phone rang, I couldn't help myself—I did my best to overhear what was said. I think that Mom and Dad were on to me though, because they kept whispering quietly into their bedroom phone. All I could hear were occasional snippets—"the Senator" and "NATO base" and something like "Rahmshtein," a word Dad pronounced like he spoke German or something. I had no idea what they were talking about, but it sounded like politics to me. Not a peep about Gary. It was hugely frustrating.

It was getting on to dusk when Dad stuck his head in my bedroom to check my homework progress. I hadn't been assigned much over the holiday weekend, but I hadn't done it yet either. Instead, I was curled up with Lucky, listening to the radio and rereading a book. Even though I know what's going to happen, rereading a good book is kind of like putting on my favorite beat-up sweater. It makes me feel all comfy and secure.

"Haven't you already read that?" asked Dad.

"Um-hmm." I was working on acting sullen, so I kept my nose buried in the book.

"A few times, right?"

"Yup."

"So, I guess you're done with your homework."

"I only have Spanish."

"And have you done it?"

"I just have to memorize some irregular verb conjugations."

"Well?" Dad was getting impatient.

224

I lowered my book, finally looking at Dad. "It's hard to do by myself," I confessed.

"All you have to do is ask, Lucy. I'm happy to help you with your Spanish homework. Give me the list."

There was no more procrastinating. I dumped the book off my lap. Lucky, disturbed from his slumber, gave me a dirty look then stretched himself and yawned, digging his claws into my leg.

"Ow! Lucky!"

Dad chuckled. "Señor Gato Suerte is your cat for sure—grumpy if you don't wake him up gently."

I grabbed my verb list, handing it to Dad. "I didn't know you spoke Spanish."

"Oh, I've just picked up a little out west. Comes in real handy."

"Do you speak anything else?"

"Pig Latin," Dad said, laughing.

"Not German?"

"German? No. Why do you ask?"

"I just wondered," I said, as innocently as possible.

Dad looked at the verb list. "Okay. Conjugate the verb 'to go.'"

"*Ir. Voy, vas, va, vamos, vais, van.*"

That was the easy one. From there on, it got a little more difficult, but Dad and I kept at it until I'd finally memorized all of my irregular verbs.

Aunt Jenny had sent us home with Thanksgiving leftovers, so we had hot turkey sandwiches for dinner. Normally, after Sunday dinner, I'd settle in on the couch to watch *The Wonderful World of Disney*. But since I was grounded, that was out, so I went back to my radio and my book. From my room, I could hear droning voices as Mom and Dad watched *60 Minutes,* the tedium broken by the sound of a ticking clock before commercials. During the commercials, Mom and Dad talked, but there was no chance of hearing them through the jangling advertisements for mouthwash and beef stew. Believe me, I tried.

Restless, I found myself glossing over pages, skimming through the book as I thought about Gary. Bored to death after one day of being grounded, I couldn't imagine what it was like for him spending two nights and a full day in juvenile hall. I didn't know whether they had a TV there, but if they did, I'm sure you never got to watch what you really wanted. And even if they had books, that was no help to Gary. I was sure he was climbing the walls by now. The thought that he might have to stay there indefinitely was horrible. I couldn't imagine facing that down. One day of limitations was enough to make me crazy. Day after day was unthinkable.

I was so deep in thought, I didn't even hear the phone ring. Mom came into my room, startling me out of my reverie.

"Lucy? There's a phone call for you."

"I'm allowed to talk on the phone now?" I asked hopefully.

"Just this one. It's Grandy." She smiled as I jumped off my bed and dashed down the hall to the kitchen phone.

Dad was still talking to Grandy, though, so I had to wait my turn, hopping from one foot to the other in anticipation.

"Yeah, Dad, she's right here in front of me. Looks like she's got ants in her pants." Dad listened for a moment, then laughed at whatever it was Grandy said back. "You bet. Okay, Dad. Love you too. Bye."

I grabbed the phone from Dad's outstretched hand and

pressed it greedily to my ear. Having not talked to anyone but Mom or Dad all day, I was hungry for the sound of another voice.

"Hey, Grandy. How do you feel?"

"Me? I'm fine, now that I'm home. Your Aunt Jenny talked your Gamma into having us stay with her another night. But all I really wanted was our own house, our own bed. You know how that is?"

It was just what I'd been thinking about—Gary, in a strange and awful place, wanting to go home. "Yeah, Grandy, I do."

"So, I hear you had quite the adventure yesterday, you and your friends."

"Dad told you?"

" 'Course he did. Said you were headed up this way when the police caught up with you."

"Yeah. Kind of. But really we were just trying to get Jake to come home."

"Well, that was mighty thoughtful of you, but how 'bout next time you let a grownup do the driving."

"Believe me. I will."

"Atta girl." He started chuckling to himself, like he'd just heard a good joke.

"What?" Whatever was so funny, I wanted him to let me in on it.

"Oh, nothing," he said, laughing even harder. "I'm just trying to picture when that police car pulled up. Bet they scared the bejesus outta you."

"Grandy!" I tried to sound stern, but his laughter was infectious, and I started to giggle too.

"I'd have loved to have seen the look on your face. You take care now, Lucy Goosey. And don't go stealing any more cars, promise?"

"I promise. Love you, Grandy."

"I love you too."

As I hung up the phone, Dad came into the room and looked at me, cocking his head and smiling.

"Feel better?" he asked.

"Yeah. I guess."

"Your Grandy's always been good at that. When I was a kid, no matter how rotten I felt, he could always make me smile. Now, how 'bout you join me in a slice of pumpkin pie with whipped cream on top?"

I couldn't say no to that.

Chapter 20
Our Day in Court

When morning came, I looked at my bedside clock and was completely freaked out and confused. It was far too late for me to make it to school on time and I panicked, dashing out of my bedroom, looking frantically for Mom and Dad.

Dad was sitting in the kitchen drinking coffee and reading the paper. He'd canceled his plane ticket back to California the night before, which was a really good sign that he was thinking about staying. He calmly looked up from the sports section, his new glasses pushed down low on his nose so he could read over them. He pushed them back up so he could see me and smiled.

"Morning, Lucy."

"I'm late for school," I said, still in a spin.

"Don't you remember? You're not going to school. Gary's hearing is today. We're meeting him at juvenile court."

That didn't do much for my panic.

"Oh. Yeah. Right."

"We don't have to be there until eleven, so slow down, have some breakfast, breathe, okay? You're going to be fine."

Dad could see right through me. He knew how scared I was.

229

"Where's Mom?"

"Dr. Oartel needed her this morning. We'll pick her up on our way there. Go on, wash up and get dressed. I'll have some French toast and bacon ready for you when you're done."

Unlike most fathers, my dad could actually cook, and French toast and bacon sounded mighty good. My ablutions were maybe not what they should have been, but I was too rushed and nervous. I raked a comb through my snarly hair, splashed water on my face, brushed my teeth, and wondered what on earth a person should wear to juvenile court. I had no clue.

On TV, courtrooms looked all formal and churchy, with wood-paneled walls and rails where the jury sat in rows, like a choir. There was always a high wooden desk and a stand like an altar where the judge and witnesses sat. The judge wore those long black robes like a priest or something, and the lawyers wore solemn suits and ties. So I figured since court was kind of like church, I should wear church clothes. Unfortunately, I had no church clothes, since we rarely ever went to church.

I stared into my closet, the smell of crackling bacon making my tummy rumble as I thought about Gary and what his morning must have been like. He wasn't getting home-cooked French toast and bacon, that was for sure. I wondered if he'd slept at all, worrying about what was to become of him. I felt a bit guilty for sleeping through the night myself and for the breakfast I was about to have, fixed by my very own dad. Finally, I realized it didn't really matter what I wore to court. This day was about Gary, not about me. So I dressed in my best new Wilmington Dry dress and figured it would do just fine.

"Well, don't you look nice," said Dad, dishing up my breakfast. "Is that a new dress?"

"I've had it since school began."

"Well, it's new to me, but then so much is."

"Like what?"

"Like Gary, for instance. How long have you known him?"

"I met him just before school started."

"Uh-huh," said Dad, setting the plate in front of me and pouring me some milk. "Well, he basically seems like a good kid, but maybe he's a little bit much for you and Jake, you know?"

"No," I said warily.

"Well, he has a very complicated life and that tends to make kids grow up too fast."

"He's really a good person. You'll see."

Dad put the milk back in the fridge, warmed up his cup of coffee, and sat with me while I ate. "You kind of like Gary, don't you?"

"Dad," I said, rolling my eyes, but I could already feel my cheeks blush, giving me away.

"You do. And that's fine. Like I said, he seems like a good kid who has more than his share of troubles. But I don't want you to get too involved. Things might not go well today, and if they don't, I don't want to see you spend your time pining for him."

"What do you mean?"

"I know you like this boy a lot. You and Jake both. Frank is going to do what he can to make things right, but there are some things that are out of his control. I don't want you to be devastated if everything doesn't turn out the way you'd like it to."

231

My French toast and bacon were sticking in my throat. I couldn't figure out why Dad was saying all this. Everything was going to be fine. It had to be. It just had to.

"Well, after Jake and I tell the judge it wasn't Gary's fault—"

"You're not going to testify, Lucy. It's not that kind of court."

"But at the police station, Frank said to Jake that the judge would hear all about how Jake ran away and Gary and I came after him."

"He'll hear it all from Frank."

"No! I want to tell the judge that it was my fault Gary took the car. I've got to."

"Don't worry, honey. The judge will know all about that."

"How will he know if I don't tell him?"

"Just trust me, Lucy. Gary and Frank have discussed everything. Now finish up your breakfast. It's getting cold."

But I knew how Gary felt about ratting on other people and was sure he hadn't told Frank the whole truth. It was a shame Dad had gone through all the trouble of making my breakfast. I absolutely couldn't eat another bite.

The courtroom was definitely a letdown. It looked more like a classroom than a church. There was no wood paneling, no jury, none of that do-you-solemnly-swear stuff. The walls were painted dull gray, and there were rows of plastic chairs bolted to the floor for us to sit in. In front of the chairs were two long fake-wood tables. Gary and Frank sat at one table, and a weary-looking woman, a social worker, sat at the other. At least the judge did have a big desk to sit at, and he did wear long black robes.

Gary looked exhausted, grimy, and, oddly enough, small. He'd always seemed larger than life to me, and his smallness in this drab place came as kind of a shock. Jake and I sat nervously beside each other, Mom and Dad by my side and Mrs. Little next to Jake, as we awaited Gary's fate. Once again, Mrs. Geary was absent. No matter what Dad said, I didn't think that when this ended, all would be well.

"Mr. Grotowski," said the judge, "is the boy's mother, Rose Geary, present in the courtroom?"

"Good question," Jake humphed, as disappointed by her absence as I was.

"No, Your Honor, not yet. She's on her way but was unavoidably detained," Frank explained.

"Well, that's a pity, because I run my courtroom like clockwork."

"Sir, if you'd just give us until noon, take a few cases ahead of us, I'm sure she'll be here by then."

"And if she's not, then what?" said the judge sharply. "No, Mr. Grotowski, I've got a full docket today and I fit this in as a favor already. You have your good friend Judge Willis to thank, but one favor's enough. You'll get no more from me. Now, Mrs. Rosen, if you'll proceed."

The social worker, Mrs. Rosen, stood to present her side of the story. After that, it would be Frank's turn. The whole thing felt like it took forever, but in truth, Gary's case was decided in less than ten minutes. The judge's next dozen cases were waiting out in the hallway for their day in juvenile court.

"Your Honor, while I don't feel that Gary Geary is necessarily destined to become a career criminal, he has been in trouble with the juvenile authorities once before and he was recently expelled from Caesar Rodney Junior High for an act of vandalism against a teacher," said Mrs. Rosen, consulting a thick file on her desk. She seemed sad to have to say those things.

"The cherry bomb wasn't his fault," hissed Jake.

"Shhh," I said.

"In addition, he has little supervision at home. His father is not around, his mother seems overwhelmed, unable to control him, and he is increasingly absent from New Castle Tech, where he now attends school."

"Why isn't Frank objecting?" whispered Jake.

"I don't know," I hissed back.

"He should object!"

"Quiet," warned the judge, glaring at us over the rims of his glasses.

"In this situation, the normal recommendation of Family Services would be to remove him from his home and place him in a stable, experienced foster care home."

"Foster care!" Jake choked.

The judge gave Jake some serious stink eye, daring him to make another peep.

"However, given the circumstances—most notably his age and his record—we've not yet been able to find a suitable home for him. As I said before, I don't feel that Gary is any great threat to society, but it seems that currently, the only place for him to stay is in juvenile hall."

I couldn't believe that this woman was actually suggesting Gary stay in juvenile hall with a bunch of real delinquents. Gary looked resigned to her opinion, like it was something he'd actually arrived at himself. Jake looked stricken, his mouth making words without any sound. The judge stared daggers at Jake, who was still trying to speak when Frank stood up to take his turn.

"Your Honor, while it's true that Gary does have a prior juvenile record, there are extenuating circumstances," said Frank, the great voice of reason.

"Huh?" puzzled Jake under his breath.

"He smashed some windows in a house that was under construction immediately following his brother Luke's death. Maybe not the best way to express his grief, but understandable. Over time his family paid for the windows, and this should have been dropped from his record. And yes, borrowing Miss Thompson's car to drive off and find his friend Jake did not show good judgment, but it does show a great deal of compassion. I won't deny that he was expelled from Caesar Rodney, and that he's been recently absent from New Castle Tech, but he's essentially been running the family business. Two weeks ago his father checked himself into the Veterans Administration hospital for treatment of alcoholism. His mother has dealt not only with that, but with the death of one son and the absence of two others. One is serving his country and the other is serving time in Leavenworth. So, yes, she is a bit overwhelmed. But the garage is the family's sole source of income, and Gary is desperately needed at home to help keep it running while his father rehabilitates."

"What about school?" asked the judge.

"I've spoken to his teachers at New Castle Tech. They're willing to allow Gary to temporarily fulfill his mechanics courses by checking over any work he does at the garage. And his academics can be handled on a half-day basis until his father returns in a month."

"I'm still concerned about parental supervision. I'm

really not happy that we're almost done and his mother is not here in court with him."

"Your Honor, there's a good reason for that."

"Well, sir, now would be the time. I'd like to hear your explanation."

"Me too," said Jake.

But Frank never had to explain, because at that very instant, the doors to the courtroom were flung open and in walked Mrs. Geary with a handsome young man in military uniform. He was a dead ringer for Gary.

The courtroom was up for grabs, with everyone talking at once.

"David?" said Gary.

"Your Honor—" said Mrs. Geary.

"Damn," said Jake.

"Jake!" said Mrs. Little.

"His brother's out of prison?" I asked Jake.

"It's the other brother."

"The Air Force brother?"

"Yeah. Holy sh—"

Bam, bam, bam! The judge banged his gavel on the desk. At least that part was just like on TV.

"Quiet, everybody, quiet!" said the judge. We all stopped yapping real quick. "Okay. You. You had better be this boy's mother, or you can both leave my courtroom right now," he said, pointing his gavel at Mrs. Geary.

"Yes, sir, Your Honor, I am Gary's mother, and I'm sorry I'm late, but I've been down to Dover Air Force Base waiting for David's flight," she blurted out nervously.

"Clear as mud," said the judge. "Who is David?"

"Oh. I'm sorry. David is Gary's brother."

"And you're here late because . . ."

"Sir, I just flew in from Ramstein Air Force Base in Germany, where I've been stationed for the past two years," said David, standing at attention. "My mother called me on Saturday and we pulled every string on earth to secure an emergency reassignment to Dover so I could return to Delaware and help take care of Gary and the garage until our father is able to come home."

"How'd you manage that?" asked the judge, impressed.

"Senator Hebner has been bringing his car to us for years," explained Mrs. Geary. "It's a vintage Mercedes and he's very attached to it. So I called and called his office until I finally got through and he agreed to do everything he could to help bring David home."

"Well, it seems between you and Mr. Grotowski, you've called in some mighty big favors. But that still doesn't tell me you're capable of supervising your own son."

"Your Honor, please, if I can just say—I know I haven't been the best mother lately." Gary looked at his mom in wonder as she spoke in a trembling voice. "We've had some terrible things happen in our family and, well, I let all that get the best of me and didn't have much left for Gary. But that is going to change, I promise you. I've lost one boy already, sir, and another is as good as gone. Please don't take Gary away from me. Please."

It was painful to watch her plead with the judge, but I absolutely had to take back everything I'd said to Dad. Even though she'd waited until the very last minute to prove it to Gary and to us all, Mrs. Geary really did care.

"Okay," said the judge reasonably. "I appreciate that. But we still have some serious issues with supervision. How is

David here going to take care of his brother and the garage from Dover Air Force Base? He can't be in both places at the same time."

"I'm a mechanic, sir. I don't have to live on base. Once I've done my maintenance shift, I'm free to go."

"Can I ask you a question, son?"

"Yes, sir."

"You're how old?"

"Twenty-two, sir."

"And you're willing to take full responsibility for your brother?"

"Sir, I take responsibility for multi-million-dollar aircraft every day."

"Your brother's not a piece of machinery."

"I know that, sir. All I'm saying is that I'm more than reliable, if that's the issue."

"That's part of the issue, but do you really think you can handle a fourteen-year-old? Do you think, when push comes to shove, that he'll listen to his big brother?"

"I can't answer that, sir," said David. "You'll have to ask Gary if he's ready and willing to obey me."

The judge pondered for a moment, then looked down at Gary.

"Son, your brother's putting himself on the line here. You understand that?"

"Yes, sir. I do."

"So if I let him have you, you're not going to be a little smart-ass, are you?"

"No, sir," said Gary, looking surprised a judge would talk like that.

"Because if I ever see you in my courtroom again, there

is no question that you'll be spending time in juvie. Is Family Services okay with this, Mrs. Rosen?"

"More than okay, Your Honor," said Mrs. Rosen, smiling.

"All right then, we're done here. But I mean it. Cross that doorway again and you've crossed me. Are we clear, young man?"

"Yes, sir," said Gary briskly.

"Okay, Mrs. Geary, take your son home."

Frank treated everybody to burgers and fries at the Charcoal Pit. Gary, Jake, and I sat in one booth and the grown-ups in the big round booth next to us. David sat with them, though I could tell he'd probably have rather been with us since the grown-ups were playing an old-fogy Righteous Brothers song on their jukebox while we were playing the Rolling Stones. I couldn't take my eyes off David. He looked so much like Gary it was amazing, but there was something in the way he carried himself that was completely unlike Gary. David seemed older than twenty-two, and it wasn't just the buzz cut or the uniform. While Gary seemed loose and a little rebellious, David seemed tight and obedient, like if he behaved just right, nothing else bad would happen to him or his family. I wondered if he was going to crack down hard on Gary and make his life miserable.

Then he looked over at me right as I was staring at him, and he smiled. He had the same blue, blue eyes that Gary had, and in his eyes I could see some of the rebel that lived beneath that stiff uniform. He'd be tough on Gary, no doubt. But he wasn't going to be a total jerk about it.

"It's gonna be out of control at school tomorrow," said Jake, sounding just a little pleased.

239

"Huh?" I said, looking away from David.

"At school. I'm sure Kwame's told everybody what we've been up to."

"Oh," I said, dismayed. "I'm sure you're right."

"Except the part about me going up to see the Amish. Nobody knows about that but the two of you."

"Really? You didn't even tell your mom where you were going?" I asked, surprised.

"Nah. It would just make her all sad and weird."

"Why would it make her sad?"

"I think she's always felt kind of guilty about me being, you know—"

"Short?" I said.

"A dwarf. She's always felt like it was her fault or something."

"I don't get that at all."

"I don't either, but I think she does. And it would make her sad to think I was heading up there just to be with more dwarves."

"Hey, you know, you never answered me," said Gary, taking a breather from his first good meal in almost two full days.

"Answered you what?" said Jake.

"When we were there on the side of the road and I asked you if you wanted me to drive you up there or not. You never answered me."

"I didn't?"

"No," I said, "you didn't. The cops came right then. Remember?"

"Oh yeah."

"So, what is it?" asked Gary. "Were you gonna make me take you up to Dwarfland or what?"

Jake looked at him, wide-eyed. Gary, like me, never called Jake a dwarf. But Jake had just done it himself, so I guess Gary figured now it was open season on the whole dwarf thing. There was an awkward moment of silence, then we all cracked up.

"Dwarfland," Jake said, choking on his cherry Coke, he was laughing so hard. "Oh, man, what was I thinking? I was on my way up to Dwarfland!"

"Hey, everybody, it's two-for-one day at Dwarfland. Bring all the kids!" I said.

"Imagine the rides in Dwarfland," said Gary, laughing his butt off.

"No one over five feet is allowed on any of 'em," said Jake.

"No roller coaster for Lucy at Dwarfland."

"You either," I said. After all, Gary's as tall as me.

We went on and on, exhausting every stupid Dwarfland joke we could possibly think of. And our answer was right there. In that moment on the side of the road, with a choice between us and Dwarfland, we all knew where Jake belonged.

Chapter 21
The School Day

We were famous, Jake and I. Kwame had made sure of that. Everybody but everybody knew we'd taken Stephanie's car, been nabbed by the police, and gone to court with Gary. The halls were buzzing with it as I put my books in my locker to head off for homeroom. Kwame walked with me, basking in my newfound glory. Just as we were almost in the door, Mrs. Meagher, my homeroom teacher, pulled me aside and told me I needed to see Mr. Offenbach.

"Why?" I asked, puzzled.

"It's about your absence yesterday," she said.

"It was an excused absence."

"Yes, but it was a doozy. Go on. He's not going to bite your head off, I don't think."

When I got to the office, Jake was sitting in a chair outside Mr. Offenbach's door, his short legs nervously swinging back and forth, his face giving none of his fear away.

"Hey," I said anxiously, sitting in the chair next to him.

"Hey," he said, staying cool.

"You think we're going to get suspended?"

"Nah. If he was going to suspend us, he wouldn't have let us come to school today at all. We'd have just stayed home."

"You sure about that?"

"No. But it sounds good, doesn't it?"

We sat there not talking for a moment, Jake's chair going *squeak-squeak-squeak* as he swung his legs.

"Jake," I said tentatively.

"Yeah."

"Can I ask you something?"

"Depends."

"Do you really think Gary likes me?"

Jake looked at me and rolled his eyes.

"Do you?"

"Lucy, for as smart as you are, sometimes you're a total moron."

Mr. Offenbach's door opened and out came Coach Bartell and Billy Stratton. Billy seemed uncomfortable, looking anywhere but at me and Jake. Coach Bartell, on the other hand, looked right at us. He was none too happy.

"Hello, Lucy. Jake."

"Hello, Coach," I said.

Jake didn't say a word. He was busy trying to stare down Billy.

"You're planning on coming to practice today?"

"Yes, sir."

"Good. Don't be late."

They walked off as Mr. Offenbach stood in his doorway, looking as solemn as an undertaker.

"Come in," he said in his low voice.

I swear he sounded like some hokey TV horror-movie host.

Jake stifled a giggle and scooched himself down off of his chair. I bit my lip and stood up, and the two of us did everything we could not to look at each other. If we had, we'd have busted out laughing, and that would have been the absolute worst thing to do because once we'd started, we'd have never stopped, and this was not a ha-ha-funny situation. Which of course made it even harder not to laugh. It's weird how that works—how the one place you want to laugh the most is the one place you really shouldn't. But anyway, we managed to sit down in front of Mr. Offenbach's desk without cracking up.

"Well, you two have had quite a dramatic weekend," he said.

Neither of us answered, still too afraid we'd start giggling.

"It's all over the school. Many versions of your adventures, in fact. I know that all of you kids think that those of us on the faculty and in the administration don't hear what you talk about, but we do. We hear everything. For instance, Mr. Little, I'd heard some time back that though you and Mr. Geary were responsible for the destruction of Mr. Haley's mailbox, you were not responsible for the incendiary device."

Jake looked up, puzzled.

"The cherry bomb," explained Mr. Offenbach.

Suddenly neither of us felt like laughing anymore.

"However, because you and Mr. Geary declined to incriminate anyone else, there was not much I could do, though I did know there were others involved. Today, Coach Bartell came in with Mr. Stratton, who very much wanted to tell me all about his true part in that little fiasco. He told me how he'd brought the cherry bomb and how he put you and Mr. Geary up to detonating it. He'll receive detention for it, but unfortunately, his confession does not absolve you or Mr. Geary of your part in it, as he thought it might. The two of you did, in fact, blow up Mr. Haley's mailbox, and nothing Mr. Stratton said changes that."

"Why would he do that?" said Jake finally, his curiosity having gotten the better of him. "Why would he try to get us off the hook now?"

"I'm not entirely sure. Guilt, maybe. Or maybe he's just got a sense of wrong and right. Which I think you have too. Both of you. I don't think either of you is a bad kid. I didn't really think Gary Geary was a bad kid. But you've all shown some incredibly bad judgment. And from end to end of this school, the two of you are going to be treated like heroes for it, which may encourage you to commit further acts of incredibly bad judgment. So, in case you should be tempted to exercise bad judgment again, Mr. Little, another bit of trouble and you will be suspended, one more and you'll be expelled. Miss Small, any more trouble from you and you'll be kicked off the basketball team. Do you understand?"

We both nodded, wide-eyed.

"I'm sorry, I didn't hear you."

"Yes, sir," we dutifully said in unison.

"Good. I'm glad we had this little talk. I hope I never see you in my office again. Now, if you both hurry, you'll just make your first class. Have a good day."

Personally, I've never been so happy to go to math class.

At lunch, Kwame and Charlene were all ears as we told them about our day in court. Well, Charlene was. Kwame was already working the details into a far more epic tale. Not that it wasn't epic enough, but Kwame just loved a good story.

"So his brother comes flying into the courtroom to save the day?" said Kwame, exaggerating wildly.

"Oh my God, Kwame, that is so corny," said Charlene.

"What is?"

"That 'save the day' stuff. You've been watching too many Superman cartoons."

"David came walking in late with Mrs. Geary and said that he'd take care of Gary. That's all," said Jake.

"But that can't be all," said Kwame, disappointed.

"Well, okay, he said he'd take care of the garage too."

"You have no sense of how to properly tell a story."

"I'm just telling you what happened."

"Yep. That's what I'm saying. You want to tell a story? *Tell* it. I swear you make it all sound like just another ho-hum day in juvenile court."

"Well, I thought it was pretty darn dramatic, David coming in like that," I said.

"Then *you* tell the story. Jake is hopeless."

"But he already told you."

"What happened, yeah, but not what I wanted to hear."

"And what's that?"

"How did it feel?" he asked.

"Like Christmas," I said without hesitation. "It felt like Christmas Day and my best birthday ever and the day I got Lucky and my dad coming home and just like one big wow!"

"Now that's more like it," said Kwame, satisfied.

"It absolutely felt like the best gift in the world," I said, finally figuring it all out.

"That it was," said Kwame with finality. "That it was."

Basketball practice was brutal after the long Thanksgiving break, made even longer by my day in court. Billy wasn't there to help out since he was serving his detention, and that put Coach Bartell in a foul mood, so he ran us and ran us and ran us until I thought I was going to die. When practice was over, we were all too tired to shower or change, so we waited in the school entryway, steaming with sweat as our rides came and we left, one by one.

Once again, I was the last one on the team to be picked up. As I waited, the cheerleaders were finishing their practice, looking as fresh and tidy as when they began. I don't know how they managed it, but I swear none of them ever sweat. They came skipping into the entryway, still clapping, stomping, and chanting in their annoyingly peppy way, waiting for their own rides to arrive. Joanne DiMotta spotted me right away, flushed and sweaty, and couldn't help her nasty self. She just had to say something.

"Wow, Lucy, that's a really nice look. What do you call that? Drowned rat?"

Kathie Chow and she giggled together. I couldn't have possibly hated them more, but I said nothing. What could I say? I did in fact look like a drowned rat, my wet hair plastered to my head, my ponytail dripping. I looked out the glass doors, hoping for my mother to come pick me up right that very second.

"But I guess your jailbird boyfriend isn't too fussy."

"Knock it off, Joanne," I heard someone say.

I looked over to the gaggle of cheerleaders to see Debbie Flack face to face with Joanne. I couldn't believe it.

"Excuse me?" said Joanne.

"You heard me."

"Oh, come on. I'm just having fun."

"I don't think so."

"Who died and made you the boss of me?" said Joanne, defiant.

"I'm the captain of the squad. If you don't like it, you can quit," said Debbie, not backing down.

They stood there, neither giving any ground, and then a car horn blew. Everyone looked to see if it was her ride.

"Oh, there's my mom. Come on, Kathie, let's go," said Joanne, all huffy.

The two of them opened the door, letting in a blast of chilly air, and ran for Mrs. DiMotta's sedan. I looked at Debbie in wonder. She looked at me and shrugged.

"Joanne's a two-faced jerk," she said. "I don't trust her any farther than I could throw her."

Another horn blew. Everyone looked. It was my mom.

"There's my ride. See you," I said, running out the door into the cold, so ready to be gone from there. Debbie didn't have to stick up for me, and I'm not really sure if that's what she was doing. It was more likely that she took every opportunity she could get to jump all over Joanne after what Joanne had done to her. Either way, I was grateful. People never cease to amaze me.

Like Dad. He amazed me too. He left and didn't even say goodbye. Well, that's not entirely true. He left me a note. But I didn't get a hug or a kiss or a "Love you, see you soon," and that's what I really wanted.

No, scratch that. What I really wanted was for Dad to stay and never leave again. But Mom said he had to go, and so he left for California on a flight that would get him to Pasadena in time to at least put in a half day's work.

"Why couldn't he stay, Mom? Why?"

The snow had given way to cold rain, and the windshield wipers beat back and forth as Mom drove me home from school.

"Your dad told me the two of you had a talk with Grandy. You remember what he said?"

"A little. Not really."

"Well, here's the thing. I hate to admit it, but your Grandy's right. Your dad has got to see this thing through. None of us like it, but he's got to finish what he started or he'll always blame you and me."

"I don't get that. Not at all."

"I'm sorry, honey. I can't help you because I don't entirely understand it either. And I sure as heck don't like it. But it's just the way it is. For now, at least."

We drove on in silence for a while, the tires from the car in front of us kicking slushy, dirty snow onto our windshield as the wipers tried vainly to keep up with the muck. The day had turned dreary and I just felt wrung out. Dad was gone, there was nothing I could do about it, and I hated that.

"Did you read your note?" asked Mom, finally breaking the silence.

"I don't care what Dad's got to say. He didn't tell me he was leaving. He didn't say goodbye."

"I know that feels lousy, and he tried to stay another day, but they needed him back at the lab."

"I need him too."

"Well, honey, join the club," said Mom, sounding just a little bitter. "But guess what—we don't have him. And I know having him here for a few days got us both thinking that we might get him to stay. But he didn't. So we're just going to have to learn to do without him again, okay?"

I nodded, fingering the folded note in my hands, and figured, what the heck—I wasn't going to throw it out the car
window or anything dumb and dramatic like that. I was going
to read it and now was as good a time as any. I unfolded the
note and read. It wasn't very long, so I read it a couple of times
as Mom drove on through the sloshy streets. It said:

Lucy Goosey.
I know you must hate me for leaving like this without say-
ing goodbye—

Well, it didn't take a genius to figure that one out.

but it couldn't be helped. I'll make it up to you when I see
you again. Or at least I'll try to. In the meantime. I just want
you to remember this—what I said about Mrs. Geary holds
true for us too: "All's well that ends well." I love you more than
I can say.
Your rotten Dad

After I was done reading, I folded it back up again and
looked at Mom. I knew she wouldn't ask me what he'd written—that was between him and me—but I felt like telling
her some of it, at least.

"He says, 'All's well that ends well,'" I said.

Mom shook her head a bit, as though she had a hard time
believing it herself.

"I hope so, Lucy. I hope like hell that's true."

After the long weekend with Dad, our house would seem
emptier now, and neither of us was anxious to get there, but
there really was nowhere else to go that wouldn't make us

feel any less empty inside. So we pulled into the entrance to The Heights and onto our street and we went home, just the two of us, alone again.

That night, I couldn't sleep. The events of the past few weeks were running through my mind like an endless movie, over and over, one scene after the next. I had gone to bed at my usual time, had heard Mom go to bed herself, and still, hours later, I couldn't make my brain stop. So I did something I'd never done before. I snuck out to go see Jake.

I got up, put my boots on, threw my coat over my pj's, hoisted open my window, and climbed out. It was strange and wonderful to be the only person out and about so late. I saw why Jake snuck out so much. It really was magical. Finally now, past midnight, the cold, nasty rain had stopped and the low clouds had blown on through. The sky was crystal clear, the moon was just a sliver, and the stars were pulsing through the darkness of space, sending their ancient light down to earth.

I walked gingerly over the slick, frozen slush, careful not to slip and fall. With the end of the storm had come a cold snap, and my breath made billowy clouds in the icy air. I made my way carefully over to Jake's, skidding only once before I reached his window. I tapped on the window lightly, but Jake didn't hear. I tapped again, a little louder. Nothing. One more time did the trick. I heard Jake hop out of bed, pad over to the window, and open it wide without even looking first to see who it was. He knew. It wouldn't have been anyone else.

"Hey. Come on in," he whispered, "and shut the window behind you. It's freezing."

I awkwardly climbed up into Jake's bedroom and shut the window as he hopped back into his bed and gathered the covers around him. It *was* darn cold.

"What's up?" he asked sleepily.

I sat on his other bed, rubbing my hands to warm them up. "Oh, you know, couldn't sleep."

"Yeah?"

"Yeah. Dad left."

"Well, you knew he wasn't gonna stay."

"I did," I admitted, "but I hoped he would."

"It sucks, doesn't it," he yawned.

"Big time. I just—I don't know."

"Feel all alone?"

"Yeah."

"I know the feeling," said Jake, smiling.

"I know you do. Out there on the road. You said."

"Here's the thing, though. It sounds kinda dumb, but I think sometimes it's easier to feel all alone. I mean, when you think you're all alone, you can mope around and be all poor, poor me, and sometimes that's easier than talking to your friends. You know?"

"Yeah."

"Like, I thought I couldn't talk to you anymore, but on the road there, with you and Gary coming to get me, I mean, duh—who else am I gonna talk to? You're my best friend."

"Me too. You're my best friend too."

We sat there for a bit, in the openness that late night brings, Jake bundled in his blankets, me wrapped up in my coat.

I was finally feeling sleepy, and Jake was getting downright dopey.

"I'm sorry about your dad," he said.

"It's okay. I think maybe he'll be back."

"I hope so."

"Sorry I didn't tell you about your mom and Frank," I said, yawning.

"It would have been weird for you to tell me."

"That's what I thought."

"Yeah, definitely."

Jake's head had met his pillow and his breathing was growing slow and steady. He was just about asleep again.

"I'm gonna go," I said.

" 'Kay," he said, barely conscious.

" 'Night, Jake."

" 'Night, Lucy. See you tomorrow."

I opened Jake's window and climbed back into the cold, cold night, crunching across the yards full of icy snow, making my way back home from the house of my best friend. And the next morning when we went to school, and the next and the next, we both would know that no matter what, neither of us was ever alone. We'd always have each other to talk to.

EPILOGUE

It's hard to believe now that all that stuff happened to us before Christmas, but it really did. And the rest of the year? Well, I'd like to say that I led the girls' basketball team to championship glory, but I didn't. We won more games than we lost, but that was it. I did better in the classroom, though, getting A's and B's in all of my subjects.

Okay—not true. Once we got to sewing, I almost failed home ec, but Kwame bailed me out, ripping apart my hideous jumper and putting it back together again in a way that made it look pretty cool. I've actually worn it a lot. He really does have a knack for that kind of thing. I think someday he'll be a famous designer, and everyone who makes fun of him now for liking "girl stuff" will be wearing his clothes. He also went to the state track meet and ran the hurdles. He didn't win, but he vowed that next year he'd turn his fourth-place ribbon into a gold medal.

Gary actually passed all his classes at the trade school and they're sending him on through to eighth grade. After seeing a news program about reading problems, his mother made a big fuss, so they tested Gary and finally figured out what he'd been saying all along—that everything turns all backward and upside down for him when he tries to read and write. It's something called dyslexia, which is a word you can't spell if you actually have it. The school got him some special tutoring, and though he'll never be a big reader, at least now he can read.

The school district said that if he wanted, he could go back to regular junior high, but he told me he likes it at the trade school. He says he's got a mechanical mind, which I sure as heck don't have. I've definitely got what you'd call a verbal mind. I'd fail miserably in a place where you had to fix things all the time, but Gary can figure out how absolutely anything works, so I guess he's right to stay at the trade school. His dad got out of the VA hospital and was okay for a while, but then he had to go back in again, so David left the Air Force and he runs the garage full-time now. Gary says honestly it's better that way, and his mother isn't so upset all the time.

Believe it or not, Mrs. Little kind of likes Gary now since the Great Dwarfland Adventure. She says that underneath all that tough outside lurks a really sweet kid whose one and only lucky break in life was meeting me and Jake. I think the opposite is just as true. We were as lucky to meet Gary as he was to meet us. Me especially.

Even though we were at different schools, Gary and I managed to hang out sometimes on weekends. The tree house where we used to go was torn down by Mr. Lukens because some parents found out about it and called it a hazard, so while the weather was still cold we started hanging out at home. Mom didn't mind having him over, and from time to time he'd even fix little things around the house for her. But I think after us all getting arrested, she never completely trusted him. So if he was at the house, she was around constantly, and we never had any time alone.

Once the weather warmed up, though, he'd meet me in the graveyard and we'd climb the maple tree and sit and talk about everything under the sun or nothing at all. He's really easy to talk to once you get past the rough exterior and the blue eyes. Just recently, while we were in the tree, he kissed me. It made me so dizzy, I about fell off the branch, and then I started laughing. The kiss made me feel silly and stupid and happy and clumsy and strange all at once. But I don't think Gary took my laughing all that well. He hasn't tried it again, and a certain awkwardness has grown between us. So I'm not sure what exactly is going on, but I still like him an awful lot. I hope he feels the same.

I hang out a lot with Charlene now too. In a way, it's kind of the same as hanging out with Kwame, not because they're both black but because Charlene and I talk about a lot of the same things that Kwame and I do: music, clothes, boys, and other girls. But there are things I talk to Charlene about that I could never talk to Kwame about. For instance, she and I both started having our periods in the spring, which is definitely not something you can talk to a boy about. And I do things with Charlene I'd never do with a boy. We make up stupid hairdos, we dance to our favorite 45s in our undies when we have sleepovers, and we even got our ears pierced at the mall last week. My jaw about hit the floor when Mom said I could. We both got small gold posts and are swabbing our earlobes with alcohol and twisting the earrings around and around, waiting the six long weeks until the holes heal and we can get ourselves some hoops. I want silver, and Charlene wants gold. We've already picked them out and are babysitting to make the money to buy them. I can hardly wait.

After basketball season, I didn't really see Billy Stratton much. He had his own stuff to do. Once he got out of his cast, he started working with Coach Bartell to get back into shape so he could make the high school basketball team, since he missed the whole junior high season. I like basketball okay now that I've actually played it, but Billy really does love the game.

He and Bebe started going steady, and she dumped Joanne and Kathie and Becky, which was good riddance if you ask me. Billy and Bebe always said hi when they saw me in the hall, and Bebe even ate lunch with us sometimes. I think it's cool that Billy and Bebe aren't so stuck on the idea that you have to be seen with certain people to be popular, even though they're both so popular they could hang out with lepers and still be popular. It must be a drag to be like Joanne and them—to worry so much what people think about you that you can't even choose your friends for what you think about them instead of what everyone else thinks about them. If that makes any sense.

And then there's Jake. Like I said in the very beginning, Jake's not around. He's in North Carolina with his dad, but not for the usual two weeks. He's there for good—or at least for good for now.

After the Great Dwarfland Adventure, Mr. Little drove up to Delaware and they all had some serious discussions about Jake's future. Jake thought his father's arrival had as much to do with his mom marrying Frank as it did his own wild behavior. He said his dad was probably afraid that Frank would try to replace him as Jake's father, which is something he should have thought about before he went and got himself a whole new family, if you ask me. Then Mr. and Mrs. Little and the school counselor had a talk with Jake, and even though his mom argued against it, she finally gave in and agreed that he should be with his dad for a while. Jake said they never asked him anything. If it had been up to him, he'd have stayed right here. But everyone went on and on about how he needed a strong male presence in his life. And even though, after everything that happened, Jake said he likes Frank okay, Mr. and Mrs. Little decided that Jake would go live with his dad for the rest of the school year. They packed him up right after Christmas and took him down south. His mother cried all the way down to North Carolina and Jake was pretty sure she cried all the way home as well.

At first I got letters and phone calls from him every day going on and on about how miserable he was. And I missed him like you can't imagine. But then he started making some friends, and his stepsister Karie, who's sixteen and just got her driver's license, lets him bum around with her and her friends, which is a miracle because just last summer Jake and Karie didn't get along at all.

He was here most of the summer, but after much more family discussion, he reluctantly agreed to go back and finish middle school down there. That's what they call junior high— middle school. It ends at eighth grade, so it's just one more year. Then he'll come back up here for ninth grade and high school—that's the deal. Jake says North Carolina's kind of an adventure, though, it's so different. His first couple weeks he had trouble understanding the accent, and people kept telling him to "just slow down" whenever he spoke. I guess we do talk kind of fast up here, but not *that* fast. It's hard to imagine that people who live in the same country and speak the same language aren't able to understand each other. I'll see for myself, though. School started early for him, so he left The Heights a couple weeks ago. But next week I'm going down to visit him for the long Labor Day weekend before school begins up here. I won't see him over Thanksgiving— he's going to the Bahamas. But then he'll be here for Christmas with his mom and Frank, so I'll see him then.

It's weird to hear him say that: "Mom and Frank." I don't know if I could get used to such a thing myself, but all in all, he's rolling with the punches. He likes having brothers and sisters, even though they're not really related to him. And I do think honestly he'd been missing his dad.

Which brings me to my dad. He did come home for Christmas last year, but then he went away again and he's not coming back. He called us just today to tell us. But it's not like it sounds. Instead, we're going there, to Pasadena, California, as soon as he can buy a house and we can sell ours. Mom's nervous, but in a good kind of way. She's never lived anywhere but Delaware and figures it's about time that she did.

At first I fought with them, begging Mom and Dad to just let me stay. I even told them I could live with Mrs. Little and Frank now that Jake's room is empty, that's how desperate I was. But they said no—I belong to them and we're stuck with each other for better or for worse.

Oh—and I have to switch schools midyear, which really stinks, but Jake says it's not so bad. He tells me you get a lot of attention being the new kid in January, everyone's so bored with each other by then. So the plan is for us to pack up and leave The Heights just after Christmas. On New Year's Day, Mom says, we'll watch the Rose Parade right from the sidewalk on Orange Grove Boulevard, soaking up the sunshine in our T-shirts and shorts.

So I'll still be able to see Jake and Gary over the holidays and spend Christmas Day with Gamma and Grandy and Aunt Jenny and Uncle Pete before we move. And next Christmas, Dad says, they'll all come see us, though how he's going to talk Gamma into getting on an airplane, I just don't know. He says we'll have a guest room and an orange tree for Lucky to climb and flowers all year long and maybe even a pool.

I'll miss everybody a ton—I mean, it hardly seems fair that I've got to move when, for the first time ever, I've got a great group of friends.

But Mom says Kwame and Charlene are welcome to come visit me anytime. Gary too, though I doubt he'll ever get the money to fly clear across the country. It makes me sad to think that right here, right now, is as close as we're going to be. I don't think he'll ever be able to come. Of course Jake will come—that goes without saying. The guest room is his whenever he wants it. Our home is his home, Mom says.

And that is the absolute truest truth. Wherever I live, anywhere in the world, my home will always be Jake's home too.

THANKS—

No one gets anywhere without a lot of help and a little luck, and I've had my fair share of both.

My deepest thanks go to my manager, Andrea Simon, who always tells me I'm a worthy writer even when I have my doubts. Huge thanks go to my agent, Jodi Reamer, who believed in this book from the get-go, and who kept me positive in the face of rejection. Enormous thanks and admiration go to my editor, Michelle Frey, the great guru of the rewrite. The book in its current state is a vast improvement over the draft I first presented to her. The final draft is a testament to her incisive comments, her constructive criticism, and her sharp No. 2 pencil.

I would like to thank my friends and early readers who encouraged me with their enthusiasm for the book: Sara Berg, Nancy Salomon-Miranda, Randy Spence, Jim Vogel, Jeff Bauer, Ron Falzone, Patty Meagher, Suzanne Plunkett, Mark Lancaster, Rose Steinhart, Jenny Barsumian Brady, Helen Fogarassy, Linda Jenkins, Dan Lupovitz, Lauri Maerov, Jim Hanson, Joe Campos, James York, Michael

Quevli, John Santacrose, Nancy Hunter, Paula Singer, Lynn Anderson, Nancy Hebner, Lyla Doyle, Pandie Anderson, Terry DeGroat, Rob DeGroat, Consuelo Campos, Alicia Hankes, Louise Smith, Marg Helgenberger, Brian Stirner, Lily Porter, Carter Mitchell, and Kendra Mitchell.

Most of all, I thank my family—Nan Nemeth, Ed Nemeth, Paula Nemeth Mitchell, Carolyn Nemeth Porter, and Dave Willis—who have always encouraged me. I'm not easy to live with when the work isn't going well, but their love and support have never faltered, and for that I am eternally grateful.

Sally Nemeth was born in Chicago and grew up in Indiana, Delaware, and Alabama. Today she lives in Los Angeles, where she is an award-winning playwright and screenwriter. Her published plays include *Holy Days, Mill Fire, Water Play,* and *Sally's Shorts,* and her television scripts—which include episodes of *Law & Order*—have been featured on every major network.

Sally grew up in a neighborhood very similar to The Heights, where her house backed up against a graveyard exactly like the one described in this book.